ABOUT RUM RUNNER

Twenty years ago, a young cop named Jacqueline "Jack" Daniels arrested one of the most sadistic killers she'd ever encountered. She has since retired from the Chicago Police Department in order to raise her toddler daughter.

But old grudges never die. They fester until the right opportunity comes along.

While on vacation in the Wisconsin north woods, Jack learns—too late—that her old adversary is out of prison. He has revenge on his mind. And he's bringing an army with him...

Outnumbered, outgunned, and cut off from the outside world, Jack Daniels is about to learn the meaning of *last stand*.

This is the 9th Jack Daniels novel, after STIRRED. More than 1 million Jack Daniels novels have been sold worldwide.

RUM RUNNER **by J.A. Konrath**
That which does not kill you, keeps trying...

J.A. KONRATH

RUM RUNNER

May 2016

Rum Runner

1 ounce light rum
1 ounce dark rum
1 ounce blackberry brandy
¾ ounce banana liqueur
3 ounce orange juice
1 ounce pineapple juice
½ ounce grenadine syrup
½ ounce 151 proof rum

Shake first seven ingredients with ice. Pour into hurricane glass. Float 151 on top. Garnish with lime and cherry.

AUTHOR'S NOTE

This book takes place during the same timeframe as my horrific suspense novel WEBCAM, written under my pen name Jack Kilborn. It also happens concurrently with the thriller short story WATCHED TOO LONG, co-written with my frequent collaborator Ann Voss Peterson. Some characters, and situations, appear in all three stories, and they overlap and crossover with one another.

You *do not* have to read all three books to find out what happens. Each of these can be read and enjoyed as a standalone. There are no spoilers.

That said, it was an exciting challenge to write three stories that interweave, and I hope readers will enjoy this experiment. If you like Rum Runner, please give WEBCAM and WATCHED TOO LONG a try. This trilogy was a whole lot of fun to write.

As always, thanks for reading.

Joe Konrath

TWENTY YEARS AGO

JACK

You look... uh... great," Detective Herb Benedict told me.

My Bonjour jeans sported a missing pocket, a tear in the knee, and so much dirt and grime the blue looked like gray. The T-shirt I had on read *Frankie Says Relax*, but it was almost impossible to see under all of the stains. One sleeve hung on by a few threads. The other was missing. On my feet were a pair of Keds that cost me a whole quarter at the Salvation Army. They were so beaten up I felt I'd been overcharged.

"This shirt smells awful," I said.

"Got it from the assistant medical examiner." Herb shrugged. "Original owner didn't need it anymore."

I couldn't tell if he was kidding, and I didn't really want to know. In my partner's hand was a wine cork that he'd blackened with the car lighter. He kept dabbing at it with his index finger and applying the soot to my face, humming something off tune but vaguely familiar. For some crazy reason I thought of that PBS painting show, with that artist who dotted his canvas with happy little bushes and trees.

"What's that song you're humming?" I asked, mostly to take my mind off things.

"*Truckin*. Grateful Dead. Jerry Garcia died yesterday."

I considered the implications. "I wonder if he's grateful."

The joke fell flat. I tried to swallow the lump in my throat, but my mouth was too dry to swallow.

Herb leaned back, appraising his work. "We need to do something with your hair."

"Why?"

"It looks too nice."

"Thanks. It's called *The Rachel*. Do you watch *Friends?*"

"It's too stylish. Crack addicts don't care about style."

I touched my hair, fluffing out the layers. "This one does."

"I'm serious, Jack. Druggies don't buy hairspray. They don't buy clothes. They don't buy food. They buy crack, and nothing but crack. You go into that drug den and try to make a buy with that hair, T-Nail is going to spot you as a narc."

I chewed my lower lip, tasted burned cork. This morning it had taken me twenty minutes to get my hair to look like this. But Herb was right. Terrence Wycleaf Johnson, known on the street as T-Nail, was a very bad man and the prime suspect in over two dozen torture-murders. My disguise had to ring true if I had any chance of getting close to him.

"Fine." I tossed my head from side to side and ran my fingers through the deliberately uneven part, messing it up.

"It still looks too nice."

I frowned. "You got any hairspray or gel?"

"I don't even have a comb. Look at me and tell me I'm a man overly concerned by his appearance."

He weighed about sixty more pounds than he should have, and his recent eating habits proved he had not yet hit his stride. His tie told colorful tales of greasy cheeseburgers, ketchup soaked French fries, and chili cheese dogs. His mustache was thick, curly, and a bit shorter on the left side.

Herb Benedict was a good cop, but he wouldn't be on the cover of GQ anytime soon. I might have told him that, but he was my senior partner and deserved some respect.

He was also the guy covering my ass.

I located the donut bag on the floor of the car. There were extra creamers in the bag, leftover from when we bought coffee that morning. I poured three into my cupped hand and rubbed it onto half my head. Then I checked my work in Herb's rearview mirror.

Yuck. Bye-bye Jennifer Aniston, fashion plate. Hello Jack Daniels, crackhead.

"One more thing, Mrs. Daniels."

Herb pointed to my left hand. I stared down at my ring. A flashy diamond and gold jacket combination. Every time I looked at it I had mixed feelings. I felt love for Alan, even though my husband wasn't the easiest person in the world to please. It sometimes amazed me that I'd ever gotten married. I spent way too much time at work, and at home I wasn't easy to live with. But there was the proof, a large garish stone flanked by so many smaller stones it looked like I had a crystal chandelier on my hand.

I tugged at the rings, surprised how easily they came off, and handed them to Herb. He tucked them into his breast pocket.

"I'll take care of them."

His tone was nonchalant, but I took it to mean he'd return them to me if I came back, or make sure Alan got them if I didn't.

"Thanks."

Herb opened up a battered plastic case and handed me the earbud radio. It was the size of a hearing aid. Tiny—but amazingly—wireless. What a difference from even a few years ago, when transmitters weighed a ton and couldn't be concealed in anything smaller than a handbag.

While Herb messed with the levels on the receiver, I put my left foot on his dashboard and tied the stained laces on my sneakers. Then I pulled up my pants leg and checked my piece, a Seecamp .32ACP tucked into a Velcro ankle holster. Six rounds, plus one in the spout. It didn't reassure me. Crack houses were like fortresses, guarded by gangbangers carrying Mac-10 submachine guns and sporting the latest in Kevlar body armor. They'd laugh at my little pea shooter.

"Testing, testing one two three. You hear me, Jack?"

"Perfectly. Sounds like you're right next to me."

My voice came up through the radio receiver, small and tinny.

"Funny, Rachel. How are Ross and Joey?"

"So you do watch *Friends*."

"Everyone watches *Friends*. The earpiece working?"

"Yeah."

I checked the mirror to make sure my hair covered the earbud, then smeared more charcoal under my eyes, giving me a haunted look. I hadn't been undercover in years, and it terrified me. That last time hadn't ended well. I wasn't hoping for a repeat.

Herb placed his hand on my shoulder.

"No heroics, hotshot. You're just there to make the buy, see if T-Nail is home. The Special Response Team will take him down."

I nodded, but it didn't reassure me. Herb was parked six blocks from the crack house, just beyond the wide perimeter of street kids acting as cop spotters. The SRT was two miles away. If I got into trouble, I'd be long dead before backup arrived.

I clenched my jaw, tried to will my hands to stop shaking. Herb must have noticed, because he put a brotherly hand on my shoulder.

"It'll be fine. A quick in and out. Like buying fruit at your local grocer."

Except my grocer didn't carry guns that could fire a thousand rounds a minute. But this was the reason I accepted the promotion to Homicide Detective. Doing traffic stops and arresting drunken suburbanites in sports bars was all part of serving and protecting, but I became a cop to catch bad guys. Real bad guys.

T-Nail was as bad as they came. In the past six months, bodies had been turning up all over Chicago with multiple broken bones and holes in their arms and legs. The M.E. theorized they'd been nailed to something, probably a wall or a floor, then beaten to death. Majority of the vics were Vice Lords and Latin Kings; gangs who belonged to the People Nation. T-Nail was a higher up in the Eternal Black C-Notes—a set from the rival Folk Nation—and the word was he'd been extending his turf. This was something the CPD Gang Unit corroborated.

Plus, the guy's street name was T-Nail. Couldn't get much more obvious than that.

The problem was there were no witnesses, no informants, no insiders to pin the murders on T-Nail.

At least, not until last night. A wit came forward—the brother of a boy T-Nail killed—willing to testify against him for that and two other murders. But before T-Nail could be arrested, we needed to confirm where he was. People and Folk kept tabs on members of the Chicago Police Department the same way we kept tabs on them, so a new face was needed. Currently, there were no women in the Gang Unit, so I was asked by my captain to go into the housing project and see if T-Nail was inside. If so, I'd signal the response team, and they'd come get him.

Simple enough.

Still, I felt sick to my stomach, and my palms were sweating so bad my fingers were beginning to prune.

"I don't like undercover work," I glanced sideways at Herb. "Scary shit." I felt weak and girlish saying so.

"It comes with wearing the badge. The day you're no longer afraid is the day you'll die."

I let the words sink in. "Thanks." What a breath of fresh air Herb was compared to my last pain-in-the-ass partner, an idiot named Harry that I'd sworn I'd never talk to again.

"Good luck, Jack."

I nodded and got out of the car, taking in my surroundings.

Chicago was hot, upper eighties, the late morning sun beating down like it was pissed off. We were parked next to a burned-out storefront on 37th and State Street, the boarded-up windows tagged with gang symbols. The sidewalk was dirty and looked like someone had taken a jackhammer to it. In front of Herb's car was an old Ford up on cinderblocks, stripped down to the chassis. Behind us was a pothole big enough to break a truck's rear axle.

Urban renewal hadn't reached the neighborhood of Bronzeville.

I tried to get into character, which wasn't the easiest thing to do. I was a white married female cop with a middle class North

Side upbringing. I didn't know poverty. I didn't know about being addicted. The only drugs I'd ever done were prescription pain relievers after assorted injuries, and a few bong hits in college when I said "yes" despite Nancy Reagan's pleas to the contrary. I had no idea what it was like to be poor, hopeless, or strung out, and my acting skills were limited to faking orgasms in my late teens.

Still, I had to be convincing. I slumped my shoulders. I dragged my feet. I put an expression on my face somewhere between "life sucks" and "don't mess with me" and began to trudge east, toward the crack house.

After two blocks I saw the first spotter. Black kid, hundred dollar Air Jordan gym shoes, wearing a drip bag on his head to protect his Bulls jersey from his hair activator. He couldn't have been more than twelve. It was a school day, but I don't think he cared.

He eyed me as I approached. Strange cracker chick, dressed like she's homeless, moving slow but with purpose. An undercover cop?

No, I'm just a crackhead. Don't go paging your boss.

"How you doing, Jack?"

Herb, in my ear.

"Why doesn't the city build new sidewalks here?" I said, navigating a section of broken concrete as rocky as any moon crater.

The spotter kid looked at me when I spoke. I put my right palm on my left biceps, gave him the universal salute. He returned a one finger greeting of his own. I shuffled past him, and he winced at my odor. The kid glanced away, his expression blank. Apparently I passed twelve-year-old muster. Score one for Herb's Make-Up Magic.

"Welfare," Herb said. "Tax payers get street repair. Public aid gets bupkis. You at the Homes yet?"

Herb was referring to the Robert Taylor Homes, a housing project stretching from 39th to 54th Street. Twenty-eight high-rise buildings, sixteen floors each, home to over twenty-thousand people, ninety-five percent of them unemployed. The structures were drab and tall and ugly, looking more like prisons than decent places to raise a family. Fencing stretched over the outside porches to prevent people from jumping. Or being thrown off. No lawns, just patches of dirt and weeds and garbage. Broken glass everywhere, dotted with an occasional hypodermic needle.

I grimaced. This was the slum. The ghetto. The place where hope goes to die.

My destination was the worst part of the neighborhood, known colloquially as the Hole. As I approached T-Nail's building, a crumbling monstrosity with nearly every window broken, I felt my heart rate kick up.

"I'm here," I said, turning onto State Street. "Looks like Beirut."

"Beirut doesn't have as many guns. Keep alert."

As if I was going to curl up in an alley and take a nap.

I headed toward the entrance. Three black guys hung out by the front door, passing a basketball back and forth. Despite the heat, they each wore Starter jackets. A ghetto blaster pumped out rap music, angry lyrics about hating the police.

"Three guards in front," I said.

They stared at me, no longer dribbling the ball. One of them reached a hand into his jacket. My feet got heavier and time seemed to slow down.

"You lost, ho?"

Young guy, not even out of his teens, ball cap cocked to the right.

"Jamal sent me," I said. I hoped the password was still good.

He squinted at me, then grabbed his groin. "Got cha-ching, or you wanna suck for the rock?"

His buddies laughed, and they all exchanged complicated handshakes. I tried to walk past, and the young guy grabbed my arm.

"Axed you a question, bitch."

I had an overwhelming urge to twist away, go for my piece. But I wasn't going to let fear control my actions. A crackhead wouldn't be scared. She'd have dealt with this shit a hundred times before. She'd be bored with it, maybe even annoyed, and anxious to get her fix.

"I got money."

He didn't move.

"You gonna let me spend it, or I gotta go someplace else?"

We stared at each other. His eyes were much older than he was.

"Six-fifteen." He released my arm.

I shouldered past, heart beating wildly. Then I swallowed, sucked in some hot city air, and headed into the crack house to find a homicidal maniac hiding among a group of soulless killers.

The front door was off its hinges, and I walked into the lobby past two African American children playing jacks on the floor with stones. The building was dark inside, the overhead lights broken, and it smelled like urine and body odor. The scuffed floor was sticky under my gym shoes. I pressed the elevator button.

"Don't work," one of the kids said.

"Never did," said the other.

I looked around for a staircase, found one, and began the trek upward. It was hot, smelly, dark, the bannister long gone, graffiti on the walls and steps. A rat ran past my feet, and I let out an involuntary shriek, grateful no one was in the stairwell to witness it.

Crackhead, Jack. You're a crackhead. You're used to squalor.

Though I wondered how anyone could ever get used to living like this.

Oh. Right. That's why they smoke the crack.

My cardio was good, so when I got to the sixth floor I wasn't winded. But a drug addict would be, so as I walked down the hall I panted and staggered a bit, holding the walls, ignoring the two gangbangers guarding the door to 615.

One was wearing a purple and gold knitted winter cap with an L.A. Lakers logo, and a matching hoodie over a green shirt. His right sneaker was untied. His partner was bare-chested with a dozen or so thin gold chains around his neck. His jeans were so baggy I didn't know how they stayed up. He had bandanas around his right ankle; purple, green, and yellow.

"What we got here?" asked the bare-chested one. He had a grill over his teeth—gold falsies with a diamond chip.

"Jamal sent me," I said.

He stuck out his chest. "Jamal ain't here."

I tried to put my hand on the door, and got roughly shoved away. The kid was late teens, and stood about my height, but he had some thickness to him.

I didn't need to pretend I was scared, because I actually was.

"Just wanna buy some smoke," I mumbled.

"Bitch want the rock, gotta suck the cock." He grabbed himself in his loose jeans, and then the duo laughed and gave each other a low five.

I considered my options. Blowing two teenagers wasn't one of them. Neither was shooting two teenagers, even though each was no doubt armed. Besides, an addict wouldn't fight back. Any show of resistance and they'd peg me as a cop.

"Get out of there," Herb whispered in my ear.

Good advice. But I wasn't ready to bail just yet.

I rubbed my wrist across my mouth, obscuring when I bit into the inner part of my lower lip.

"I give you head, I get it free?" I said.

"Free? Nothin' is free. You gonna suck off both me and my boy here, then you can buy some rock."

"'Kay," I said, opening my mouth, making sure they saw the blood.

"Shit! Bitch got the herpes, Cleve!"

Cleve gave me a shove. "Get that nasty shit away from us, ho."

I spit on the floor. "You gonna let me in?"

They both stepped away from the door, hands up as if afraid to touch me. I turned the knob and went inside.

The room was dingy, smoky, and smelled like burning ball point pens and piss.

Crack. I'd busted a few dopers in my time, knew the stench.

There was a black girl on the couch, puffing away on a sooty glass pipe, and in the near doorway a gangbanger was having sex with another girl while she bent over, her jean skirt up around her hips. She seemed oblivious to the guy slamming into her, and her eyes had the glassy look of a sleepwalker.

A kid in reflective sunglasses and a Bulls cap, the tags still hanging from it, sat on a ratty lounger in the corner of the room. He had a Walther MP submachine gun in his lap, and was watching cartoons with the sound off. He jerked his thumb to another doorway, and I bowed my head and walked over. Inside was a guy behind a desk, purple bandana on his head. Another stood alongside the door, wearing camo pants and an El Rukin fez. Both were armed. So far, no one I'd encountered looked more than twenty years old. And none of them was T-Nail.

"Whachooneed?" the desk guy asked.

"Rock."

"How much?"

"Quarter."

He opened a drawer, took out a tiny baggie that was about one centimeter square. Four tiny rocks, each the size and shape of aquarium gravel. I tugged twenty-five dollars out of my front pocket and placed it on the desk.

No one moved. The silence stretched.

Finally, Bandana guy held out the bag for me. When I reached for it he pulled away.

"Never seen you 'round here before."

"Other supply dried up."

"Who you buy from?"

"Terrell in Bridgeport. He's not around."

Bandana smiled. He knew what I knew; T-Nail had murdered Terrell and taken his territory.

"Smoke up," he said, tossing me the drugs.

I caught the baggie in a fist, then turned to leave.

Camo Pants was blocking the door.

"Don't you wanna smoke up here?" Bandana asked.

"Forgot my pipe." I tried to keep the fear out of my voice. Junkie who just scored wouldn't be scared. She'd be eager. "Got one?"

"Pretty thang like you can borrow mine."

I turned back and Bandana was holding out a glass cylinder the size of a cigarillo. Silver stuffing—steel wool—was shoved into one end.

In case something like this happened, I had a contingency. A few weeks ago, some uniforms had confiscated several ounces of fake crack off some scam artists selling in Lincoln Park. Chunks of dried, powdered milk stained with coffee. I had some of these fake rocks in my back pocket. If needed, I could smoke them.

But how could I get the fake stuff from my pocket while being scrutinized by two sets of eyes?

I reached for the pipe, taking it between my two fingers, and then detected movement behind me.

"You a cop?" asked a low voice. Real low, with a scratchiness to it. Like a bear had learned how to talk.

I looked.

T-Nail.

I recognized him from his mugshot taken years ago. He'd changed. More specifically, he'd grown.

When T-Nail had been pinched for dealing weed, at age 15, he'd been five foot ten and a hundred eighty pounds. The giant before me was at least six-five. Barrel-chested, legs like tree trunks, biceps the size of bowling balls. He wore a black leather vest, his gang colors and symbols stitched into it. His beard was splotchy, like mange, hair unable to grow on large patches of scar tissue. Rumor was a rival threw a flaming cup of gasoline in T-Nail's face, and T-Nail beat the man to death while still on fire.

"Ain't no cop," I said.

"Either of you clowns pat this bitch down?"

Bandana and Fez each shrugged. T-Nail pimp-walked over to me, one hand on his crotch. He put a hand on my neck, so enormous he could almost completely encircle it. With his other hand, he groped my shirt, my breasts, my waist. Without breaking eye contact, he dropped to one knee, putting him at almost my height. When his hand touched between my legs, I thought about pissing. First, because it would stop him from frisking me. Second, because my bladder felt ready to burst from fear.

"You're T-Nail." I said, my voice shaky.

His hand brushed over my ass, then moved to my thighs.

"You know me?"

"Heard of you."

"What you hear?"

He touched my knees. In a few more seconds he'd reach the Seecamp in my ankle holster.

"Hear you nail people to the floor."

His blank expression didn't change. But unlike the other gang members I'd encountered on this little adventure, his eyes weren't dead. They were alert.

I was scared, and he liked it.

"You heard I nail peoples to the floor?"

I nodded.

"Caught this Vicky Lou on my turf few weeks back. Got me a nail gun. Put one here." He squeezed above my left kneecap. "And here." He pinched my right.

His grip was so hard I whimpered.

Herb would be calling the SRT. They'd be on their way. But it would take them two minutes to secure the outside building, and another minute to get upstairs, longer if T-Nail's gang put up resistance. T-Nail had more than enough time to kill me, or worse, before they showed up.

"Wasn't to the floor. It was old school Roman shit. Up against the wall. Crucifixion style." T-Nail tightened his grip.

"I just want my smoke," I managed to whisper.

"So smoke, bitch."

I brought the glass pipe to my mouth, held it in my lips, and with trembling hands tried to open the baggie.

T-Nail removed his hands from my knees—

—and delicately took the bag from my hands.

With small, precise movements, he shook out the rocks onto his palm, selected one, and pushed it into the steel wool of my pipe. He pushed hard, so the glass clinked against my teeth. Then he stood up, towering over me, his hand going into his front pocket.

He took out a Zippo, which had a yellow smiley face on it, and flicked on the flame. His other hand wrapped around my neck, so hard he lifted me up onto my tiptoes.

"Marco, tell the boys we got a raid coming. Carl, reach down and take this cop's tiny gun out of her ankle holster." T-Nail smiled, and it was an ugly thing. "After she done smoking, we gonna smoke this pig."

HERB

Panic. Like a jolt of liquid electricity flushing through Herb's body, fueling every worst case scenario at once.

Jack was more than a co-worker. More than a partner.

She was his friend.

And he had to get to her. Fast.

Herb stuck the *Starsky & Hutch* style cherry light to his roof, hit the ignition, and floored the accelerator, sirens wailing and tires screaming. He fishtailed out of his parking spot, adjusted for the drift, and beelined for the projects as he fumbled for the CB.

"SRT, we've got a 10-1 in progress at 5326 South State Street. What's your twenty, over?"

"Two minutes out."

"Make it one," Herb told the Special Response Team as he jumped a curb.

When he reached the Hole he screeched brakes, watching as the C-Stone soldiers guarding the entrance scattered like roaches when the refrigerator is pulled back. He parked, unholstered his SIG Sauer, racked in a 9mm round, and ran for the front door as fast as his chubby legs could move.

JACK

Hand trembling, I put the glass pipe to my lips.

T-Nail held up a lighter. His expression was one of vague amusement.

I poked the pipe into his eye, hard as I could.

He fell to his knees, and I dropped into a squat, freeing the Seecamp.

The gangbanger guarding the door ran through it, so fast his camo pants were a blur. Bandana, behind the desk, flung open a drawer.

"Hands up!" I ordered, thrusting my gun forward. "Face the corner!"

There was a split second of indecision, but incredibly he obeyed.

"Palms on the wall!"

Then T-Nail, still on his knees, stared up at me, his left eye swollen shut and crying blood. But his expression was oddly calm.

In one hand was the crack pipe.

In the other was a silver-plated fifty caliber Desert Eagle, pointed at the floor.

"Drop the weapon!"

"You gonna shoot me with that tiny little gun, cop lady?"

"I said, drop it!"

"Is that a .32?"

"I'm counting to three. One..."

My heart was beating so hard I could barely hear. I was gripping the small Seecamp with both hands, but couldn't stop it from quavering.

"How many bullets in that little thing?"

"Two..."

The left corner of his mouth turned up in a cold smirk. "How many rounds do you think it'll take to put me down? More than you got, I think..."

"Three!"

T-Nail raised the .45.

It took all seven bullets to drop him.

A moment later, Herb ran into the room, heaving. Between great gulps of air he managed to say, "Sorry... sorry... I'm late..."

But I wasn't listening.

I was staring down at the man I just shot. Herb's words from earlier bounced around in my head.

The day you're no longer afraid is the day you'll die.

I wasn't going to die that day. Because I was terrified.

Terrified I'd killed someone, and wouldn't be able to live with myself.

And then I was doubled over and throwing up.

PRESENT DAY

JACK

We were sitting on my couch, watching two-year old Harry McGlade Junior pull off his Mickey Mouse diaper and wave it like a flag as he ran around in circles, cheering triumphantly.

"Just like his old man," Harry McGlade Senior said.

"The nudist streak?" my husband Phin asked. "Or the diaper?"

"I'm man enough to admit to both."

The three of us stared as Harry Junior toddled over to my ficus tree and began to urinate into the pot.

"Good boy, Junior!" Harry beamed. "No pee pee your pants!"

I glanced at Samantha, playing quietly with a set of blocks. Though a little younger than McGlade's prodigy, Sam was already potty trained. Smart kid. Well behaved. Adorable. She had Phin's dirty blond hair and intense eyes.

A perfect kid. I should have been happy.

Phin had his arm around me, idly stroking the back of my neck. I shifted, drawing away from him.

"You here?" Phin asked.

That was our code for, "Are you living in the moment?" Phin knew I had bad memories, and sometimes they popped up and wouldn't go away. It's hard to be hopeful while looking at your baby when all you can see is blood from your past.

That was a daily problem I struggled with. But I hadn't told Phin about the other problem.

The bigger one.

"We can talk later," I said.

"Or we can talk now."

I looked at Harry.

"Is this some sex problem thingy?" he asked. "Because maybe I could help. I've had every kind of sex problem. Sores? Discharge? Something stuck where you can't get it out?"

"Are we having a sex problem?" Phin asked me.

I caught a curl of sarcasm. We hadn't had sex in a while. Every time he reached for me, I rebuffed it.

A few months ago he stopped reaching for me.

"You guys having backdoor issues? If you want to tap that dumper, Phin, the key is lube," Harry made a fist and stuck a finger of his prosthetic hand into it, indicating difficulty. "And lots of it. And Jack, try to push out while he's getting up there."

"Speaking of dumpers," Phin said.

Harry followed his gaze, saw his son was attempting number two in my ficus pot. "Whoops. Code brown. Sorry, Jackie. I need a sink and some soap." He stood, scooped up his child, and carried him down the hallway.

Phin turned to me. "If you're sick of work, why do you keep inviting him over?"

"I didn't invite him. Harry invited himself. You let him in."

"But you are sick of work."

"Work is work."

"You hate it."

"We need the money."

"It's more than that. You miss being a cop."

"No." That wasn't true. "Yes. The private sector sucks." Since retiring from the Chicago PD, I'd joined Harry's private detective firm. He'd been my partner in our rookie years, before Herb, and was a major PITA back then. He still was a pain in the ass, but I guess I'd become somewhat immune to McGlade's eccentricities.

"You miss the streets. The excitement."

"I miss being relevant."

"Being a mother isn't relevant?"

"Of course it's relevant." I turned away from him. "I don't want to have this conversation now."

"You never want to have this conversation."

"So how about respecting that?"

"How about you respect our marriage and talk to me?"

I folded my arms over my chest, staying silent.

"I get it." Phin said. "Your boring little life with me and Sam can't compete with you running around, chasing serial killers."

"Now you're being a dick."

I stood up. Phin caught my wrist, and I reflexively twisted out of it and fell into a defensive stance. As if we were about to spar.

"Really, Jack? I'm the enemy now?"

I took a deep breath, let it out slow. "I really don't want to talk about this with Harry here."

"It's okay!" McGlade yelled from the bathroom. "I can't hear you!"

Phin was as good at ignoring Harry as I was.

"Is it some medical thing you're not telling me?" He looked concerned.

"No."

"Menopause?"

"Kiss my ass."

"You're fifty, Jack. It would explain the hormone swings. The lack of a sex drive. The anger."

"I'm not angry," I said through my teeth.

"You sound pretty angry!" Harry called from the bathroom. "Hey, do you have more towels?"

"The cabinet," I yelled back.

"I used those already."

Phin made a face. "There were five towels in there, McGlade."

"This bowel movement was supernatural. It's like the *Amityville Horror* of baby shits."

"Check the hall closet," I said.

"Thanks. Also, I owe you a new bathroom rug."

"Tell me the problem, Jack," Phin said. "Please."

Tell him the problem? How was I supposed to do that, when I didn't know for sure? I'd been stressing over it for months. And the stress brought guilt, the guilt brought worry, and the worry brought more stress.

"Is it our sex life?"

I didn't answer.

"Jack?"

"I'll tell you," I said. "I just need some time."

Harry yelled, "Do you have a long handled mop?"

"Seriously?" Phin called back.

"Some got on the ceiling."

"I got this." Phin stood up. For a moment, it looked like he was going to hug me.

I stiffened. He walked around.

I watched Phin head down the hall, and I slumped back down on the couch. This was a bad situation. Bad bad bad. And I didn't see any easy way out.

Our sex life was part of it. But it was a symptom, not the underlying problem. I hadn't been in the mood. I felt blah. Unmotivated. Decidedly unsexy. Phin was younger. And he was a guy. He wasn't going to wait forever. Like any man, he'd eventually cheat.

Maybe he was already cheating. I wouldn't blame him.

That should have scared me. Not caring if Phin slept around wasn't a good sign. I should have leveled with him. Told him my feelings.

But how was I supposed to tell my husband, the father of my child, that I didn't know if I still loved him?

TERRENCE WYCLEAF JOHNSON

After the three hundredth chin-up, the man known as T-Nail dropped to his cot.

His upper body was burning with lactic acid, his muscles on fire from the work out, his shirt soaked with sweat.

His lower body, as usual, had no feeling at all.

Catching his breath, he stared at his useless legs. He wore an XXL shirt, necessary to cover his massive chest, and his biceps still stretched out the seams.

For bottoms, he wore a medium, and they were baggy as hell. The twigs inside were no larger than the bones beneath the skin, the muscles long ago wasted away. They were the legs of a child.

The legs of a cripple.

For twenty years, T-Nail did solid time. He hustled for the Folk Nation while inside. Drugs. Booze. A numbers racket. Even paralyzed, he commanded Respect with a capital R. He had homies who had his back, and everyone owed him favors.

Even though he was paralyzed, he was feared.

Because of that fear, no one messed with him. Not the People, or the chollo sets, or those Aryan ass crackers with the Nazi ink. Everyone showed respect. T-Nail smoked up when he wanted. Got his drank on. Ran his game and ran it tight. It wasn't freedom, but T-Nail got by.

Ceptin' for hoes. His dick was as useless as his legs.

In one way, it made the time easier. Didn't have to resort to no homo shit to keep his wick wet. Been so long, he couldn't even remember what coming felt like.

Or what walking felt like.

"'Sup, homes."

His cellie, a lifer from the Maniac Latin Disciples, came into the cell with an exaggerated p-walk. But he wasn't pimpin'.

"You got it," T-Nail stated what he already knew.

"Cost a carton of squares," he said, grinning, "but I got the goods."

He pulled a rusty old length of iron pipe out from inside his pants, holding it out to T-Nail like he was about to knight him.

"Cool." T-Nail hefted the iron bar. The weight was good. Solid. This would work.

"You... you sure you want to do this?"

"You shading me?"

T-Nail searched the man's face for defiance. He only saw fear.

"No, man. No way. But this shit is hardcore."

"I'm hardcore."

"For real. You... you need help?"

More fear there. And something else. Unease. This man had seen violence. Done violence. But he didn't want to be involved with what was coming next.

T-Nail shook his head. "I got this."

"Okay. Shit. You doin' this now?"

"No time like the present."

"Well, damn. Been a pleasure doing time with you, yo."

The Mexican offered a fist bump. T-Nail returned it.

"Gimme two minutes, then call the bulls," T-Nail said.

"You got it, homes."

"Don't leave me hangin'. There's gonna be blood."

The Mexican pounded his chest, threw up a gang sign, and left T-Nail alone in their cell.

T-Nail pulled up his left pants leg. He stared at his withered, toothpick leg, letting his revulsion grow.

Can't walk.

Can't fuck.

Been locked up for two dimes.

Long time.

Half a lifetime.

No possibility of parole.

T-Nail used his hands to lift his leg up to the bed. He stretched it out, putting the ankle on the frame, and thought about his trial.

You did this to me.

You cop bitch.

Shot me with that teeny tiny little gun.

Didn't have the guts to kill me. To put one in the brain pan. To put me down for good.

Naw. You went and crippled a brother.

Crippled him, then locked his ass up and threw away the goddamn key.

She got to testify in disguise. Dressed in a wig and sunglasses. In a goddamn court of law. Didn't have to give no name. Some bullshit about protecting undercover officers.

For twenty years, T-Nail had called in countless favors to find out who she was.

For twenty years, he paid and bribed and threatened everyone he could to get a name.

But the cop bitch was a ghost.

Until last week.

Got your name now, bitch.

Got your name, your record, your address, your blood type, your family, your whole damn life. I finally know who you are.

And I am gonna make you suffer.

T-Nail raised the rebar.

He didn't hesitate.

He never hesitated when it came to violence.

Didn't matter if he was nailing some snitch to the wall, or doing it to himself.

What needed to be done, got done.

He brought the bar down with all of his strength, right below his knee.

WHACK!

Heard his own bone snap. Watched it bend inward at a forty-five degree angle.

This gonna be you soon, girl. 'Cept you gonna feel it.

WHACK!

His leg bent further.

Gonna do all sorts of creative shit to you.

WHACK!

The flesh on his shin split, and the broken bone peeked through, sticking out an inch.

You and your husband. Phineas.

WHACK!

The blood was really spurting now, pumping with his heart-beat. T-Nail tucked the rebar under his mattress, then reached down and grabbed his ankle.

You and your daughter. Samantha.

He pulled, hard. The fractured bone came up six inches, jutting out of his flesh like a bloody white spear.

I'm gonna hurt you more ways than you can count, Jacqueline Daniels. You're going to feel pain on a world record level.

"Guard!" he screamed. "Broke my muthafuckin' leg!"

Then he waited to be taken to the infirmary, holding his leg above the knee so he didn't bleed to death.

Many times, in the past twenty years, T-Nail had thought about dying.

But now…

Now he finally had something to live for.

"Shoulda killed me when you had the chance, bitch."

PHIN

There was baby shit everywhere. The sink. The floor. The walls. It was an apocalypse of feces.

Phin's face pinched. "Jesus, McGlade. It looks like a cow exploded."

Harry had his son sitting in the toilet. Not *on* the toilet. In it, like it was a bathtub. McGlade was bouncing him up and down, trying to rub Junior's butt on the seat to scrape some of the mess off.

"Father to father, here's a tip: Prune juice and bran flakes shouldn't be mixed."

"Who could have guessed."

Phin had brought the mop with him, and got to work on the floor. All he succeeded in doing was smearing it into long, brown streaks. He was amazed that anyone, anywhere, ever had more than one child. Phin loved Sam, but he was so past the poopy diaper stage, and had no desire to revisit it ever again.

"So, what's going on with you and Jack?"

"She's been… tense lately."

"I told you. You gotta use lube if you want to get anywhere near her backdoor."

"Enough with the butt jokes. Especially while I'm mopping up after your child."

"Sorry. I do it for attention. I was adopted, you know."

"I know."

Harry flushed the toilet. Junior must have enjoyed the swirling water, because he cackled in obvious glee.

"You know what you guys need? A vacation. Get away from everything. Have some quality time together. Dump the kid and take off."

Phin had suggested that to Jack, several times. Drop Sam with her mother, go someplace. Reconnect. Rekindle the romance. Enjoy one another.

But Jack hadn't wanted to leave Samantha. Samantha came first. Always. So Phin focused on being a good parent, a good provider, a good protector, even as their marriage eroded.

"Jack doesn't trust Sam with others."

"Why not?"

"Luther Kite."

Luther was the latest in a seemingly endless string of maniacs who had it out for Jack. His whereabouts were unknown.

"I hate that guy. But no one has seen him for, what? Two years? Maybe he crawled into a hole and died."

"Convince my wife of that."

"Okay. You want me to do that now, while you finish up with Junior?"

"No."

"So take Sam along. Find some resort that has one of those kiddie jails."

"Kiddie jails?"

McGlade nodded. "Like casinos. You drop your kid off in some hotel-run daycare, you and Mom can get your freak on, booze it up, zone in on the baccarat action, then pick up your bundle of joy at the end of the day."

"Aren't those daycares run by stoned teenagers who don't give a shit and just plop the kids in front of a TV for eight hours?"

"That's a stereotype," Harry said. "Sometimes the TVs don't work."

"So anyone could walk off with my child."

"No. You and the kid get matching wristbands."

"You think a wristband is going to stop a determined criminal?"

"They've also got locks and stuff. Probably."

"What about guns?"

McGlade frowned. "I'm pretty sure the hotel babysitters don't have guns."

"Someone comes in with a gun, points it at the stoned teenager, demands to take a child."

"You're dark, man. You think of some really dark shit."

"It's a bad idea, Harry."

"How about fatso? You trust him?"

Harry was referring to Jack's other ex-partner, Herb Benedict.

"Herb's on vacation."

"Where'd he go?"

"Nowhere. It's a staycation. He's catching up on *The Walking Dead*."

"Is the new season out?" Harry asked. "I tried to record it, but my DVR is full of clown porn."

"I don't know. I'm not really into zombies."

"Then don't ever sleep with Harry Jr.'s mother," Harry said, giving himself an invisible rim shot with sound effects.

"I won't."

"Seriously. Don't. It's not a jealousy thing. Sex with her is truly awful. Toss a bologna sandwich on your bed and have a go at that. It'll have more enthusiasm. And be warmer."

"Duly noted."

"Salami works, too."

"What can I say or do to get you off the topic of having intercourse with lunch meat?"

Harry rubbed his nose on his sleeve. "So that's it? You hide in the house with your daughter for the next twenty years?"

Twenty years? At the current rate, Phin didn't think the marriage would last until spring. Jack froze whenever he tried to touch her. She couldn't relax. Not even at night. Sam had a perfectly good bedroom, but she still slept in their bedroom, which put an even tighter damper on their sex life. Jack would spend the night tossing and turning, wake up tired and pissy, and Phin couldn't think of anything he could do to help her.

"Do you love them?" Harry asked.

Phin didn't hesitate. "Yes."

"Are you happy?"

"I'm happy they're safe."

"It's not what I asked."

He shrugged. "Right now, it's all I got."

"Fair enough. I know a good cryonics lab. Got a deal with them to freeze my head and my junk when I die. You can freeze Jack and Sam for a hundred years, thaw them out when the world is a better place."

Harry took Junior out of the toilet, wrapping him in the last clean towel. Phin tossed the other dirty towels, and the mop, into the bathtub to wash later.

"Or, there's another alternative," Harry continued. "You go somewhere no one knows about. No credit cards. Pay cash for everything. No cameras at every stop light. No Internet. Somewhere no one can find you."

"No place like that exists."

"Actually," McGlade said, his smile as wide as a zebra's ass. "It does."

T-NAIL

Jesus," the prison doctor winced at T-Nail's leg. "You did this falling?"

T-Nail shrugged. "Doing some chin ups. Landed bad."

"This is... this is one of the worst compound fractures I've ever seen. I don't know if the leg can even be saved."

"So cut that shit off."

"We're not equipped for that here. I... I'm calling the hospital."

"Doc, I ain't in no pain, but I'm kinda light-headed."

"Let me check your O2 levels." He clipped some electronic gizmo to T-Nail's finger. "You're hypoxic. We'll get you started on oxygen." The doctor put a mask up to T-Nail's face, looping the elastic around his ears. "Just breathe normally. We've got the bleeding under control. You're going to be okay. They'll be able to take care of you in the ER."

T-Nail looked at Chalmers, the guard who brought him here. "Looks like we're going for a ride, Chalmers."

The oxygen mask hid his grin.

JACK

"A cabin in the Wisconsin north woods," I repeated.

"It's more than a cabin, Jack," Harry said. "It's the only house on a private lake. No one else is around for miles. I bought it a few years ago, when I had some dealings with several shady characters who shall remain nameless, and I thought I might need a safe house."

"You got involved with the Mafia."

"If I go into detail about my business dealings it could end in subpoenas and/or concrete shoes for you. Let's just call them shady characters."

"So you bought a hidey-hole."

"This place is entirely off the grid. Wind turbine power. No phone. One road in, one road out. Great security. All set up under a fake name."

"Sounds like prison."

"Far from it. There's hiking. A hot tub. Pool table. I've got a million DVDs and games up there. Private lake is a few hundred meters away, and you can fish. Food for a month. And a full security package. Cameras. Weapons. It's really secure. The cabin could weather a siege if it needed to. But it won't need to, because no one knows where it is."

"Why haven't you ever told me about this?" I asked.

"Deniability," Harry said. "That way, if someone tried to find me through you, you couldn't give them anything. They could torture you for weeks and weeks, but I'd be safe."

"You're always thinking."

"I know, right?"

"What if I needed to call someone?"

"That kind of defeats the purpose of a safe house, Jack. Cell reception is spotty, but there is partial coverage. If you really need to make a call, there's a town half an hour north, near the Minnesota border. Spoonward. Population under five hundred. Quaint, in a Mayberry RFD kind of way. But with 4G and WiFi. Buy a disposable cell at the Walmart, and you're off the grid."

I batted it around between my ears. A change of scene would be nice. Getting away from society. The tranquility of the woods. A chance to actually relax.

Phin raised an eyebrow. "What do you say, Jack?"

"I'm on the fence."

"Also, there's porn," Harry said. "Lots of porn."

"I'm not sure your porn is a selling point." Phin glanced at me. "Besides, I don't think we'll need it."

I kept my face neutral. If porn helped us rekindle our spark, I was all in. I hadn't felt sexy in a long, long time.

"Do you have the *Marriage Saver App* on your tablet?" Harry asked.

"I don't want to know what that is," Phin said.

"But I'm going to tell you anyway. You brought up porn."

"No, *you* brought up porn."

"The *Marriage Saver App*," Harry pressed on, "is a video showing a close-up likeness of a celebrity, moaning. You strap your tablet over your partner's face while having sex. So it seems like you're with someone hotter."

"Nice," I said. "Sounds like the perfect way to connect."

"Got one that looks like Scarlett Johansson?" Phin gave me a playful wink.

"I do," Harry nodded. "Both with long hair and short hair."

Two could play this game. "How about one that looks like Robert Downey Jr.?"

"I've got all of *The Avengers*," Harry said. "The Samuel L. Jackson simulation swears at you for five minutes then pulls out a gun and threatens to blow your fucking cock off. I'm not into dudes, but I've used it on a partner once or twice. The man's star power arouses me."

"If we go, what about Samantha?" I asked.

"I'm more than willing to watch your daughter while you're gone," Harry said.

"No. Seriously."

Harry frowned. "I'm sensing you don't think I'm a responsible parent."

I pointed to Junior, sitting on the floor. "You're letting your son play with your gun."

"I took out the bullets. I think. And he's not strong enough to pull the trigger."

"You're a terrible human being," I said.

"Yeah, I know. How about Tangi? I have custody of Junior for the rest of the month, but maybe I could get her to watch the kids for a week."

"Your baby mama?" Phin asked. "She's as irresponsible as you are, Harry."

"That's impossible."

"She left your child in the back of a cab," I said. "And forgot about him for five hours."

"Those Persians returned him."

"She let him stick a fork in an electrical outlet."

"That was my watch. And I have a circuit breaker. He just got a strong shock."

"Didn't Junior swallow dishwashing soap while she was drying her hair?" I asked.

"Yes. But dishwashing soap isn't poisonous. And she told me his puke was pretty much all bubbles. It practically cleaned itself up."

"You two shouldn't have had children."

"And yet, we did, and he's fine."

Junior had taken off his towel and had his head caught under my couch.

"Not happening," I said.

"How about Mom?" Harry asked, pulling his son free.

"Mom is on one of her cruises."

"One of those Viagra buffet things? Where all the old people have nonstop sex?" Harry frowned. "Why do they even stop at ports? No one gets off the ship. They all stay in their rooms and play with each other's wrinkles. It's one big geriatric booty call. Didn't she break a hip on the last one?"

"Let's change the subject," Phin said. "I don't like picturing your mother having sex."

"Why not?" I asked. "Because when a woman gets past a certain age, she isn't a sexual being anymore?"

"I didn't say that."

"Maybe it's the sound," Harry said. "All those brittle old bones creaking and popping. It's like squeezing a bag of chips." He hooded his eyes. "So I've heard."

"At least someone in this family is getting some," I said, happy for Mom.

"Like it's my fault?" Phin said. "You try to kiss an ice tray, see how that works for you."

"I'm telling you guys," Harry said. "The Marriage Saver app. You could be Channing Tatum, and you could be Natalie Portman. Or vice versa. Whatever weird gender shit you're into."

We both told Harry to shut up.

"How about Val Ryker?" Harry said.

Phin nodded. "That might work."

I narrowed my eyes. "You want to have sex with Val Ryker?"

"Not on the app. Val could watch Sam. She's a cop. She's a friend. She's responsible. We both trust her. Sam would be safe. Just as safe as she is with me and you."

"And she's in Wisconsin," Harry added. "You could drop her off on the way to the cabin."

I let it sink in. It was a lot to ask Val, but I watched her niece a while back when Val was having some trouble. So she sort of owed me a favor.

"Plus she owes me a favor," Harry said. "She owes me like ten favors. I think she's got a little crush on me."

"Don't we all," Phin said. "What do you think, Jack?"

I stared at Sam. She'd stacked up ten blocks and glanced back at me for approval. I smiled, and her chubby fingers went for number eleven.

It was such a worn-out cliché, but I loved her so much. I could look at her, and see me.

But when I looked at me, I didn't see anything. Somewhere, in the last two years, I'd disappeared. All I once was, all I used to be, had been replaced by Diligent Guardian of Sam.

That wasn't a complaint. It was a job I gladly embraced. Nothing I'd accomplished in my past was as important as that little girl sitting on the floor, playing with blocks.

I glanced at Phin. He, too, was watching Sam. And he had the same look of marvel in his eyes that I probably had.

I wanted to reach out to him. To hold his hand.

But I was afraid I'd forgotten how.

"Okay," I said.

Phin raised an eyebrow. "Okay?"

"I guess I could call Val, see if she's free. I'm not sure. I think I need to sleep on it."

"No rush," Phin said. "It's not like we have to leave right away. We have time to think about it."

T-NAIL

The ambulance wasn't in no hurry. T-Nail couldn't look out the window in the back door because it was too high up, so he couldn't see how fast they were going. But it didn't feel fast from his spot on the stretcher.

Just like in the hood. What's the rush? One more busted-up gangsta. Maybe, if we're lucky, he dies and we don't have to waste time on him.

Nothing had changed. Tech had gone from cassettes to mp3s, from paper to ebooks, from cell phones the size of bricks to handheld computers with touch screens. But 911 was still a joke, and brothers still got no respect.

"Hey, Chalmers, this really necessary?" he said through his oxygen mask, extending his arm as far as the cuffs allowed.

"Those are the rules, Terrence."

"You gotta chain a human being to the bed? It's degrading."

"Rules." Chalmers looked away.

T-Nail looked at the second guard in the back of the ambulance. "How about you, Neville? Why the bracelet? You afraid of me?"

"Naw. It's for your own protection," Neville said. "We wouldn't want you hurting yourself."

The prison guards shared a snicker. The paramedic, a black guy, joined in.

"Kicking a man when he's down," T-Nail said. "I get it."

Chalmers got serious. "Hey, Terrence. I don't know if the doc said anything, but I think it's only fair to tell you… it doesn't look like you'll ever walk again."

More laughter.

"You guys are hysterical. You should be on TV."

Then all four tires blew out, and the laughter stopped.

"Check it," Chalmers told Neville after the ambulance skidded to a halt. The guard went to the front of the ambulance, and stopped halfway when the *POP POP POP!* of gunfire was heard.

"Shit! That's shooting! Someone's shooting at us!"

"You guys lost your sense of humor real quick," T-Nail said.

Both men took their guns out, and Chalmers fumbled for his cell phone.

Half a second later the back window smashed inward. T-Nail watched the canister drop inside, and he closed his eyes tight.

Someone yelled, "It's tear gas!"

Coughing and swearing and retching and random shooting from the bulls ensued. T-Nail breathed easily through his oxygen mask, waiting for this shit to work itself out. It only took thirty more seconds for someone to unlock the back door, gasping for fresh air.

The guards and medic flopped outside and got themselves shot. From the sound of it, about a hundred times.

That was followed by the familiar sounds of a beat down, and then T-Nail's cart was being wheeled out. He peeked open his eyelids, saw bangers all around him. And it wasn't just brothers representing. Of the dozen-plus guys, there were also some Latinos, and two white dudes. The Folk Nation had gotten a lot more diversified since T-Nail had been running things.

He locked eyes with every soldier, saw the respect there. Kids, most of them. Not a single familiar face from the old crew. Streets were hard. Thug life had taken them out of the game.

Neville and the paramedic were dead. Chalmers seemed to be hanging on, shot up and beaten but still moaning.

T-Nail took off his oxygen mask and took his first breath of freedom in over two decades. The night was warm, the stars out.

T-Nail couldn't remember the last time he saw the stars. Staring up at them he felt....

Nothing.

T-Nail knew his emotions had been paralyzed years before his legs, and all that sentimental shit like love and hope and faith had vacated the premises long ago. He'd been dead inside since he was a kid, after his father was killed. Or maybe he was just born that way. It was what it was, no use dwelling on it.

His gang had hit the ambulance on an empty stretch of highway somewhere between the prison and the hospital. This was southern Illinois, miles and miles of cornfields. He squinted up the road, saw a shorty packing up the spike strip they'd thrown. It had been a good plan, well executed.

T-Nail looked around for his General, Del Ray. They'd never met before, only communicated through third parties. Del had worked out the whole escape in just a few hours. He'd informed T-Nail his fracture had to be bad enough to warrant a trip to the ER. Knew there had to be enough blood loss to require an oxygen mask. He'd studied for it, prepared every detail, and it came off flawlessly.

But T-Nail spotted him from his description. Del Ray was standing to the side of the ambulance. He was in his mid-twenties, had a Dr. J afro, and was bare-chested except for a furry looking vest.

T-Nail had heard rumors about the vest. He hid his surprise that Del Ray had worn it.

Del sidled up to him, and they did a C-Note handshake.

"Welcome back, War Chief," Del said.

A shorty handed T-Nail his old colors. A leather vest with his rank on the lapels and gang symbols on the back. T-Nail stretched out his arms, allowing himself to be draped in it.

Tight, but still fit. Like an old pair of kicks.

"Gat," T-Nail said.

Del Ray handed him a .45 Glock. "It's giggled-out, yo."

T-Nail squinted at the gun. The rear slide plate had been replaced with a so-called *giggle switch,* which allowed the semi-auto to spray rounds like a machine gun.

T-Nail took aim and shot Chalmers fifteen times in less than a second, turning his feet into hamburger.

"Hey, Chalmers," he said above the guard's screams. "It's only fair to tell you… it doesn't look like you'll ever walk again."

He handed the gun back to Del Ray.

"We got to put you back inside," Del Ray told him, pointing his chin at the ambulance. "Got a doctor waiting for you."

"Got eyes on the cop bitch?"

"Burbs. Sent a team to check it out. Should hear soon."

"Good."

"We'll dump the meat wagon and the bodies in Gary. Take time for the po-po to figure out what happened."

T-Nail nodded. Del Ray was smart. Genius level. He was the mastermind behind a new way to cook meth, which cut costs and increased output. He was a wizard with firearms and explosives, taking the war on the streets to whole new levels. And the brother knew computers and electronic shit like nobody else.

But Del Ray also had some… peculiarities. His furry vest wasn't made of fur.

It was made of human scalps.

Rumor was, Del Ray had some Sioux blood in him. But that alone didn't explain it. T-Nail would hurt people to show power, or send a message, or punish. Inflicting pain was no different than swatting a mosquito. But Del Ray took trophies. To remember the moment. That was seriously twisted.

T-Nail was put back into the ambulance, along with a still-alive Chalmers, and the bodies of the dead. Del Ray rode in front.

"You… gotta…" Chalmers paused to moan. "Take… me… to a… hospital."

"I got a better place to take you, Chalmers. It's called hell."

As the bull screamed, T-Nail broke all of his fingers. But his heart wasn't really into it.

He was too preoccupied thinking about Jacqueline.

JACK

Sleep eluded me.

I stared at Phin, snoring softly in bed. His face was completely relaxed when he slept, in a way it never did during waking hours. It made him look younger. And something else. Something I didn't want to admit.

When he was asleep, my husband looked peaceful.

Awake, he always had a measure of urgency about him. Even when he acted calm. Phin was ten years my junior, but lately he didn't appear to be. Lately he looked old and worn out.

Was that a recent thing?

I thought back to when we first became friends. Me, a cop. Him, dying of cancer, engaging in various illegal activities to make money because he didn't think he'd see next summer. I knew he'd robbed, and used the money on drugs, to make the pain go away. Though we rarely talked about it, I suspected he'd committed even more extreme crimes. Crimes where people died. Phin had a moral core, and the people he'd killed weren't innocent, but it weighed on him the same way the deaths I was responsible for weighed on me. Taking a life, even an evil life, was the stuff of nightmares.

But even back then, living day-to-day as a hired thug, battling stage 4 pancreatic cancer, he hadn't seemed as stressed as he'd been for the last two years.

Since moving in with me and having Samantha.

I swung my legs over the side of the bed, careful not to disturb him, and walked over to the bed where Sam slept. My little girl wore vintage *She-Ra Princess of Power* pajamas; a gift from Harry, who seemed to constantly troll eBay for nostalgic crap. She looked like she always looked, whether awake or asleep. Innocent. Perfect. Angelic.

I knew deep down I loved her like every parent should. Fiercely and unconditionally.

So why did I have to keep reminding myself that?

I squinted in the darkness of the bedroom, trying to see myself in her. My genes. My dreams. My future.

But all I saw were my chubby legs and double chin.

Since retiring from the Chicago Police Department, I'd been mostly taking it easy, and the weight was sneaking up on me. Harry and I were partners in a private detective firm, but most of my work involved sitting; in cars, on chairs talking to clients, in front of the computer prowling the Internet. I couldn't remember the last time I'd been to the gym. Or the *dojang*. Phin had put a mat in the garage, and I'd been teaching him a bit of taekwondo, but it seemed that whenever we began to work up a sweat, something child-related would interrupt us.

I put my hand on Sam's chest.

Felt her heart.

Wondered why I couldn't feel more.

Postpartum depression?

No. This wasn't chemical. This was situational.

Once upon a time, I was relevant. Criminals feared me. Men wanted me. I was dangerous. I was sexy. I was a force to be reckoned with. But taking pictures of cheating spouses didn't hold the same satisfaction as putting away a murderer. Especially since the cheating spouses were getting laid, and I wasn't. It had been so long, I'd practically forgotten what Phin's cock looked like.

Hell, when was the last time we'd even kissed?

Any third party looking at my life would think I'd fully embraced domestic bliss, from the suburban picket fence outside the house to the apron stained with congealed applesauce. But I didn't feel bliss. I felt disconnected. Almost confined. Which made me feel guilty. Which made me feel more disconnected, and more confined.

With Phin and Sam, I knew I'd been given a second chance. A do-over. They were my reward for a life spent on the street, catching bad guys.

So how come, instead of feeling like I was being rewarded, I felt like I was under house arrest?

Noise, from the window leading to the backyard. A soft thump. I immediately switched from self-pity mode to self-preservation mode. In two steps I was next to my nightstand, pulling open the drawer, gripping my .38 Colt Detective Special. Phin immediately jackknifed into a sitting position, sleep still in his eyes even as he pulled his 1911 out from under the mattress.

"Noise," I whispered. "Outside."

Phin picked up his iPad with his free hand and checked our security system while I crept up to the window and peeked through the side of the shade.

My backyard was well-lit, almost to the level of a soccer stadium. We had motion detectors and cameras covering every inch of the property. I didn't see anyone.

"Holy shit," Phin said.

"What?" The hairs on my arms stood up in alarm.

"That's the biggest damn squirrel I've ever seen."

He showed me his tablet, which was zoomed in on a squirrel sitting atop our plastic garbage can. And it was, indeed, a big one. Though not over eighteen inches, which was the size we'd set the perimeter alarms for.

"Wow," Phin said. "Check out the size of his nuts."

Our intruder had two acorns in his paws.

"Funny."

"Those nuts are so big he'll never fit them in his mouth."

I sat on the bed and put my gun back in the drawer.

"I used to be able to make you smile," Phin said.

He didn't reach for me. I guess he knew better.

"I'm not in a good place," I told him.

"I want to help you get to a good place."

I didn't answer.

"Assuming you want my help."

I knew that was a cue to snuggle against his body. But I didn't want to give him false hope.

Shit. How had it gotten so bad between us?

A minute passed. The silence felt loud.

"You been up all night, Jack?" he finally asked.

I noticed his use of my first name. When our marriage was good, he called me *honey* or *hon*. A tiny little term of endearment that I hadn't really paid much attention to.

Until he stopped.

Phin hadn't called me *honey* in months.

"Most of the night," I answered.

More noisy quiet.

"Been thinking about Harry's offer? Cabin in Wisconsin?"

I nodded.

"Are we going?"

I didn't want to leave Sam. But I didn't want things to stay like they'd been. Or get worse. Something had to be done. Inaction hadn't improved us, so I either had to take action, or give up.

I was pretty good at navel-gazing and moping. But giving up wasn't something I did very often.

"I guess I'll call Val in the morning, see if she can babysit."

DEL RAY

The paramedics and guards had been stripped and dumped at an old warehouse, teeth and fingertips removed to make ID'ing the corpses harder. The ambulance went to a chop-shop in Joliet, to be sold in a million pieces. Del Ray had been checking the police chatter on an app, but no word yet about the escape.

Perfect plan, perfect execution.

T-Nail was in the clubhouse den with the gang doctor, patching up his leg. Del Ray felt good that he was able to help an OG. T-Nail was old school, and deserved respect. But it remained to be seen how he'd fit in with the new clique. During his time inside he'd been consulted on big issues, but Del Ray had been running the game for the last few years. If T-Nail wanted his territory back, the manifesto said he'd get it. He could elect to take a less active position, which would probably be best for everyone. Or, if T-Nail wanted to rule as War Chief again, Del Ray would have to ease him back into the groove.

But the best case would be if T-Nail stepped down. Things had changed. It was the new mack's turn to shine.

His cell buzzed, and Del Ray answered without talking.

"She got up late, talked to her man."

"The equipment work?"

Del Ray had put together the laser microphone himself. It was a long range listening device that sensed the vibrations caused by sound waves when pointed at glass. When people spoke indoors it could translate the sounds bouncing off the window into words. Del had ordered his team to set it up outside the cop's window.

"It was like butter, dog. You want to hear?"

"Yeah."

Del Ray was subjected to some stupid shit about a squirrel, before getting to the part about Harry and Val and a cabin in Wisconsin.

Was the happy family planning a vacation? If so, that would be good. An earlier report showed that the cop's home security was tight. Cameras. Sensors. Alarms everywhere. She was a seriously paranoid bitch. But if she left home, grabbing her would be easier.

"Keep me posted," he told his men.

Del Ray put away his phone and walked into the den. The doc had finished patching up T-Nail, who was sitting in one of the leather theater recliners. In his left hand was a bottle of Hennessy XO. In his right was a barbell, which he was pumping. Dude had a chest and arms like Terry Crews.

"Cop may be taking a trip. We can hit her on the road. Even if she's armed, ain't no thing."

T-Nail pulled at the cognac, drinking a quarter of the bottle in a few gulps. "Get my wheelchair."

"I got something better. Some real Tony Stark shit."

"Tony who?"

Del Ray checked himself. They probably didn't show movies in the joint.

"Lemme show you."

He jogged over to the garage door, and went into his workshop. The project he'd been working on for the past week had only been completed a few hours before the escape, and Del Ray considered it one of his finest inventions. He sat down in the device, strapped himself in tight, and hit the on switch. Then he scooted over to the door, went through sideways, and rolled into the den.

"I call this the Gyro," he told T-Nail.

"It's an electric wheelchair."

"My brother, this ain't a wheelchair. It's a pimped-out all-terrain vehicle. Titanium frame. Kevlar fiber sling. Top speed of thirty miles per hour on the straightaway."

Del Ray took the Gyro through the paces, starting with a tight spin.

"Mecanum wheels. So it moves any direction. Sideways." He demonstrated. "Diagonal. Goddamn figure eights if you feelin' it."

The Gyro slid across the floor like butter on a hot skillet, going whichever direction Del Ray pointed the joystick.

"And if you want to get through a small entrance, or play a little B-ball..."

He hit the conversion button, and the Gyro straightened itself up, picking up its rear tires and stretching to standing height.

"This is why I call it the Gyro," he said. "Balancing on two wheels, without the gyro inside it would fall over. But the sensors are accelerometer based, so it won't tip. Like a Segway."

"I want to try."

Del Ray switched back to sitting position, then motored next to T-Nail. He unbuckled himself.

"Handles are up here," he said. "You can lift yourself in."

T-Nail easily hoisted his frame into the Gyro, his muscles rippling. He adjusted his considerable bulk, settling in.

"The buckles keep you tight when you're in a standing position. In the back are a second set of wheels. They work on stairs and other bumpy conditions, like sand and dirt."

T-Nail began to circle around the room, getting the hang of the controls.

"The batteries last for eight hours. I put a holster on the right side. Got a giggled-out Glock with two hundred rounds in the drums. And on the left side, I got something special."

T-Nail checked under the armrest, and pulled out the nail gun from the custom holster.

"Pneumatic," Del Ray said. "The hose is fed from an air compressor in back. It'll work even if the power is off. Try it out."

T-Nail pulled the trigger, and a 20d nail shot into the tile floor, embedding itself four inches deep.

Del Ray didn't expect to be thanked. Men didn't thank each other. But there was no shake. No nod. T-Nail didn't even look at him.

"Where's my room?" was all he said.

"Down the hall, first door on the right."

He sailed over to his Hennessy, grabbed it, and motored away.

Del Ray frowned. Doing time for two dimes no doubt sucked dead donkey ass, but that was no reason to be such an ungrateful SOB. Del Ray put some long hours into the Gyro. He didn't need a hug, but what kind of brother doesn't even offer a fist bump?

He went back to his workshop, grabbed a bottle of tannic acid powder, and began to dust the new scalp he'd gotten last week. Untreated, it would rot and stink. Had to be cured like leather.

T-Nail hadn't said shit about the vest, neither. Del Ray hardly ever wore it in public. After all, it contained DNA evidence for more than two dozen murder cases. Getting caught with it could mean life in the slam. But he wore it, proud as his colors, for T-Nail. And didn't get a damn word of praise.

"Brother might start feelin' unappreciated," he said to himself, working the tannin into the skin.

But Del Ray still wanted to give T-Nail the benefit of the doubt. The man had a rough day. Hell, he had seven thousand rough days. Twenty years behind bars was a long time.

Maybe, when Del grabbed the cop and her family, T-Nail would be a little more appreciative.

Del Ray ran his fingers over his vest. Lots of dead peeps. But none were white women.

The concept intrigued him.

"Maybe it's time to embrace some diversity."

After all, Del Ray didn't want anyone thinking he was racist.

PHIN

Jack was finally asleep. Phin swiveled out from under the covers, walked silently past his daughter, and left the bedroom.

Mr. Friskers, Jack's cat, was sitting in the hallway, his eyes reflecting the little light coming in from the kitchen window. He stared at Phin, and Phin stared back. The cat was notorious for not liking anyone, and attacking without provocation. It had yet to attack Phin or Sam, but it had done a number on their former basset hound, Duffy, who had since gone on an extended visit with Jack's mother in Florida. Phin would have preferred keeping the dog and ditching the cat, but Jack's mother had refused the cat.

Yet another concession.

He strolled past the living room, into the garage, and over to the red tool cabinet. Three feet high, twenty drawers, it was one of the few things in the house that was uniquely his. Not by choice; Phin was no more a handyman than the average Joe. But when he married Jack and moved in, and they delegated responsibility, household repairs and general maintenance fell under his watch.

The garage was dark, but his eyes had adjusted enough for him to maneuver without tripping over anything. He padded over to the chest, felt for the tactical flashlight on top, and hit the low beam button. Phin pulled out the third drawer, found a cardboard box of wood screws, and set it on the cabinet.

He opened the box, shining his light on the vial. Glass, no larger than his thumb, filled with a white powder.

Cocaine.

He hadn't done coke in years. It seemed like a lifetime ago. He could still vividly recall the rush it gave him. The feeling of invincibility. How it reduced every care and concern to background noise. At the time, Phin had told himself it was palliative. He'd been dying of stage 4 pancreatic cancer, nearly hobbled by unrelenting physical and emotional pain. Risk, sex, and drugs were how he dealt with it.

He hadn't done anything truly risky in years.

Hadn't had sex in months.

And he couldn't even remember the last time he'd snorted any coke.

But a month ago, after a stupid argument with Jack that ended with him going for a drive to cool off, he found himself in Chicago, at an old haunt, and ran into a dealer he used to know. Phin bought the blow, but didn't do any. When he got home, he put it in the tool chest, and hadn't touched it since.

But he hadn't forgotten about it.

Two weeks ago, he'd gone into the garage and stared at the drawer it was in.

Last week, he'd crept into the garage at 4 A.M. to look at it.

Now, Phin reached for it, holding it in his fingers.

Kicking his old coke habit hadn't been pleasant. It was an easy drug to get addicted to, and a hard one to quit.

I'm a husband and a father now. No sign of cancer. I live in the suburbs. Maybe I'm having some relationship trouble, but a cocaine monkey on my back isn't the way to fix it.

So why did I buy it?

Why did I hide it?

Why am I here looking at it?

Phin wasn't sure if it was a reminder of how things used to be, or a portent of things to come.

He closed his eyes. Thought of Samantha in her crib, asleep. Thought of her mother, the woman he loved and would always continue to love, even though she was slipping away from him.

Phin wondered if Luther Kite was the problem. Jack hadn't been the same since Michigan. Phin, Harry, and Herb had a pretty rough time there, but Jack had it the worst. Knowing that Luther was out there in the world was no doubt gnawing at Jack's soul. He was the reason for all the home security. And for Sam sleeping in their bedroom. Maybe Luther was also the reason Jack had switched off, emotionally.

The past was a bitch that did its best to fuck with the present.

The coke in Phin's hand was a perfect example of that.

He placed the vial back in the box of nails, shut the drawer, and went back into the house.

Went back into the bedroom.

Kissed his sleeping daughter.

Kissed his sleeping wife.

Climbed into bed.

Closed his eyes.

Twenty minutes later, he was back in the garage, cutting a small pile of coke with a utility knife blade on the side of a Trix cereal box. He snorted the line using a plastic straw from one of Samantha's sippy cups.

The rush hit, hard.

Phin's body shook with pleasure, and he laughed, for the first time in as long as he could remember.

JACK

I peeked at the clock. A little after 8 A.M. Sam was sitting up in bed, holding a toy helicopter, one of those Fisher Price models where every detail was big and round and child-friendly. She stared at me, then dropped the toy on the floor.

"Fly," she said.

I walked over to her, put my hand on her head. "It doesn't fly, dear. It's a toy."

"Hebbi-cob-der."

"Yes. A helicopter." I picked it up and spun the plastic propeller. "But it can't really fly. It's pretend."

I made a *foop foop foop* blade sound and circled the toy around Sam's head.

She seemed unimpressed. I couldn't blame her.

"It's an analogy for life," I said. "Something looks like it should do something, and you get really excited about it, but instead it disappoints you."

"Trix," Sam said.

"Good idea."

I picked her up, carried her to the kitchen, expecting to see Phin. He wasn't there, but I heard sounds coming from the garage. I sat Sam at the kitchen table, in her booster seat, and got her a plastic bowl. The Trix box wasn't in the cabinet.

"How about oatmeal, Samantha? We're out of Trix."

"Pbbt," she said.

"I agree. I'll pick some up later. Do you want oatmeal?"

"Bacon."

I went to the fridge, found the cooked bacon in a Tupperware container.

"Do you want it heated up?"

"Nope."

"Cold?"

She nodded, smiling.

"Do you also want a dinosaur for breakfast?"

Sam laughed. "Mommy, you can't eat dine-sore."

"You're right. No dinosaur, then."

I wondered if every mother felt like she had the smartest, most adorable child in the world. Probably. But they were mistaken, because I had her.

I couldn't find the straw for the kiddie cup in the sink, so I fished a clean one out of the dishwasher, set Sam up with some cold bacon and green Hi-C—the breakfast of champions—and then poured myself a cup and went to look for Phin in the garage.

He was on the judo mat, shirtless, covered with sweat and beating the crap out of the heavy bag that hung from the rafters. He had my training gloves on, throwing punches so fast they were a blur.

My man was formidable. And still in great shape. Broad shoulders, tapering to a toned stomach. A lot of definition in his chest and biceps. He hadn't put on, and kept on, baby weight like the other person in this marriage.

I watched him for a moment without him noticing, feeling a little like a voyeur. Phin was younger, attractive, still had that bad boy vibe that drew me to him in the first place. I was so used to seeing him holding Sam, walking around with a diaper bag, I'd almost forgotten this side of him.

He stepped away from the bag, gave it a shoulder-high kick, his bare foot slapping the canvas—

—and leaving a red streak.

I looked at his foot, saw it was bloody.

The mat was also bloody.

"Your toe," I said, and Phin whirled on me fast, a snarl on his face, and I reflexively put up my guard.

When he realized it was me, his features softened.

"Morning, Jack."

"You broke your toenail."

Phin looked down, saw the blood oozing from his big toe. "Shit. Didn't even notice."

He walked past me, glazed with sweat and smelling like guy, and went to the gym locker. He found a roll of gauze, then put his foot up on the shelf and began to wrap his toe. I noticed the box of Trix on his tool chest.

"Got hungry?"

"They're not just for kids, you know."

"I've heard."

Phin tied off the makeshift bandage. Then he walked up to me, staring at me hard as he took my Hi-C. He finished it in three big gulps. Then he whistled a few bars to a Helen Reddy song that he knew I hated.

You and Me Against the World.

When was the last time that had been true?

"Want to go a few rounds?" he asked, his breath washing across the top of my head.

"Sam's eating bacon."

"Excuses, excuses."

"She could choke."

His eyes twinkled. "On bacon that you cut up to the size of postage stamps?"

"Are you making fun of my parenting skills?"

"Do you even remember how to throw someone?"

I grabbed his wrist, twisted, then threw him over my hip. He flipped onto the mat, and I turned and knelt on him, straddling his head between my legs. My heart rate had doubled, and I felt my face flush.

"Now what?" Phin said, grinning. "Are we sparring? Or something else?"

I stared down at him, and for some reason thought about Sam's toy helicopter.

"Mommy, why are you sitting on Daddy?"

Sam was in the doorway, holding her cup.

"Mommy and Daddy are wrestling," Phin said. "We used to do it all the time, but haven't in a while. Isn't that right, Mommy?"

His tone seemed playful, but I sensed the sarcasm underneath it. And it hurt.

I stood up, and Phin rolled gracefully to his feet. He scooped up Sam, gave her a raspberry on the neck, and then carried her back into the house.

I picked up the plastic cup he'd dropped when I flipped him. Then I went to the tool cabinet, grabbed the Trix box, and one of Sam's plastic straws, and followed them back inside.

Phin had seated Sam back in her booster chair, and they were sharing the bacon. I poured some Trix on her plate, put the box back in the cabinet, and watched them eat.

This was the life I'd chosen. And it was a good life. It hadn't worked out like I'd expected, but what in life ever did?

I knew I had three choices.

Don't do anything.

Try to fix what was wrong.

Or divorce.

I picked up the phone and called Val. To see if she could watch Sam for a few days.

She could.

So Phin and I would have some alone time at Harry's cabin in Wisconsin.

We'd either figure out how to save our marriage, or we'd figure out how to share custody of our daughter.

I rubbed my fingertips together, stared at the faint traces of white powder that had been on the cereal box, and frowned.

I would give us a try. But I wasn't optimistic.

And there was no way in hell he'd get visitation rights if he tested positive for coke.

T-NAIL

It had been a rough night.

The mattress on his new bed was too soft, and T-Nail had slept on a blanket on the floor. He was used to his cellie snoring, but the clubhouse was eerily silent. The smell of his room wasn't right, and it seemed too big. The brandy he had didn't taste anything like the prison hootch pruno he'd come to rely on. And coupled with the rich food he'd eaten—burgers and pie—T-Nail now had a really bad belly ache.

Being on the outside would take some adjustments.

The new wheelchair was cool. Almost too cool to actually exist. Del Ray had gone above and beyond. T-Nail knew he owed the man. And Del knew it, too. He showed total respect, but T-Nail saw underneath it. Resentment. Distrust. Pity.

T-Nail didn't like being pitied. He shanked a guy in the showers, second year in, because the man had complained to the bulls that they didn't have wheelchair ramps in the shitter. T-Nail didn't want to be treated any different. He might have been paralyzed, but he wasn't weak, and he didn't want to hear none of that *special needs* bullshit.

T-Nail would rather get the shit beaten out of him than be shown special treatment. People were bastards, but there wasn't nothing crueler than sympathy.

It came down to two rules to live by.

Take more punishment than the other guy.

Give more punishment than the other guy.

He remembered his blood-in for the C-Notes; the beating he had to take to join the gang. Thirteen years old, facing a gauntlet of eight guys, all trying to knock him down. They called it a rum runner, because by the time it was over, a brother couldn't stand up straight, just stagger around like a drunk. But T-Nail didn't drop. He took every punch and kick, refusing to go down even as his fellow gangstas broke his nose, busted four ribs, and knocked out three teeth. It was the bloodiest rum runner the block had ever seen, and gave T-Nail more street cred than any shorty that came before, or since.

To hell with sympathy. T-Nail demanded respect.

He sat himself up on the floor, pulled himself to his new chair, and reached for the support bars.

Yeah, Del Ray had done a real good job.

This chair was solid, and T-Nail was able to fold the seat back and do a hundred dips, breaking a sweat, exercising until his arms shook. He sat down, strapping himself into the chair, and then wheeled toward the bathroom. T-Nail hadn't checked out the facilities last night; he'd already been dealing with too much to dwell on his bodily functions. But he ate and drank, which meant he produced waste, and that had to be dealt with.

He rolled in through the door, impressed how the Mecanum wheels let him enter sideways.

Then he took a look around and stopped being impressed.

The shower was normal, except for a chain to reach the spout, and a waterproof chair. The toilet, he forgave. It had safety rails on two sides, attached to the wall, but a lot of shitters had those. Next to it, was a sliding board, and T-Nail knew that was pretty common knowledge; paraplegics needed to slide from their chair to the john.

But then it got real.

There was a whole shelf of handicapped supplies. Latex gloves. Jars of Vaseline. Catheters, from tiny ones up to those jumbo Texas-sized muthas. Colostomy bags. Boxes of suppositories and enemas and other freaky ass stuff that T-Nail had never seen before.

He felt the rage bubble up, start to boil over. All this embarrassing shit, out in the open. Not even in a cabinet. Just sitting out there, for all the soldiers to see. Showing them how infirm their War Chief was. How he was weak. Lesser than they were.

Bullshit on that. T-Nail pulled out his cell and called Del Ray.

"Bathroom. Now."

Then he pulled off his leggings, and his underwear, and waited for his second in command to show up.

"I'm here, dawg."

"Then get your black ass in the shitter."

Del Ray entered. He stood at ease, hands behind his back, staring T-Nail in the eyes.

"Got a whole wall full of supplies here. You seem to have an unhealthy interest in my bodily functions."

"Did some research. Didn't know what you needed."

"I'll show you what I need."

Without using the safety rails or the sliding board, T-Nail lifted himself from the wheelchair to the toilet, and lowered himself until he could balance.

"This is called the Crede method," he said, pressing and tapping on his side, pushing against his bladder. He pissed into the bowl. "And this," he said, raising a finger, "is all I need for the rest."

He massaged his rectum and held his breath, pushing hard and bearing down until the shit came out.

Del Ray watched without blinking.

"Has your curiosity been satisfied?" T-Nail asked.

Del didn't seem embarrassed, or even phased. "The cop is on the move."

"When?"

"This morning. She's going up to a cabin in Wisconsin. Town called Spoonward, population four hundred and sixty. Out in the boonies, one police chief and two officers. She's dropping the shorty off with friends, spending some alone time with her hubs."

"Got the address?"

"Address, GPS, and satellite pics. She left an hour ago. Got a team following. What's the move?"

T-Nail sucked in a long, deep breath, and let it out slow. "I want to declare war on this bitch."

"All-out war?"

"All-out war. How many soldiers can we send in?"

"Without suspending any operations, about fifty."

"And if we suspend some operations?"

Del Ray hesitated, then said, "A hundred."

T-Nail nodded. "I want more than a hundred. I want the town of Spoonward shut down and cut off. I want her and her man surrounded. I want to own that territory like it's our turf."

"It will cost us."

T-Nail grabbed Del Ray by his neck, jerking him down to his level.

"Tell me, General; how much did twenty years of my life cost?"

Del Ray maintained his cool. "We'll get it done."

"I know we will."

"And her kid? Want to hit the shorty, too?"

T-Nail considered it, then answered.

"Anything else?" Del asked.

"Get all this bullshit out of my bathroom. Don't want to see none of it again. Dismissed."

He released Del, and the man left.

T-Nail wondered how long it would be until Del Ray made a move against him. He figured he'd have to kill the younger man sooner or later. Too much pride there. Too much ambition. With luck, it wouldn't be necessary until they'd finished dealing with the cop. T-Nail had been out of the game for a long time and needed Del to get him back up to speed. Be a pain to start over from scratch. He'd also have to start testing the soldiers, gauging their loyalty. Wasn't nothing he hadn't done before. Any good leader had to check the rank now and then.

T-Nail closed his eyes. A peace, one he had never known, settled over him. Very few War Chiefs, in the history of the game, had ever declared all-out war.

It felt good. Real good.

It would not feel good for Jacqueline Daniels.

JACK

Phin drove. We'd recently bought a Mitsubishi Outlander, and he didn't look good driving it. He looked like he compromised.

I was the one who made him compromise, because it had the best safety rating out of the SUVs we could afford. And, for some reason known only to astute psychiatrists, I resented Phin for giving in so easily.

Could that be part of the problem? He'd been tip-toeing around me since we had Sam, and I didn't want a pushover as a partner.

Maybe that was the reason I didn't mention the cocaine. Maybe I was actually happy he found his spine again.

At the same time, doing drugs around our daughter was unacceptable.

Shit. When did life get so complicated? It was almost easier chasing serial killers.

Sam slept in the back seat; car rides always did that to her. Phin irritated me by fiddling with his iPod shuffle as he drove. I tried to read an ebook, kept losing my place because the music was driving me batty, and eventually settled in to stare at the boring scenery as it passed. Southern Wisconsin, like most of Illinois, was flat plains, about as interesting as watching water boil or glue dry. We passed a gas station, and I told Phin to stop so I could go to the bathroom. When he did, I purposely didn't go to the bathroom, just to see if he noticed.

He filled the tank, got coffee, and didn't notice. Or he noticed, and didn't care.

We got back on the road. The bad music and mind-numbing view dragged on and on. Phin made it even more irritating, by humming slightly off tune. I was practically sitting on my hands to avoid leaning over and punching him.

He glanced at me, perhaps misinterpreting the displeasure in my eyes as passion, and said, "Ya'aburnee."

"What?"

"I saw it on the Internet. It's Arabic."

"What does it mean?"

He smiled. "It means, *I want you to bury me.*"

"And what does that mean?"

"It means, dear wife, that I love you so much, I want to die first. Because if you died first, I wouldn't be able to handle it."

Dumb expression. I wondered if he was still high.

Sam woke up, a few minutes before we got to Val's. As always, she woke up rested and happy, two things that seemed to elude me lately. She asked for some pretzels, and her cup, and enjoyed those as we pulled up past Val's stable and to her two story home in the woods of Lake Loyal, Wisconsin. Phin parked, turned around to unbuckle Sam, and I got out and walked to my friend's front door, giving it a firm knock.

"Val!"

I forced a grin. It was nice to see Val, but we weren't there to visit. We exchanged a brief hug, and Phin came up behind me and shook Val's hand.

"Sam, do you remember Val?" I asked my daughter.

Sam buried her face in her father's chest.

"Stranger danger!" Sam yelled. "Stranger danger!"

"It's okay, Sam," Phin put Sam down. "She's not a stranger. She's a friend."

Val crouched down to Sam's level. "Last time I saw you, you were only one."

They reacquainted themselves, and Sam quickly accepted her and begged to ride one of Val's horses. As the discussion ensued, a moving truck pulled onto the front lawn. David Lund, Val's boyfriend, exited the cab, wearing a worn leather jacket and a Lake Loyal Fire Department ball cap.

"Great to see you again, Jack," he said, smiling.

"You too, Lund. This is my husband, Phin."

Lund extended his hand and Phin shook it. Jack wondered, quite inappropriately, if Phin could take him in a fight. Probably. Even a domesticated bull was still dangerous.

"A pleasure," Lund said.

"Thanks for watching my little girl."

"She's in good hands." Lund knelt down to Sam's level, like it was the most natural thing in the world. "Hey, Sam, my name is David. Did you know there are bears out here?"

Sam's eyes got wide and she shook her head.

"Just a second. I'll show you." He reached into the truck cab and pulled out the largest teddy bear Val had ever seen. It was practically Sam's size and wore a red checked bow around its neck. "This bear is for you. What should its name be?"

"Harry."

"Because he has so much hair?"

"Because he looks like dickhead."

Lund raised an eyebrow. "Did she say *dickhead*?"

"That's her name for Harry. I may have used it a few times around the house, and it stuck." I squinted at the toy. "You know, the bear does sort of look like McGlade."

Val raised an eyebrow at the bear, then asked, "So, do you have all the rules written down?"

"Rules?"

"You know. Food. Bedtime. Baths. Allergies. All the stuff I need to know."

I shrugged. "She's highly flammable, so keep her away from open flames."

"Huh?"

"And don't give her any helium," Phin said. "She might float away."

"No helium," Lund was pretending to jot it down. "Check."

I patted Val's shoulder, as she looked confused. "Seriously, Val. Just ask Sam what she needs. It's not like children are so fragile they'll break from the smallest thing."

"I knew that."

"Do you guys want to come in for coffee?" Lund asked.

"Sure. Come in," Val added. "I'll throw on a pot. Shouldn't take long."

I shook my head. "We've got to get going. Got a lot of hours ahead of us."

"Whereabouts you going?" Lund asked.

"Spoonward. Near the Minnesota border."

"Way up in the woods. Beautiful country. But be careful. Hunting season just started. A lot of jackasses out there shooting anything that looks like a deer. And after a few beers, everything looks like a deer." He cocked his head. "You hear that?"

Rifle fire, less than a few miles away.

"That means no antler hat, young lady," Phin said, giving Sam a tickle. "Promise me."

"I promise, Daddy. No taddle hat."

Phin gave her a hug and told her he loved her. "Bye, sweetie. Be good for Val and David."

"I will. Love you, daddy."

"Val," Phin nodded at her. "Lund." They shook hands again. Then he walked back to the car.

"She'll be fine," Val said.

"I know. That's not who I'm worried about." I glanced back at Phin.

"That'll work out."

Lund picked up Sam and Sam's little suitcase. "How about we go inside and I show you our house?" he asked as he took her inside.

I watched. I'd been without Sam for short periods since I brought her home. But this was the first time I was trusting her with people other than Phin or my mother.

For some reason, Val looked as anxious as I felt. I wondered if it had to do with Lund.

"You having doubts, too?" I asked.

"Maybe there are always doubts."

"Maybe. That would kinda suck."

Val laughed. "Yeah, it would. Go work your stuff out, Jack. You'll do the right thing."

"So will you. And thanks for the favor."

"My pleasure. God knows you've always been there for me."

"I don't know what cell reception will be like up there, but I'll get into town and call every day. Either we'll pick her up on Wednesday," I exhaled. "Or I'll pick her up on Wednesday."

Without my husband.

SERGEANT HERB BENEDICT

Herb was an old school living dead fan, going back to the genre's creation by filmmaker George A. Romero. He saw *Night of the Living Dead* at a drive-in when he was a kid. Also saw the theatrical releases of *Dawn of*, *Day of*, and *Return of*, and dozens of Italian rip offs. He never told anyone, not his best friend Jack, not his wife Bernice, but he once went to a DragonCon cosplaying Ed from *Shaun of the Dead*.

Well, not really. But he'd considered it.

When *The Walking Dead* came on the air, in all of its gory glory, Herb was in fanboy heaven. Maybe it was the fact that, as a Homicide Sergeant, he had to deal with real death all the time, so the harmless make-believe of the living dead was a welcome stress reliever. Or maybe there was something inherently cool about being outnumbered and surrounded by a group of blood-crazed monsters while fighting to survive.

Whatever the case, Herb was hooked. So he burned one vacation week per year binge watching zombies.

Which was why his phone was off.

Which was why he didn't get the message that Terrence Wycleaf Johnson, known on the street as T-Nail, had escaped from a maximum security prison last night.

Which was why he didn't warn his best friend, Jack Daniels, that hell was coming for her.

PHIN

Expressway.

No scenery to speak of. Nothing to look at.

Just miles and miles of road, of other cars, of occasional billboards.

Jack hadn't said anything since Val's. She was either lost in thought, or bored with him.

Or both.

Sensing the music was irritating her, Phin turned it off. Instead he listened to the white noise of the engine, the purr of traffic as it passed. Counted the road signs pointing to McDonalds, which seemed to be at every exit. Lost count after eight.

Checked the GPS. Still two hundred miles to go.

Two hundred more miles of uncomfortable silence.

He considered the coke in his pocket.

Checked the gas gauge.

They'll need to fill up soon.

Went back to counting road signs.

• • •

The memory, more than two years old, settled over him like a shroud as he drove.

Phin had seen the box in her hand. Had seen the engagement ring he'd bought her. The one she'd rejected earlier. He had asked, she had refused, and Phin had thought that was the end of it.

But it wasn't.

She had told him, "I need you to drive me someplace."

He'd raised an eyebrow. "Where?"

"City Hall. If we get the marriage license today, we can be married by tomorrow."

Phin wasn't sure he'd ever known true happiness. But in that moment he did. It made him feel both heavy and light at the same time. Like he was more than he'd ever been.

"I'll go put Samantha in her carrier."

"Wait. First, I need you to put this on me." Jack had held out her left hand. "Please."

Phin had gone to her. Considered getting down on one knee, but decided he wanted to be face-to-face. Eye-to-eye. Close enough to smell her breath, to memorize every curve and line of her face, to take a mental picture he knew he'd always carry with him.

"Jacqueline Daniels, will you make me the happiest person on the planet?"

"No," she had said.

"No?"

"I'll marry you, Phineas Troutt. But it won't make you the happiest person on the planet." Her eyes had begun to tear up. "You'll have to settle for second happiest."

Phin had settled for it. Slipped the ring on her finger. Kissed her like it was the first time and the last time.

He knew they'd be together forever. Knew it more than he'd ever known anything.

True happiness. What a lucky son of a bitch I am.

• • •

"What happened to us?" he asked.

Jack didn't answer. Didn't look at him.

"If we're done, tell me," he said. "I'll move out. Give you a no-fault divorce. I'm not going to take Sam away from her mother. I'll see her on weekends."

The words hurt, deeply, but he kept his voice steady.

The sights of autumn all around them. Stubbled fields, with copses of leafless trees, cotton clouds pinned to blue sky everywhere. A mile passed. Two.

"I don't know what it is," Jack finally answered.

"I've been patient."

"I know."

"What are you feeling?"

"I don't know."

"Do you still love me?"

She finally looked at him. Her eyes were sad.

"I don't know."

• • •

Phin whistled that Helen Reddy song he knew Jack didn't like. *You and Me Against the World.*

Jack ignored him.

He did it louder, watching her peripherally.

She gave him her shoulder.

After a few bars, Phin gave up.

• • •

Phin thought about the cocaine again.

Jack wouldn't try it. Ever. She hadn't even gotten drunk since Sam was born.

Her depression might have been chemical. But she refused to try chemistry to correct it. Never brought it up during routine doctor visits. Never sought therapy. Never discussed it.

She was a shell that used to be Jack. Or a robot impersonator, who used up all of her energy being a mother, with none leftover for anything personal.

Phin had stayed the course. He loved Jack, and Sam. He liked being a dad, and was good at it. He was lonely, but he'd been lonely before meeting Jack, so it was a state he understood.

He couldn't fix Jack.

Jack had to fix Jack.

But Phin was beginning to think that maybe she never would.

• • •

This was the wilderness. Real wilderness. Evergreen trees so dense they blotted out the sky, home to wild turkey and mule deer and cougar and bear.

The unpaved private road they'd taken was overgrown with weeds, unpaved and rough enough that four wheel drive was needed. They bounced and jolted for half a mile, going no faster than ten miles an hour, before reaching McGlade's cabin just off of Lake Niboowin.

At first, Phin didn't see it. The woods were dark, the house was brown and made of logs, blending almost seamlessly into the surrounding foliage. But his eyes caught the straight lines and right angles and it seemed to suddenly appear, like an image in one of those Magic Eye posters from the 90s. A ranch, a big one, rough-hewn log walls, no windows at all, peeling brown paint on the front door and garage door, no driveway, the grounds overgrown. It looked old, abandoned, and as unwelcome a cabin as Phin could imagine.

"Yuck," Jack said, breaking a two hour silence.

"Maybe the inside is better."

"Does Spoonward have any motels?"

They'd passed the town twenty minutes ago, and he hadn't seen any. But in fairness, it had only taken a few seconds to drive by. There probably wasn't much to see in a town of five hundred. Phin recalled a library, a bait shop, a small police station, and a sign for Walmart.

"Probably," he said, erring on the side of optimism.

He parked, turned off the engine, and they got out. The air smelled fresh. Not the floral kind of fresh that companies bottled to spray on clothes or in rooms, but fresh like unspoiled nature. Cool and clean with notes of pine and lake.

On top of the house, stretching above the tree line, was a huge wind turbine on a steel tower, spinning silently in the breeze.

Dead leaves and fir branches crunched underfoot as he walked to the front door. Phin examined it, and saw stainless steel beneath the peeling paint. The lock and hinges were heavy-duty, and still had some shine to them. This wasn't decrepit; just made to look that way.

He fished McGlade's key from his pocket, and it turned easily in the deadbolt. The door was solid, surprisingly heavy, and as he opened it Phin was hit by a waft of must; that unique smell proving no one had been there in a while. He squinted into the darkness, then felt along the inside wall for a light switch.

It didn't work.

Phin turned to tell Jack the electricity might be out, but didn't see her.

His wife was gone.

That was when he heard the gunshot.

DEL RAY

"Stop here," Del Ray told the driver.

The bus pulled onto the shoulder and rolled to a stop next to a billboard for a Walmart. Del Ray pressed the walkie-talkie app on his cell.

"Team Alpha, go."

He watched through the tinted glass window as his team exited the van that had parked behind him. Each wearing a DayGlo orange vest, the silkscreened *Wisconsin Public Works* logos on the backs made to look faded. One guy went to work with a jackhammer, ripping into the asphalt, while three others set up pylons and *Detour* signs.

Del Ray opened his laptop, using his cell's WiFi hotspot. On Google Maps he checked the only other road leading into Spoonward, and then texted Team Beta.

ETA?

The reply came back within a few seconds.

5 mins.

Del Ray felt T-Nail's eyes on him, from his seat in the rear of the bus. He purposely ignored the cripple; there was no need for scrutiny or lectures when this mission had been planned to the tiniest detail. They were riding with enough ordnance to take over a small country. Two buses, five vans, a dozen cars. Food, water, toiletries, and tents if it took longer than a single day. There was even a back-up plan if it all went to hell.

He texted Kangol, his number one lieutenant, who'd gone on ahead with Team Beta to deal with Spoonward's pig situation.

ON SCHEDULE was the reply.

Then he gave Team Gamma a simple three word text:

START THE BURN.

They had enough combustibles to burn half the state down. And that was the plan; to use a forest fire as a distraction. Throughout history, many great generals used distractions. Not only did it draw attention away from the main goal, but it seriously taxed manpower.

Next he texted Hackqueem, leader of Team Zeta, no doubt the weakest link in this particular chain. It took over a minute for his soldier to respond.

Got delayed. On it.

Del Ray frowned at the response, and considered calling to get more details. But he didn't want to look weak in front of T-Nail, so he let it slide. Best to deal with it later.

Finally, he texted his spotters, who had followed Jack and her husband to the cabin.

Pinned down came the reply.

"Why we stopped?" T-Nail said. Loud enough for the whole bus to hear.

Del chose his next words carefully. He couldn't disrespect a general in front of the men. That would be insubordination, and gave T-Nail instant cause to retaliate. At the same time, these men were actually Del Ray's men. At least they were up until last night when they assisted in T-Nail's jackrabbit parole. Del didn't want to look weak in front of them.

"Move along," he called to the driver. Then he turned to T-Nail. "LTE hot spot connection problems. Works better when we're stopped."

He figured T-Nail didn't know shit about cell phones or signal strength, so it was a subtle way to show the men how much of a dinosaur T-Nail was. Yeah, he was OG. But there was a reason there weren't many original gangstas left; they went extinct.

The bus pulled back onto the highway, and Del Ray and T-Nail stared at each other.

Both refused to blink.

JACK

The sonic boom of rifle fire startled me, and I reflexively ducked. Whoever was shooting, they were close. I heard Phin yell out my name, and then he was sprinting toward me, a .45 in his hand, his face pinched in a grimace.

I held up a palm before he reached me, shaking my head.

"It's okay," I said as he came to a stop in front of me.

Three more gunshots rang out in the west, then another in the east. Phin stared at me like I'd told him two plus two equals eight.

"It's hunting season. Remember?"

His cheeks puffed as he blew out a breath, and he flicked his safety and stuck the 1911 in the waistband of his jeans, against his back.

"Let's check the house out," Phin said.

I crossed my arms. "I want to go home."

"We said we'd give this a try."

"I changed my mind."

Phin's face remained impassive. I felt myself get angry because he didn't get angry. I knew I was acting like a jerk. He knew I was acting like a jerk. But he didn't react to it, which made me want to act like an even bigger jerk. I was aware of it happening, and I couldn't stop myself.

"It's a long drive back," he said, his tone gentle. "Let's spend the night here, we can leave in the morning."

"We're going now."

Why wouldn't he blow up at me? Was he made of stone?

"I know you've been feeling bad," Phin said. "Michigan. Leaving police work. You aren't happy, and you blame yourself. But I don't blame you. You're wounded. I'm sticking around until you heal."

"What if I don't heal?"

"I can't fix you. Only you can. All I can do is be there when you do."

"When did you become so whipped?"

Phin shook his head. "I'm not playing this game, Jack." He turned around.

"That's right. Walk away. Why finish something you started? You weren't even there to see your daughter being born."

When he looked back at me, I saw the steel in his eyes. The Phin I used to know. Ice cold and capable of anything. I knew I'd pressed the right button. That's who I wanted to fight with. Not Mr. Understanding.

"I wasn't there," Phin said, lowering his voice, "because Harry and I were prisoners of a psychopath who took turns torturing us. And that wasn't the first time your past came back to hurt me. The shit I've gone through to be with you—"

"So you're saying I'm not worth it."

"I'm saying that your old job, which is apparently the only thing that ever gave you a sense of self-worth, has hurt everyone you know."

"Maybe you should just leave, Phin. You're not man enough to be with me."

"Man enough? Was Latham man enough? Was Alan? So far I'm the only one who has managed to survive a relationship with you. And my reward for sticking around and staying alive is you acting like a bitch."

"So leave if I'm such a bitch."

Phin stepped closer to me. His jaw clenched, and all that came to my mind was sex. How messed up was that? I was driving away the man I loved, and for some sick reason it was turning me on.

"I'm not going to leave, Jack. Because I'm not going to leave our daughter in the hands of someone so mentally unhinged."

That cooled me off really quick. What might have been a cathartic argument went sour.

"You think I'm an unfit mother? You're a bank robbing coke head, and I'm the bad parent?"

Phin clenched a fist, raised it, and punched a birch tree behind me. There was a *thump*! and yellow leaves fell onto us.

"You used to be a decent person," he said, his tone even as blood dripped from his knuckles. "I know Michigan messed you up. I know these last few years haven't been easy. But you won't get counseling, you won't take meds, and you aren't getting better."

"So leave," I told him through clenched teeth.

"I'm not going to leave."

"But that's what you're good at, isn't it? Life gets hard, drop out. Go rob and steal and whore around and snort shit. That's how you deal with things, remember?"

"Well, maybe if I did leave, I'd have a chance. Because anyone who gets close to you winds up dead."

I blinked.

Shit. He was right.

Maybe I wasn't just pushing him away because I felt bad about myself.

Maybe I was pushing him away to protect him.

I wondered what to say next, but Phin was already storming back toward the house.

An owl hooted.

Gunfire rang out in the distance.

I felt like crying, but I couldn't remember how.

POLICE CHIEF SCHUYLER

John Schuyler frowned at the time. Officer Kinsel was twenty minutes late, and the later it got, the less time he'd have on the lake before sundown. His game fish of choice, the elusive muskellunge, had been biting. Musky would sometimes gorge themselves before the winter freeze, and Schuyler had caught two in the past week. Both were under regulation size. He was hoping to hook one last keeper of the season while it was still warm enough to do so. It had been an Indian summer, no snow yet, and every second Kinsel putzed around was a second Schuyler wasn't throwing out a Suick, trying to entice a lunker to bite.

He tried the radio once more, got static, and spit some Copenhagen chaw juice into an empty Coke can on his desk. His secretary, an ancient woman named Mabel who'd been working there for longer than Schuyler'd been alive, had left an hour ago, and the station was empty and quiet. Tourist season, such as it was, had ended months ago. The rest of the year, their one jail cell remained mostly empty, except for the occasional local DUI. The staties took care of major accidents and highway problems, DNR took care of hunting and fishing, the county took care of anything else that might crop up, and Schuyler and his staff binged on Netflix, and liked it that way. Spoonward was a small, peaceful town where everyone knew everyone, and the last violent crime they'd had was back in 1953 during a particularly harsh winter. Ms. Michele Sewell killed her husband, Robert, with a shotgun while he slept, claiming she couldn't last one more night in a tiny, snowbound cabin with someone who snored like, to quote the murderess, "a chainsaw cutting asphalt." She was committed to an institution, where it is said she lived out the remainder of her life crocheting doilies.

That was Spoonward. Even murder had sort of a homey, feel-good tint to it. So it was of great surprise to Chief Schuyler when three African American youths came into his office wielding firearms.

"I'm sure whatever the problem is, we can work something out," Schuyler told them, hands over his head. They didn't have to disarm him, because he didn't wear a pistol. He wondered if they were drunk or high. He recognized gang colors on their clothes. Probably drove down from Duluth.

"How many cops in this hick town?"

"Three, plus Mabel. She's the secretary."

"Old bitch with glasses?"

"She wears bifocals," Schuyler said. "But she's only sixty. And she's not a bitch."

"Already got her," the guy said. "And that fat one."

"Officer Kinsel?"

"Apparently you don't need to pass a physical to be a pig up here."

"What do you mean you *got* them?"

The youth didn't answer. He looked to be still in his teens, but he had old eyes. Schuyler's brother, Dave, had eyes like that when he'd gotten back from Desert Storm. Dave had seen things, done things, and wound up not being able to live with himself. He ended it all in the garage with the Chevy on and the door closed.

"Where's the last cop?" the kid said. "You said there were three."

Schuyler thought about his other officer, Barbara Knowles. She lived with her disabled brother, who made fishing lures that looked like swimming muskrats.

"It was just three," Schuyler said. "Me, Mabel, and Kinsel. What happened to them?"

The youth nodded, and the other two grabbed Schuyler's arms, holding him steady. Then he reached into his baggy pants and took out a pair of tin snips.

"We gonna see how many fingers you willing to lose before you tell the truth."

It took eight fingers.

"You lasted longer than I thought," the kid said. "I'll tell Officer Knowles you tried."

Then he put a bullet in Schuyler's head.

PHIN

Using the tactical penlight on his keychain, Phin pushed open the ridiculously heavy door and ventured into the dark house, searching for a fuse box. He found the circuit breaker panel on a wall in the kitchen and switched on the power.

Without waiting for Jack, Phin took a tour.

In typical Harry McGlade fashion, the cabin was ridiculous. Though the exterior cleverly imitated the appearance of an old, unused house, the inside was opulent and over-furnished, with technology and security to spare.

Four bedrooms, three and a half baths, each with a urinal.

A sprinkler system to prevent fires.

A stockroom with enough non-perishable food to feed two people for a year.

A video surveillance room, with twelve monitors each serving a dedicated camera, covering the perimeter and every entryway.

A mini infirmary, with a padded examination table and enough drugs and medication for an army regiment.

A pool table, foosball, a Playboy pinball machine, five giant televisions, an extensive Blu-ray library, a beer and wine cellar, a full bar, and a Jacuzzi.

"Take a look at this," Jack said.

Phin followed her voice, and ended up in a room at the end of a hallway. He whistled. Firearms lined every wall, floor to ceiling.

Revolvers, semiautomatics, rifles, shotguns, machine guns, ammo by the crate.

"Is that a flamethrower?" Phin asked. The tank had X15 stenciled on the side.

"Yeah."

"That's legal?"

"Flamethrowers aren't considered firearms, so they aren't regulated. No license or BTFA or NFA permit needed."

"Useful if you want to roast marshmallows from fifty feet away."

"I doubt that was Harry's intention when he bought it."

"And what the hell is that?" Phin pointed to something resembling a shotgun, except it was over three meters long. "That can't be real."

"It's a punt gun," Jack said. "They used them at the turn of the century for hunting ducks. One shot can take out a whole flock."

"What does it fire? Cannon balls?"

"A two gauge shell." Jack pointed her chin at a box of ammo. Phin had originally thought it was a case of antique flashlights, and they looked so old he doubted they'd even still fire. Each shell was a foot long, silver, and wide as a soda can. Phin sometimes wondered if Harry was overcompensating for something.

"Dinner?" he asked.

"I guess."

Phin reached for her hand. She pulled away.

"Jack..."

"Don't."

"This is why we came here. To figure things out."

"I'm tired. Let's eat and watch a movie."

He searched her eyes. "It's like I'm watching you drown, and can't do anything to help."

Jack held his stare. "Then just let me drown."

"You're hurting the woman I love."

"Phin, honestly, I'm not sure the woman you love exists anymore."

"What happened to *you and me against the world*?"

"I never liked that song."

"It's not about the song, Jack. It's about us."

"Let's just eat and talk tomorrow, okay?"

He resisted the urge to touch her again, and said, "Okay. I'll grab some food from storage. I think I can make a decent chili from what I saw in there."

Phin walked off.

Took a hit of cocaine.

Gathered up some dehydrated meat, beans, and assorted cans of tomatoes, onions, celery, a brick of Velveeta, and some corn chips.

Wondered why anyone, even a doomsday prepper stockpiling for some imagined nuclear Armageddon, would buy four hundred cans of Chef Boyardee lasagna. Phin never liked it as a kid; it always reminded him of brains. And what was up with the two cases of ketchup?

Knowing Harry, he probably filled a bathtub with the stuff for some kinky sex thing.

Phin snorted more coke, then went into the kitchen to look for spices, trying and failing to forget about the asshole he'd married.

They ate in silence.

Watched a Sandra Bullock movie on DVD.

Went to bed.

When Jack finally fell asleep around 2A.M., Phin got up and did a line of coke. His nose started to bleed, and he went into the kitchen to look for paper towels. Found several rolls in the cabinet under the sink, next to an old Polaroid camera and a box full of instant snapshots. Phin wiped away some blood, then packed his nose with two strips of paper towels. Against his better judgment he flipped through a few of Harry's photos. As expected, they were sexual in nature. Lots of crazy stuff, including several naked selfies. Phin congratulated himself on his correct assumption; McGlade did buy the punt gun as overcompensation. But at least the dude was getting some.

He left the kitchen and searched through McGlade's extensive collection of adult movies, found something not-too-weird, watched ten minutes and jerked off, thought about playing some pinball but figured it would wake Jack up, sniffed more coke, did a hundred pushups, ate some leftover chili, and set up the table to shoot some nine ball.

After he broke the rack, Jack wandered into the game room. She was wearing one of his old tee-shirts, and looked half asleep.

"I got up to check on Sam," she said.

"Sam's not here." Phin sunk the one ball.

Jack yawned. "How long have you been playing?"

"Just started."

"So, what have you been doing?"

"Ate," Phin said, lining up the two. "Exercised. Watched some porn. Whacked off."

"That all?"

Phin sniffed, wiped his nose to make sure the bleeding had stopped. "That's all. You up for a game?"

"No."

"This used to be our thing."

"I know."

"We used to have fun together."

"I know."

Phin missed the shot, and sank the cue ball. He chalked the stick, and without looking at his wife he said, "I'm trying real hard, Jack. But I'm not liking you very much lately."

"I don't like myself very much lately."

He placed the cue, sunk the two in the corner. "If you aren't going to make an effort, why did you come up here with me?"

"I don't know, Phin. If you don't like me, why are you staying with me?"

"Because I love you."

"I'm... broken. And I don't know if I can be fixed. It's like I've been putting my feelings on hold, and now all the pain and horror of the past has finally caught up with me, and I have nothing left for anyone but my daughter."

"She's our daughter. I'm in this, too."

"How am I supposed to care about you when I don't care about myself?"

"Start small." Phin held out the cue. "Play a game with me."

For a moment, Jack seemed like she was going to accept the offer. There was a hint of it. In her eyes. In her posture. But instead she said, "Your nose is bleeding," and then left the game room.

Phin blew his nose into his tee shirt, snorted more cocaine, missed his next four shots, then broke the cue over his knee in frustration.

He marched into the bedroom.

"I know you're going through some shit. I've gone through some shit, too. And now, you're putting me through more of it. You can't even play a goddamn game of pool? Really, Jack? After all we've been through, that was too much to ask?"

Jack shifted in bed, but didn't respond.

"I'm hiking into town. I'll be staying there until you decide if you want to be a part of this marriage, or if you're so far gone you're willing to throw it all away."

Jack remained quiet.

"I'm leaving. Don't you have anything to say?"

Phin listened to her breathe. After several long seconds she whispered, "I didn't mean to hurt you."

"You didn't," Phin said. "The woman I fell in love with left me over a year ago. And she didn't fight hard enough to come back."

Phin found his jacket, pocketed his cell phone, and left the house, heading toward Spoonward. He walked to the main road, saw a sign for a motel eight miles north, took another bump of coke, wiped the tears off his cheeks, spat on the ground, and went to find a room for the night.

He'd left in such a rush of bad feelings and cocaine impulsivity, he'd forgotten to take his .45 with him.

T-NAIL

Spoonward was his.

The two roads leading in and out of town were covered. Law enforcement had been removed. They had formed a wide perimeter around the cop's cabin, watching her with night optics, planning the final details.

At 4 A.M., T-Nail had been ready to give the attack order. Then the cop's husband, Phineas, walked out the front door.

`Should we take him down?` Del Ray texted.

T-Nail despised texting. He was willing to admit he'd fallen behind, technology-wise, while in the slam. But the amount of time these kids spent on their mobile devices was infuriating. T-Nail believed he could single-handedly murder half of his team before any of them looked up from their cell phones to see what was going on.

Still, texting was silent. They were out in the sticks, no one around for miles, but ringing phones and talking could alert the enemy of their presence. So as much as he loathed it, T-Nail texted a reply.

`No. Follow him.`

Del Ray's response came so quickly, T-Nail wondered if he'd already written it and was just waiting to press SEND. `Do we take the cop?`

T-Nail glared into the darkness. He wasn't sure where Del Ray was, but the General was overstepping his boundaries. T-Nail alone would give the order, and no one was to question him. Had

Del asked that question while in the same room, T-Nail would have broken his nose.

`We wait to see where the man goes.` T-Nail texted, his fingers too big for the touch screen, hating how long it took to make sure there were no typos.

`Got a team on him. We're waiting on your signal.`

Insubordinate moron. Of course they were waiting on his signal.

T-Nail took a deep breath. The air had an unfamiliar taste. He missed the smells of Chicago; car exhaust and Lake Michigan and garbage in alleys. Gunpowder. Crack smoke. The sour, oily scent of the El train when it passed. Wisconsin smelled wrong. Too clean. Too foreign.

Pressing the button on his chair, he extended himself to a standing position. The men around him cast surreptitious glances, trying not to stare. He moved forward, his wheels easily navigating the forest floor, crunching over pine needles and rocks and dead branches. T-Nail stopped when he had a clear line of sight on the cop's house. He raised up his night vision goggles and zoomed in.

The house was still

He switched to thermal. It didn't work as well as Del Ray had boasted. But he eventually found a small, pink line in the eastern corner of the house.

Jacqueline Daniels, lying in bed.

It had been twenty years since he'd last seen her. A long time. She'd be an old lady now.

That made T-Nail an old man. An old man, about to settle an old score.

For two decades, she'd been allowed to live her life, while he'd been denied living his. Free to go where she wanted. Do what she wanted. Eat what she wanted. Fuck who she wanted.

Walk where she wanted.

Enjoy your legs, cop. They're going to be one of the first things I take from you.

But they won't be the last.

How much suffering could T-Nail inflict on Jacqueline and her family to make up for all he'd gone through?

T-Nail had no idea.

But he was anxious to find out.

DEL RAY

His thumbs were a blur on his touch screen.

He went into town.

Del waited for T-Nail's response.

Waste him.

Del Ray texted the team that followed the husband, giving them the go ahead.

And the cop? he texted back to T-Nail.

Kill the signal. We take her. Now.

JACK

The phone woke me up.

Phin wasn't in bed next to me, so I grabbed my cell, hoping to see his name come up. But instead of Phin, it was Tom Mankowski, a detective at the 26th who used to work for me. I blinked at the time. 7:16 A.M.

An emergency?

"This is Jack."

"Loot, sorry to call you so early. It's Tom Mankowski."

"I'm not a lieutenant anymore, Tom. What's up?"

"I just found out about it, and haven't been able to get in touch with Sergeant Benedict. Did he call you already?"

"Herb's on a staycation. He turned his phone off. Found out about what?"

"Last night, Terrence Wycleaf Johnson escaped from prison."

That was a name I hadn't heard in a long time. "T-Nail."

"Two guards and three paramedics are missing."

"What happened?"

Tom ran it down for me.

"Sounds like he had help. Has the ambulance been found?"

"No."

A chill ran over me as the paranoia took root. I'd been so worried about being visited by Luther Kite, I hadn't given much thought to other monsters from my past who might come calling. T-Nail was a very bad man. No conscience, no boundaries, as ruthless as a person could get. But unlike the other serial killers I'd dealt with in my former job, T-Nail was also a chief member of one of the largest gangs in the country. If he wanted to make a play for me or my family, he'd have unlimited resources.

"Have you talked to anyone in the gang unit? Are they making a move?"

"I just heard about it on the blotter, immediately called. Want me to send a car over?"

"No need. We're up north. Harry's got a place near a lake. I'm pretty sure we're okay. T-Nail never even learned my name. I testified undercover."

"Where are you? Wait, don't tell me. I'm working a case, and electronic security is a lot less secure than I had thought."

"The Snipper?" I asked. I'd been following the case in the papers.

"Yeah. Got me and my partner running in circles. Don't know if you've heard, but there's been a second murder."

"Describe the scene," I said.

Tom ran through the highlights. Or, more accurately, the low points.

"It sounds like a sex crime," I said.

"No semen. No evidence of rape."

"Were her breasts mutilated like her mouth and vagina?"

"No. Untouched. Like the last one."

"Was the bra left on?"

"Yeah."

I thought it over. "Men sexualize the female breast. Unusual that the killer left hers alone."

"Are you thinking the perp might be a woman?"

"I'm thinking that even though it looks like a sex crime, the killer may have an agenda that isn't sexual. Have you run a ViCAT report on the vic's name? You can also run an alert to inform you automatically if anyone inputs new data. It's likely the killer is looking for a new victim. If the pattern is followed, there will be harassment first. Maybe you'll catch a break."

"Good idea. You have a second to spitball?"

"Sure." This was a lot easier than talking about relationships.

Tom gave me his theory on who the killer might be. I admired his insights. Tom was a good cop.

"Identity is more than how we view ourselves," I added. "It also colors how we view others. We're pack animals. We tend to want to be around people like us."

"And what if we can't find anyone like us?"

"Then we try to change them so they are."

It felt good to be talking shop, but when I spoke those last words, I realized the obvious.

That was what I'd been doing to Phin. I was unhappy, so I was trying to make him unhappy. By pushing him away, proving I was unworthy of his love, I could justify rejecting myself.

Maybe I had Post Traumatic Stress Disorder. Or postpartum depression. Or a midlife crisis, exacerbated by a new baby and a drastic job change.

Maybe I had all that, and even more.

But making Phin hate me wasn't the way to deal with it. I should have been doing the opposite.

If I just stopped fighting and let him love me, maybe I could learn to love myself again.

I needed to call Phin. To apologize. To beg him to forgive me.

I just hoped it wasn't too late.

"Tom, I gotta run. Thanks for the call."

I waited for a response, but didn't get one.

"Tom? You there?"

I looked at my cell, saw the call had ended. Did Tom hang up? Had the call been dropped?

I dialed Phin.

Nothing happened. I squinted, looking closer at the screen.

No Service.

Getting up from bed, I began to walk around, holding my phone in front of me like Diogenes, searching for a signal.

No matter where I walked, bars refused to appear.

Then I heard a beeping. A beeping that wasn't coming from my cell.

It was coming from the control room, where Harry had all of his security and surveillance equipment. I jogged over to it, going inside, focusing on the glowing monitors.

I counted thirty armed men, with guns, moving toward the house. Harry's cameras were hi-definition, and in the dawn's early light I could see the colors they wore.

Purple. Orange. Green. Caps and bandanas tilting right.

Eternal Black C-Notes.

T-Nail had found me. And he'd brought an army.

Fear squeezed me all at once, making it hard to breathe. But my first concern wasn't for my safety. My first concern was Phin. Why had I let him leave? Did they have him?

Was he already dead?

I checked my cell phone again. Still no service. I'd had some experience with cell phone jamming before, and I knew I was being shut out. And Harry, in his infinite wisdom to keep his secret hideout a secret, didn't have a land line or Internet access. There was no way I could contact my husband.

But Phin was a badass. Except for an old mob guy named Tequila, and a spy named Chandler, Phin was the toughest person I knew. He wouldn't go down easily.

I pushed him out of my mind, convincing myself he was fine until I learned otherwise.

Then I pushed the fear deep down and went to go arm myself.

I knew what T-Nail wanted.

He wanted me.

And he wasn't getting me without a fight.

PHIN

It had taken him two hours to get to town, and less than five minutes to walk through it. Spoonward's Main Street could have fit neatly inside of Soldier Field. It consisted of a bait shop, a tiny police department, a library, a diner, a gas station, a post office, and a tiny building only open Tuesdays and Thursdays that housed a lawyer, two doctors, and a dentist.

Phin attempted to use his cell map to find a motel, but couldn't get a signal for the GPS. So he followed a road sign to the twenty-four hour Walmart, hoping it would have a payphone.

His immediate not-very-profound thought was why the hell did this small town need a Walmart? Maybe it was one of those cases you read about where a Walmart came in and drove all the mom and pop stores out of business, making it the only place left to shop. Phin admitted some surprise when he approached the parking lot, which held close to a dozen cars. Some had to be staff, but even a few customers at five in the morning in a town this tiny suggested that maybe Sam Walton was onto something.

Upon entering the first set of doors, Phin saw a soda machine, a Redbox for movie rentals, and one of those claw games where you wasted fifty cents to try to grab a stuffed animal worth a quarter.

No pay phones.

Apparently the universe didn't want him to find a motel.

Phin didn't believe in fate. He rejected destiny the same way he rejected religion; it was baseless superstition with no empirical proof. But for some reason he was penetrated by the fear that something terrible was about to happen to Jack.

Something that would be his fault. Because he'd walked out on her.

Phin quickly wrangled the feeling, trying to make sense of it. Which was easy to do.

This wasn't some ungrounded premonition.

It was guilt.

Since leaving Harry's cabin, all during his long walk on dark, empty roads, Phin had been hating himself and his actions. He'd allowed his temper to get the better of him.

No, that was actually a lie. Phin had been angry with Jack for months. He'd always managed to maintain his cool.

The problem wasn't anger. The problem was cocaine.

He'd reached for it out of unhappiness, and it gave him the false bravado to leave the woman he loved, when she needed him most.

Yes, Jack was broken. And maybe she'd never be fixed.

But he was the King of the Assholes for giving up on her. She might have had a few personal issues making her tough to deal with sometimes, but Phin had more than a few issues; he had a lifetime subscription to the Bad News Gazette. His life was a photo essay of bad decisions and sketchy actions. But Jack still loved him. Trusted him. Stood by him. Had a baby with him.

And he'd gotten high and walked out on her.

Why? Because she'd been distant? Because their sex life had dried up? Because she wasn't the Jack he used to know?

Sure, all of that was true. But it was easy to love someone when everything was going right.

A strong relationship, the kind Phin wanted, meant still loving someone when everything went wrong.

He needed to tell this to her. To apologize. To beg forgiveness. Jack hadn't been the same since Sam was born. But as long as Jack would have him, Phin would support her and be there for her and love her.

Phin dug the vial of coke out of his pocket, dropped it in the nearest garbage.

I'm going to be the man Jack married.

I'm going home.

He turned back toward the parking lot, and was so into his own thoughts he failed to immediately notice the seven armed men converging on the front door. Five black guys, one white, one Latino, each of them with bandanas up over their faces and automatic weapons in their hands.

A robbery?

Then the nearest raised his gun and fired at Phin from twenty meters away.

Before the shot went off, Phin was diving and rolling into the store, coming up on his feet, sprinting down the grocery aisle. As he ran, he reflexively reached behind him for a pistol he'd forgotten back at the cabin.

It was, in a way, pretty funny. Phin didn't have a concealed carry permit, or even a firearm owner's ID, but he always kept a weapon on him when he went out, on the off chance he ran into trouble. And when it finally did happen, when the secret wet dream of every guy with an NRA bumper sticker came true and an armed assailant opened fire in a public place, Phin had been too pissed off and coked up to remember to bring his gun.

Fail.

More shots from behind him, and Phin cut left and almost ran over a confused-looking teen girl wearing too much eye makeup and a stud in each nostril. In her hand was—predictably—eye shadow.

"What's going on?" Her eyes were wide with obvious fright.

"Robbery. Seven men with guns. You need to hide."

Phin tried to get around her, but she latched onto his wrist.

"Help me. Please."

Phin pulled free, but the teenager was right on his heels, following him through the toy aisle. He searched the overhead signs, looking for sporting goods. Someone in the front of the store yelled, "Don't! Please don—" and was cut off by a gunshot.

Had they killed him?

That didn't make sense.

During his stretch as a criminal, Phin had robbed a fair number of people. Most of them were drug dealers. For those robberies, Phin had been armed, because his targets had been armed. It was risky, from a life-threatening standpoint, but safe when it came to getting arrested. Those crimes were never reported. There was zero chance a pusher would complain to the cops, demanding they find the man who stole all their smack. But there were a few times when Phin had been desperate enough to rob a bank—something he did via the drive-through window with road flares and a digital clock rigged to look like a dynamite time bomb. He'd never been armed for those crimes. Armed robbery tended to make the police keener to find the suspect. Murder trumped even that. If you wanted a guarantee to be hunted by the authorities forever, killing someone was the way to go.

If this was just a robbery, no thief with half a brain would start shooting people. That was the zenith of stupid.

If this was just a robbery.

But what if it wasn't?

The assailants all dressed like gangbangers. Phin had been an equal opportunity jacker, and had made enemies of many gangs of every possible affiliation. These were wearing Folk Nation colors.

Were they here for him? Could they have found him and tracked him to Wisconsin?

What if this was a hit?

Movement, ahead and to the left, and then Phin saw a red laser dot glowing on the floor just a meter ahead of him. Phin skidded to a stop and ducked behind a display of Star Wars T-shirts just as a gang member turned down the aisle. Phin got under the metal clothing rack and shoved, hard, upending it onto the man, blanketing him with XL droids and Wookies.

The *TD-TD-TD-TD-TD!* of submachine gunfire shredded the shirts, rounds pinging into the ceiling, and Phin backpedaled, the girl grabbing onto his belt and getting tugged along like a caboose.

I need a weapon.

Phin's everyday carry—other than the 1911 he'd left at the cabin—consisted of an Emerson Kershaw folding knife with a three-and-a-half inch tanto blade, an Olight flash that put out twelve hundred lumens, a Zippo, a tactical pen with a glass breaker and hidden handcuff key, and a Bowen belt knife. All useful items with varied self-defense applications. But they meant getting up close. Pointy hand-to-hand weapons weren't too helpful against Scorpion submachine guns that could fire nine hundred rounds per minute.

But this was a Walmart in Wisconsin. There was a good likelihood it carried ranged firearms. A rifle or shotgun would make things a little more even. Phin scanned the overhead signs, searching for the Sporting Goods aisle.

That's when the girl he was lugging along tripped.

She didn't let go of his belt and almost brought him down, falling to her knees.

Then she began to bawl.

Loudly.

Phin took a quick three-sixty look around, spotted a dressing room in the middle of the store. Bad hiding place; it was too obvious, only had one entry point, and provided zero cover. But next to it, attached to a column, was something useful.

He helped the girl up and pulled her to the dressing room area, then released her wrist and unbuckled the fire extinguisher from the column. Phin pulled the pin, yanked the scrunchie from her ponytail, and quickly sprayed CO_2 around them. Big white clouds billowed up to shoulder height, and he led the teen toward the back of the store, covering their movements with clouds of gas. Then he stretched the hair fastener around the handle of the extinguisher to keep it squeezed, and threw it as far as he could.

In the Electronics section, Phin saw an employee cowering behind the register. An older woman, chubby, her hands covering her head as if the roof was coming down.

"Does this store sell rifles?" Phin whispered.

She didn't move, and her eyes had a faraway look.

More shooting, from where he'd thrown the fire extinguisher. At least two guns, possibly three. He couldn't see them, but they weren't far.

He glanced around, hoping to spot a fire exit, and his eyes settled on an oversized cardboard Blu-ray display of Matt Dillon, from some show called *Wayward Pines*. Phin ushered the teenager behind the counter, next to the employee, and covered them with the cardboard, putting it over their heads like a lean-to. It muffled the girl's sobbing a little, but anyone walking by would hear it and discover them.

Matt Dillon couldn't save those people. Phin couldn't, either. But they weren't his responsibility.

"Sporting goods is that way," the employee said, poking her hand out from under the cardboard and pointing. Then she said, "Please. Save us."

He tried the phone on the counter. Didn't hear a dial tone.

"How do I get an outside line?"

"It's broken."

"Stay hidden. Keep quiet. Maybe they won't find you."

That was all Phin had to offer.

Then he ran, hard, along the back aisle, past DVDs and video games and TVs and camping gear and fishing poles, and reached his destination moments later. The gun case. Phin wasted a few seconds looking at the long arms, then remembered that guns didn't kill people. Bullets did. So he searched for ammunition, figuring he'd pick the weapon based on the rounds stocked.

All he saw were boxes of .22lr.

In Phin's mind, twenty-two long range was plinking ammo; good to practice with because it was small enough to shoot for extended periods without hand fatigue or ringing eardrums, and cheaper than dirt. While one of the most popular calibers, the cartridges were also one of the tiniest, about the length of four Tic-Tacs, and only slightly wider. He'd never used it for defense. When Phin bought .45 ACP ammo, twenty-five rounds of Hornady cost about $25. The fifty round box of .22lr Remington Thunderbolts he stared at was marked $2.79.

He wasted ten precious seconds searching for something larger, failed, and reached for the Thunderbolts, four boxes fitting easily into his front pocket. Then he went back to the rifle case and tried to determine which could hold the most bullets. Phin's experience with .22 long arms was limited, but he knew the four basic types of action. Pump action, like a shotgun. Lever action, like Chuck Connors used on the old TV show *The Rifleman*. Bolt action, the preference of snipers. And semi-automatic, which spring-fed the next cartridge into the chamber without having to do anything manually.

Phin's eyes settled on a Marlin 795 semi-auto rifle with a ten round magazine. He broke the glass with the pointed handle of his tactical pen, grabbed the firearm, and jogged over to another column to relieve it of its fire extinguisher. After dousing the sporting goods area with a white cloud of CO2, he hunkered down next to some plastic sleds and began to load the magazine. The rifle was small and light, feeling like a child's toy in his hands. He slapped the full mag in, pulled the bolt to load the first round, and squinted into the fog, looking for bad guys.

The fog made them easy to find.

Phin had never understood the point of laser sights on a weapon. If your aim was lousy, you should practice until it wasn't, not rely on a dot. Lasers alerted your target, and also gave away your position. Phin only needed to follow the long red lines cutting through the carbon dioxide, which might as well have been arrows pointing toward his attackers. He raised the rifle, stock tight against his shoulder, aiming at the nearest. Then he paused.

Phin had spent the last two years raising a child, and that tended to soften the edges of even the hardest man. Bringing a life into the world, knowing all that went into doing so, made ending a life harder. Killing wasn't ever easy. Even in a kill-or-be-killed scenario. Phin had been avoiding violence for so long, he wasn't sure he still had it in him.

The gangbanger was about fifty meters away. Straight line of sight.

Phin thought about Samantha.

He wanted to see her again.

He *needed* to see her again.

He fired twice.

The Marlin had almost no recoil, and the gunshots were about as loud as hand claps. Phin hadn't been able to clearly see his target, but his guess where the man's head was at proved correct when the guy dropped his gun and it stayed dropped.

One down, at least five to go.

Phin watched the red beams, but they were choppy and kept disappearing. Merchandise was in the way. He stayed low and moved to another, larger aisle, getting on one knee and waiting for the next target to round the corner. But instead of proceeding, the guy backtracked, taking off in a jog. Phin took a millisecond before deciding to pursue, running with his head down, heading for the long lane and a straight shot. He fell to his knees, sliding across the tile floor, smoothly aligning the sights and double-tapping at the retreating figure.

This one didn't go down. Instead, he turned and emptied his magazine in Phin's direction. His aim was off, but he exchanged magazines within a few seconds, and Phin stared down the metal sights of the Marlin long enough to see he was wearing a flak jacket.

A high powered rifle, with the right ammo, could possibly penetrate body armor.

A .22 rifle could not.

Phin adjusted his aim, concentrating on keeping the gun steady, noticing in an almost detached way as his opponent's laser sight streaked up the floor and raced toward him. Just as the red dot reached Phin's feet, Phin exhaled and squeezed the trigger.

For a tiny little bullet, the .22lr did a good job of tearing out the man's throat.

Society now had one less problem to deal with. Phin still had four.

He stood, searching for more red lights, and heard screams. Two female screams, coming from the electronics department.

Phin reminded himself they weren't his responsibility. Jack and Samantha were. He owed those strangers nothing, and owed his family everything. Helping them was risky, and selfish.

"Please don't hurt me!"

A slapping sound.

A wail of pain.

Phin pulled his attention away from their problems and stared down the aisle. It was a forty meter sprint to the front doors. One gangbanger was obviously back in Electronics. One was in the grocery aisle on the other side of the store. Phin didn't see the remaining two. But he liked his chances at getting away.

I'm not a hero.

I can easily justify saving my own neck.

I've done some bad things, and I can still live with myself.

If those women die, they die. It isn't on my hands.

I have my family to think of.

He ran for the exit. Hit the door at a full sprint, bouncing through, then the second door and he was in the parking lot, heading for the road. He focused on an image in his mind, an idealized thought of Jack holding Sam, both smiling, urging him to come home to them. The relief he felt getting out of that Walmart was like escaping captivity, and the cool breeze that stung Phin's cheeks was magical.

Then the night spit rapid-fire bullets at him, chewing up the parking lot asphalt to his left. It was coming from behind. Phin dove right, bringing the gun to his chest, skinning the leather off his jacket shoulder, then quickly crawling behind a parked Honda for cover. He chanced a look around the bumper, saw the banger alongside the store, sliding another magazine into his machine gun.

They'd had a seventh man covering the exit. Phin had been stupid; so eager to get away that he hadn't used his head, and the mistake had almost killed him.

He raised the rifle, fired twice, missed both times. The wind was effecting his aim.

More shots, peppering the Honda. Phin hid behind the tire, reloading, considering his options. The man shooting at him didn't look older than twenty. He'd probably never been in a firefight. None of these guys had, hence the need for laser sights. The drive-by/spray-n-pray school of murder banked on the fact that if enough lead was thrown at a target, a few shots would hit home. That worked in the hood against unarmed victims. It didn't work when your opponents also had guns. This moron still hadn't gone for cover, probably thinking his bulletproof vest made him invincible.

Phin stood, sighted left to adjust for the wind, and fired one round per second, using the brick dust pinging off the wall behind the target to help him zero in. On shot number seven, Phin hit the shooter in the nose, and he dropped like a marionette with its strings cut.

Should have gone for cover.

Phin took off again, exiting the parking lot and heading for the road, letting adrenaline power his footfalls.

Being alive, getting away, felt good. Phin knew about the euphoria associated with surviving a near death experience, because he'd lived through a few horrible things. Things that still gave him nightmares. Things that made him even more determined to reunite with his family.

Phin didn't think about the people he'd left behind.

Until he did.

The teenaged girl wearing too much make-up to look older.

The chubby cashier, who was probably grateful Walmart came to town and employed her.

Not my responsibility.

Phin was a survivor. His risk-taking days ended when his cancer went into remission. The surest path to getting through a crisis was to get away from it. As far away as possible. Cemeteries were full of heroes.

I am not a hero.

Jack is the hero of the family.

Jack is the one who puts herself in harm's way to help others.

I am not Jack.

I'm no different than the three men I've just killed.

Phin stopped.

Because that was a lie. He *was* different than the men he'd killed. He had to be. Jack wouldn't have loved him if he wasn't.

Phin didn't lack empathy. He was using his questionable moral compass as an excuse for the real reason he didn't want to try and save those people.

I'm afraid.

Phin had never been truly afraid before. He'd stared down stone cold killers. He'd spat in cancer's face. He'd engaged in behavior that any reasonable person would run from, and hadn't even blinked.

But his life didn't belong to only him. Not anymore. He was part of something bigger.

He was part of a family.

And that was positively terrifying and absolutely amazing.

What makes life worth living is the wonderful fact that we have so much to lose.

Phin wanted to be the man that his wife and daughter deserved.

And that man would never run from people who needed help.

That man would help them.

Phin turned around and stared at the Walmart. The fear was still there, a fist squeezing his stomach.

He told the fear to fuck off. He had people to save.

Phin sprinted to the kid he'd killed, trading the Marlin for a Scorpion submachine gun and two full magazines, and then rushed back inside the store.

A shooter, next to the checkout lanes, raised his weapon.

He was quick.

Phin was quicker. His new Scorpion had select-fire for semi-auto and full auto, with no in-between option for a three round burst like an M-16. So Phin went full, lining up the dot rather than steadying the iron sights, the gun bucking in his hand like a pissed off stray cat, erasing the kid's head in a *poof* of blood and bone faster than it took his heart to lub-dub one last time.

Phin dropped the empty mag, slammed home a fresh one, re-charged the bolt knobs by giving them a slight tug, and wondered if he should reconsider his opinion on laser sights. He ran to the man he'd killed and relieved him of three more mags and his bloody flak jacket. Phin shrugged out of his leather coat, Velcroed the vest into place, then ran toward the Electronics section through the dissipating carbon dioxide gas, wary of red beams. When he got to the counter where the women had been hiding, the Matt Dillon standup was face-down on the floor, and they were gone.

On the floor was a small smear of blood.

Phin held his breath, trying to hear his surroundings above his thumping heart.

There. Somewhere behind him. A girl crying.

He followed the sound, scanning for baddies. There had been six inside, one outside, which left three more.

Phin didn't notice the shooter until he'd been shot six times in the back.

In one of his unluckier moments in life, Phin had been beaten with a baseball bat. It hurt. A lot.

Getting shot while wearing a vest hurt almost as much.

Phin fell onto his face, the wind punched out of him, in so much pain he couldn't tell if the Kevlar had stopped the rounds or not. Agony be damned, he flipped over onto his back, unable to scream in pain because his lungs were empty, and raised his Scorpion to face his shooter, who was rushing his way.

Phin blew out the man's knees, burning through the full mag in less than two seconds.

The gangbanger fell, his gun skittering across the floor in front of him.

Bright motes danced around the edges of Phin's vision because he still couldn't suck in a breath. He ejected the empty magazine and tried to force in a fresh one, but it wasn't fitting correctly.

The banger began to crawl for his dropped gun, dragging his bloody legs behind him.

Phin flopped onto his side, finally able to suck in a breath. It came in a stuttering, agonizing gasp, and Phin still didn't know if he was bleeding and didn't waste time to find out. He continued to struggle with the mag until he realized he was trying to jam it in backwards.

The banger reached his Scorpion, raising it up.

Phin aligned the mag properly, released the bolt knob, and fired at the same time his opponent did.

The gangbanger took the rounds in the face.

Phin took them in the chest.

Everything went bright, then dark, then bright again, and Phin found himself on his back, staring at the ceiling. Then the pain came. Full body pain, like he'd been thrown into the back of a cement mixer with a pallet of bricks. Without lifting his head, he gently ran his hands over his torso and then checked his fingers for blood.

Incredibly, there was none. It didn't feel like it, but the vest had stopped every bullet. He turned his head and spat. No blood there, either. Maybe he'd actually survive.

Another scream, from the back of the store. Phin rolled over with a wince, got to his feet with a groan, and then picked up the nearest Scorpion. He charged a new mag and headed toward the sound, coming to an abrupt stop in the Automotive section. It took Phin a moment to wrap his head around what he saw.

The older cashier was on the floor, her jaw open and crooked, blood leaking out of the gaps where teeth used to be.

The girl sat next to her, her eyes streaked with black make-up.

The two remaining gangbangers were taking off their pants.

Phin didn't announce himself. He didn't give them any chance at all to surrender.

He just shot both of them in the backs of their heads, execution style.

They dropped, and he went to the women. In shock, but alive. He asked for their phones, got no response, and went through the girl's purse. No signal on her cell phone, but she had keys to a Chevy.

Next, Phin patted down the dead gangbangers. He found two cell phones. Again, no bars. A back-up SIG Sauer P238 in .380. Three full Scorpion magazines. A Krieger switchblade. A set of brass knuckles. Cigs, weed, rubbers. As he searched them, he asked the women about the law in town, why the cops hadn't shown up yet.

They clung to each other, not answering.

Phin helped them up. They needed a hospital. He could drop them off using the girl's Chevy, then borrow it to get back to Jack.

They moved slowly through the aisles, like a broken, six-legged animal, moaning and hobbling.

Phin came across three more dead employees, and another dead gangbanger, one he'd shot earlier. He picked up one more magazine for the submachine gun and another cell, no signal.

Maybe it was a coincidence that nobody's phone worked. Maybe this part of the country was one of the few dead spots left when it came to cell coverage.

But Harry had told them the town had coverage. Which made Phin wonder.

Was someone preventing calls? Is that why the police hadn't stormed in yet?

Phin knew about cell phone jammers. He'd dealt with a situation like that once before. Is that what was—

The girl holding Phin's shoulder squeezed, hard. He turned to look, saw the terror on her face as she stared off into the distance, just before the bullets stitched up her body and jerked her head back.

She fell, and Phin raised the Scorpion, looking around for the shooter, and spotted him just as the red dot caught Phin in his right eye. Before he could duck, the man's weapon sprayed.

But Phin wasn't hit. At that very moment, the panicked cashier ran directly into the line of fire. Her body spun—a full pirouette that almost seemed graceful except for the ribbons of blood spraying everywhere—and when she fell Phin dropped to one knee and cut down the shooter, taking off part of his head.

Phin did a quick scan around for more assailants, didn't see any, and turned his attention to the girl.

She was still.

CPR wasn't an option.

Phin checked on the cashier. There would be no life-saving measures there, either.

He looked at his own hands, which were shaking and spattered with blood that wasn't his, and a clipped sound came out of him that almost sounded like a dog whimpering. Phin sucked in a stuttering breath, blew it out through clenched teeth, and took a moment to center himself, because he knew if he tried to walk his legs would give out. When he managed to regain control, he knelt down and gently closed the girl's make-up streaked eyes.

Still no police. No paramedics. No ambulances. No National Guard, or Army, or Coast Guard, or Foreign Legion. No one to help.

Phin was all alone.

He wandered up to the eighth man, wondering how he'd missed him. It didn't matter. Phin had counted wrong, and people had died. Nothing he could do about it now. Phin checked the gangbanger's cell, saw no signal, and almost tossed it away when he noticed it had a text message on it. Phin read the exchange and felt his whole body get very cold.

He went into town.

Waste him.

And the cop?

Kill the signal. We take her. Now.

Phin scrolled up to a picture. It was of him, Jack, and Samantha at the house, getting into their SUV that morning, before they left for Wisconsin.

Phin didn't stop to think.

He ran.

JACK

The manual for the X15 flamethrower was surprisingly thin, and on a whim I leafed through it. McGlade apparently hadn't read the instructions, because he wasn't supposed to leave the tank full of gas or pressurized with CO_2, yet he'd done both. I'd never fired a flamethrower, and knew I never would, so I set it aside and began to load a duffle bag with other things.

I took the bag back to the control room, sorting through weapons while watching the security monitors. The house was surrounded—at least three dozen men—but no one had attempted a breach yet. I found a volume knob and turned it up, listening to ambient forest noise mixed with voices too far away to make out.

I loaded a twelve gauge Mossberg 590, which conveniently had a bandolier sling already containing shells. That's when I saw T-Nail.

At first, I was surprised because he appeared to be walking, and last I'd heard he'd been paralyzed from the waist down. Then I noticed he was strapped to some sort of upright motorized wheelchair. I fiddled with the control panel, and was able to use a joystick to zoom in on his face.

He'd gotten old.

But then, so had I.

He still had that same look in his eyes. They were just as intense as the last time I'd seen them, in court over two decades ago. Prison apparently hadn't reformed him.

I put on a nylon fanny pack with a full hundred-count box of .38 ammo. I also added a retractable asp baton, a set of brass knuckles, and a Kimber pepper spray gun. The pack was heavy, but my hips were wide enough to keep it from falling down.

Thank you, Samantha.

One eye on the monitors, I noticed T-Nail wasn't the one giving orders. I zeroed in on a younger, slighter man wearing a fur vest who seemed to be running the show.

Interesting. I wondered how T-Nail felt about that. Locked up for decades, taking direction from some kid half his age.

I buckled on an ankle holster that held a subcompact Hellcat 389, and pulled my jeans down over it. On my other ankle I Velcroed a six inch Buck knife. Harry had ample rifles to choose from in his armory, and I'd gone with a Bushmaster Predator with a Nightforce NXS scope. Five extra mags, thirty rounds each, went into a backpack. Finally, I strapped on my shoulder holster, with my Colt Detective Special. Even over the Kevlar, it felt like old times.

When I stood up, in full gear, I weighed thirty pounds more.

A tiny part of my brain wondered if this was what I'd wanted. It seems, for the past two years, I'd been waiting for death to come calling. Now it finally had.

I wasn't good at waiting.

But I hated fighting even more.

The chili I'd eaten last night seemed to be alive in my stomach, sour and angry and looking for a way out. My palms were wet, my throat too dry to swallow, and I'd begun to breathe through my mouth in what could only be called a pant. Not seeing Sam again, not seeing Phin again, had gone from an abstract, intangible worry to a real thing that I had to immediately deal with. And I had no idea how it would pan out.

McGlade had built a fortress. But T-Nail had brought an army.

And I stared at the monitors as the army began its attack.

Their first act was taking away my vehicle. Or rather, they slashed the tires, smashed the windows, and set it on fire.

Then they attacked the front door. It began with kicks, followed by shoulder smashes. When that didn't produce results, they tried a handheld battering ram. I could hear the blows through the monitor speakers, but when I turned down the volume I couldn't hear anything inside the house. They were swinging the heavy hunk of metal with some serious, but McGlade's door was so thick it was practically sound-proof.

It also seemed to be bulletproof. I watched, half-amazed, as a gangbanger approached with a 9mm handgun and emptied the magazine.

The door held.

The next guy swaggered over with a large revolver—looked to be a .357 Magnum.

Six shots, and the door held. The paint had been chewed off, but the steel beneath didn't even appear to be dimpled.

The next contestant, who was white (it was a small reassurance to know that the C-Notes had embraced racial equality), had a shotgun, and he unloaded on the door. When it didn't make more than a dent, he was so irritated he spat on it.

Current score: Gangbangers, zero. McGlade's Wealthy Privilege Paranoia, five.

The next attempt made me lean up to the monitor, gripping the desk.

They had a grenade.

I racked a shell into the shotgun, ready for the breach.

The breach didn't come. When the explosive went off and the smoke cleared, McGlade's door had an indentation at the bottom, but it remained closed and sealed.

T-Nail seemed irritated by the delay, but the guy in the fur vest looked pensive. As the gang took a break, I familiarized myself with McGlade's security board, finding a button called BLUEPRINTS. When I pressed it, one of the monitors showed the house layout with an architectural draft superimposed over it. Sort of like a Google Map, which labeled the streets as well as showing a satellite view. This schematic had lines leading to definitions of equipment and armaments. The front door, according to the plans, was fireproof, bulletproof up to 15,000 foot-pounds, and could withstand a Category 5 hurricane.

It would have been laughably overkill, if I hadn't just had a street gang try to get in using grenades. A minute earlier and I would have mercilessly chided McGlade for his extravagant waste of money. But now I was ready to kiss his lumpy ass.

I looked at the garage door specs, and it was rated as high as the front and rear doors. There were no windows, but there was something called *balistraria*. Eight of them, on several of the walls. It wasn't a word I'd heard before, and I couldn't look it up without 4G or WiFi. I made a mental note to physically check it out later, and then zoomed in on a written list labeled OFFENSE.

Harry apparently wasn't content to just sit there, waiting for the enemy to figure out how to get in. He'd come up with some ways to fight back. I looked at a dial labeled SPRINKLER that had a LED gauge next to it which read 155°.

I hit the dial and watched the monitors. A moment later, everyone jumped up like they'd been simultaneously electrocuted. It was followed by yelling, waving arms, and a mass exodus off the property. As the camera lens misted up, I realized what I'd just done. Harry had installed sprinklers on the grounds. But rather than use them to care for his lawn, they sprayed scalding water.

It wasn't as gruesome as pouring molten lead off a castle wall, but it was just as effective. The last one to get away was T-Nail, his wheelchair having gotten stuck on a fallen log. Having been burned once or twice in my life, my mom-genes switched on and I turned the water off before he was parboiled. Sympathizing with the man who wanted to kill me probably wasn't wise, but I wasn't the type to steam a disabled man alive while I watched on a video monitor.

I hiked up the volume on the outdoor speakers. There was a cacophony of voices, most of them swearing, coupled with wilderness sounds like birds and the wind.

As the gang regrouped, I left the control room and went to check on the integrity of the front door. As I'd hoped, it was secure in its jamb. I needed to check if it could still open, for when Phin returned. I knew he would return. The only thing that would stop Phin was death.

Which was a problem. A better strategy than coming to my rescue was to scope out the situation, then go and get help. But Phin wouldn't be able to resist checking to see if I was okay. He wouldn't get help. He'd barricade himself in here with me.

Strangely, that's what I wanted more than anything. To hold him. To kiss him. Even if it put both of us at risk.

The heart was stupid. I could have made love to Phin anytime in the last six months, and I'd chosen not to. And now, when I was surrounded by a gang trying to kill me, I longed for his lips on my body.

Maybe my heart wasn't the stupid one. Maybe it was me.

I unlocked the door, gave it a swift tug.

It opened.

No one was out there.

I locked it again. Then I went back to the control room, watching the monitors.

My man would return.

If he wasn't already dead.

Please. PLEASE. Don't let him be dead.

HERB

Sergeant Herb Benedict was in his easy chair watching Netflix and wondering if anything could be worse than zombies conquering the world when something worse walked into his living room.

"When I see you sprawled out like that, I find myself looking for a tiny Princess Leia on a chain leash."

Herb frowned. His wife Bernice had broken the one solemn vow of a staycation; no outside calls or visitors. And of all the people to break that vow for, it had to be Harry McGlade.

"Where's my wife?" Herb asked. "I'm going to tell her to find herself a good divorce attorney."

"I don't think she's home. I let myself in. Your front door lock is like a child's toy. You don't even have a deadbolt. And I don't mean to be the bearer of bad news, Jabba, but your neighborhood isn't the best." Harry lowered his voice to a stage whisper. "I think I saw a minority outside."

"Racism isn't funny, McGlade."

"It's kind of funny. In an ignorant, fear-based kind of way. Besides, we're all genetically suspicious of people who look different than us. The PC crowd demands diversity, but they still put their wallets in their front pockets when they see someone of color in the same Starbucks. Basically, all people suck."

"Why are you in my house?"

"Because you won't answer the phone."

"I'm on vacation, and don't want to be bothered. Especially by you."

"What if I brought you éclairs?"

Herb's anger subsided a tiny bit. "Did you bring éclairs?"

"No. Because I know you don't have the will power to fight your diabetes on your own."

The anger returned. "I don't have diabetes."

"That's the diabetes talking. I can smell your blood sugar from here. Smells like Butterfingers."

The more Herb engaged him, the more McGlade would make fat jokes. So Herb clammed up and waited to hear the reason this idiot stopped by. Then he could kick him out and go back to *The Walking Dead*.

"You've got something stuck in your moustache," McGlade said, rubbing his own upper lip. "I think it's a whole turkey leg."

Herb refused to be baited.

"And an ear of corn."

I'm a rock, Herb told himself. *Rocks can't be insulted.*

"Okay, no more jokes," Harry said. "I saw a pair of women's shoes by the door, but Bernice isn't here. Answer me honestly; did you eat your wife?"

Rocks don't react.

"There were bones on the kitchen table. Could be pork. Could be human. Was it homicide? Or hamicide?"

Rocks are solid. Patient and unmoving.

"I can't hear you," Harry said. "I'd come closer, but I don't want to be sucked into your orbit."

Even rocks have a breaking point. "Tell me why you're here or I will get up and get my gun."

"Do you need help? I've got a jack and a crowbar. I also know a place that rents block and tackles."

Herb heaved his bulk out of the chair and took two threatening steps toward Harry, who held up his palms in supplication.

"It's Jack! She might be in trouble."

Herb halted. "Talk."

"She and Phin went up to my hideout up in northern Wisconsin near Lake Niboowin. They've been having some problems in the marital department. I think it's a butt sex thing. Anyway, I got a call this morning from Tom Mankowski. Terrence 'T-Nail' Johnson escaped from prison last night."

Herb processed the info quickly, and his automatic reaction was, "Ah, hell."

"I haven't been able to get ahold of Jack or Phin. Cell, texts, email. No answer."

"You try a land line?"

"Don't have one. Place is off the grid. Has its own well, house runs on wind power."

"Internet?"

"Which word in *off the grid* is perplexing you? It's a hideout. It's supposed to be cut off from the rest of the world."

"There a local Sheriff?"

"Police chief. Called. They said they'd check. That was an hour ago. Haven't called back."

"Staties?"

"I'm a PI, Herb. I don't have any sway there. Now maybe they just turned off their phones, and Phin is prying open that backdoor and doesn't want to be disturbed while he's uprooting mudflowers—"

"How did you get to be this old without someone shooting you?"

"—or maybe they're in trouble. We can figure it out on the way."

"On the way?"

Harry grinned. "Pack up your Lunchables, tubby. We're road tripping to Wisconsin."

T-NAIL

Rage.

T-Nail had been living with rage for so long, he'd turned it into fuel. Rage blazed inside him, pushing him forward, driving him to live another day just to quench it. But it was unquenchable.

The hot water had stopped, but every inch of his upper body continued to pulsate with first and second degree burns, steam billowing all around him in the cold November air. He eyed the back of his hand, staring at the blisters as he pushed his joystick forward. The wheels continued to churn mud, preventing him from moving. Because the chair didn't have a manual override when he could power it by hand, he was stuck there until someone came over and freed him.

Injury.

Insult.

Rage.

T-Nail closed his eyes, the lids beginning to swell. He imagined nailing Del Ray to a wall, then getting up close and personal with a utility knife and a ball peen hammer. There would be screaming. And begging. And no mercy.

He was so into the fantasy that he didn't even notice when some of his men came by and pushed him out of the trench his spinning wheels had dug. When he opened his burning eyes and realized he was moving, the rage intensified. The soldiers pushed him up to Del, who watched with an expression that might have been amusement. He had a few puffy spots on him, but for the most part didn't look like he'd been scalded at all.

"Explain what just happened," T-Nail said, his voice low.

Del Ray held his stare. "Any wheel can get stuck in the mud, T-Nail. Even all terrain shit. But if you'd switched the Gyro to a sitting position, you probably could have pulled out."

T-Nail felt eyes on him. His men, staring, waiting to see who was alpha. Angry as he was that he'd gotten stuck, T-Nail let it go for the time being. Right now he had to establish dominance, after looking like a damn fool who'd been—literally—spinning his wheels.

"Your crew was sent here to scope out the place," T-Nail said. "And now all of my men have gotten burned, because you didn't see this coming."

"I saw the sprinklers. I didn't know they were for defense."

"What were they for, then? To water the dead leaves?"

A few chuckles from the soldiers. T-Nail pressed on.

"You were supposed to watch the cop. We could have snatched her in Chicago. But instead, she came up here to some kind of goddamn fortress. Did you spook her somehow?"

"Naw. She's just on vacation."

"She went on vacation to a house with no windows, metal doors, and boiling water shooting out of the ground? She's hiding. How'd she find out?"

"I don't know."

"You set up the surveillance. You set up the attack. You failed, Del Ray. You failed me, and you failed my homies here. You feel me?"

Del Ray didn't answer.

"Back in the old day, we'd rum runner your ass for this colossal clusterfuck. Hold up your hand."

T-Nail raised his palm up as an example, as if he was giving an oath. Del hesitated, and T-Nail saw fear there. But he also saw defiance.

T-Nail knew how to deal with defiance. The moment Del lifted his hand, T-Nail drew his nail gun and shot him through the palm, quick as a cobra strike. The younger man howled and doubled over, tugging the nail out and dropping it to the ground.

Alpha established.

"You have two hours to figure out a way to get into that building," T-Nail ordered. "Now somebody get me some goddamn burn cream."

HERB

Welcome to the Crimebago Deux," Harry said.

He pronounced it *crim-ee-baygo*, playing off the name Winnebago, which is what the vehicle was. A motorhome McGlade had outfitted in ways only McGlade could, which is to say it was ostentatious, impractical, and expensive.

"It's a portable crime lab on wheels," McGlade boasted. "It's also fully armored without sacrificing any luxury or drivability."

"It's red," Herb said.

The entire recreational vehicle was painted candy apple red.

"I'm getting older, and sometimes I forget where I park. This makes it easier to find."

Herb eyed its length, which was at least six meters. "Yeah. I imagine you lose this all the time."

"Want to see the engine?"

"Not really."

"It's a hybrid. The Crimebago Uno got a quarter mile to the gallon, so I had to fill up every twenty minutes. But this one gets almost half a mile, while also powering the home entertainment center, the dishwasher, and the vibrating massage chair. Don't sit in the vibrating massage chair, Lardzilla. It isn't rated past three hundred pounds."

Herb was going to tell McGlade where he could stick his vibrating massage chair when someone yelled, "HOMEBOY!"

Herb squinted into the recesses of the Crimebago, and saw a rubber chicken in a cage.

But it wasn't a rubber chicken. It was moving.

"That's my new pet," Harry said. "His name is Homeboy."

"HOMEBOY!" the thing squawked.

What Herb had thought was a rubber chicken was actually a parrot. At least, it looked like a parrot from the neck up. Its head boasted a traditional curved black beak covered with poofy green, yellow, and blue feathers. But the rest of its body—chest, back, legs, wings—was plucked bare. It looked like a pink, dimpled, underfed roasting turkey wearing a parrot mask.

"Handsome bird," Herb said.

"Homeboy was a rescue. He was confiscated in a drug bust. His former owners cooked meth, and I think he got hooked on it. So now he pulls out his own feathers. Some sort of nervous disorder."

"Couldn't you buy him a little sweater or something?" Herb said, eyeing the naked animal.

"I did. He didn't like it. He prefers *au naturale*. I got him because I thought it would be fun to have a pet that could talk."

"HOMEBOY!" yelled Homeboy.

"Does he say anything else?"

"METH!" said Homeboy.

"Just that," Harry said, shrugging. "I think the meth broke his little bird brain."

"METH! METH! METH! HOMEBOY! METH!"

"He's nice," Herb said.

Homeboy screamed, so loud it made the hair on Herb's toes stand up.

"He also screams," said Harry.

"METH! AAAAAAAAAAAAAAAAAARG! METH!"

"I don't have any meth, little fella." Herb reached a finger up to the cage, but McGlade pushed his hand away.

"He bites," McGlade said, showing black stitches on three of his fingers. "He doesn't like being touched. Or quick movements. Also, try to avoid direct eye contact."

"AAAAAAAAAARG! HOMEBOY! AAAAAAAAAAAAARG!"

"It's important to have pets," McGlade said. "They enrich our lives."

"AAAAAAAAAAAAAAAAAAAAAAARG!"

"He's certainly enriching mine right now," said Herb.

"If you want to, you can feed him peanuts. Just keep your fingers outside the cage."

McGlade fished a nut out of a plastic bag on the table and held it up to the bars. Homeboy bent down for it, then fell off his perch and hit the bottom of the cage with a big *THUD*.

"Did you save the receipt?" Herb asked.

"I tried that. They won't take him back. He bit off part of the ear of the guy who was fostering him."

"METH! METH! METH! AAAAAAAAAAAAAAAARG!"

"How long do parrots live for?" Herb asked.

"Fifty to sixty years."

"How old is Homeboy?"

"Three."

"HOMEBOY! AAAAAAAAAAAAAAARG! HOMEBOY!"

"This makes me very happy," Herb said.

Homeboy righted himself, then climbed the inside of his cage using his beak and claws. He took McGlade's peanut and began to nibble on it, holding it in one foot.

"Well, that's sorta cute," Herb admitted

Homeboy lifted up his tail and squirted about half a liter of poop out of his ass. It plopped onto the newspaper lining his cage, and some splashed on Herb.

"You should wash that off," McGlade said. "Parrots are teeming with bacteria."

Herb found his way to the bathroom, and used liquid soap to get the guano off his shirt. Then he washed his hand thoroughly, following it with a healthy spritz of sanitizer gel.

"You try the bidet?" McGlade said when Herb came out.

"What bidet?"

"I got one of those Japanese toilets, with all the functions. It shoots water up your butt. It's practically a religious experience."

"What church do you go to?"

"I'm serious. You'll never feel cleaner in your life."

"I'll check it out," Herb said, making himself a promise that he'd never check it out.

"You should. You know how you buy a jar of peanut butter, and when you get to the very bottom the only way to get that last little bit out is to use your finger? Well the bidet is even better than a finger. Shoots up there and completely clears you out. My colon is so clean you could eat out of it."

"AAAAAAAAAAAAAAAAAAAAAAAAARG!"

"I'm going to call in," Herb said. "Check with the gang unit, see if anything is happening."

"Sure. I'll give you the rest of the Crimebago tour when you're done. But note the defibrillator on the back wall. I just bought it, because I knew you were coming along."

Harry held out another peanut to Homeboy, who reached for it and fell onto his head. Herb whipped out his cell and walked to the back of the RV. He was on hold for five minutes before being put through to Detective Alanzo in gang enforcement. Alanzo was third generation cop, the kind who busted his ass to make dad and granddad proud.

"Got all kinds of Folk movement," he told Herb. "Spotters saw two buses leaving the city."

"How many?"

"Close to a hundred. Word on the street is war, but no one knows who against. People Nation is rallying, but emissaries say it's an out of town gig."

Herb felt his stomach twist. A hundred? Could that be right?

"If you hear about the target, call me."

"No prob, boss."

"Thanks, Detective." Herb tried Jack again, got voicemail. Then he turned to Harry, who was wiping bird shit off his pants using his bare hand. "Are you sure your place is safe?"

"It's completely incognito. My name isn't even attached to it. No way anyone could find it."

"Good."

"Unless they followed Jack there," Harry added.

Not good. Not good at all.

"But it's safe?"

"It's a safe house, kemo-slobby. I spared no expense. It could weather a siege against fifty guys."

"How about a hundred guys?"

McGlade blinked. "You serious?"

Herb nodded. Harry looked thoughtful, which was an unique look for him.

"Maybe," Harry eventually said. "Depends what kind of firepower they had. I mean, nothing is truly impenetrable. Ask the Alamo survivors."

Good point. "Well, let's get going then."

"We will. But we got some stops to make first."

"What kind of stops?"

Harry winked. "You think I'm going into battle with just you on my side, Puff Fatty? We're picking up reinforcements. But first, we need to hit my storage locker."

"What for?" Herb asked.

"Crowd control." McGlade grinned so wide it looked like his face would split. "I got an idea on how to even the odds."

PHIN

He pulled over alongside the road on the crest of a hill, a few hundred meters from the dirt road that led to Harry's cabin. After reigning in the panic he'd experienced at the Walmart, Phin had regained the capacity to reason and forced himself to come up with a plan. It involved some 140x binoculars liberated from the sporting goods section, as much Scorpion ammo as he could gather up, various hats and bandanas, extra Kevlar vests, and a Dodge pickup truck courtesy of a dead gangbanger.

Phin raised the binocs to his face and peered at the parked vehicles below, a pimped out Toyota Supra and a beater Ford Mustang parked along the left-hand side. Four men stood next to the cars. They wore gang colors, and machine guns hung at their sides.

Spotters. They'd be waiting for their posse from Walmart to return. They were in front of the dirt road turnoff that took them to Harry's place. The sky beyond them was so overcast it almost looked like smoke.

Phin took out the dead banger's cell phone and texted `HE'S DEAD`, wondering what they'd do when they got it. Maybe leave their post.

The text failed to send. Either the gang had jammers, or they'd taken out the nearest cell tower. Maybe both. Phin had tried several landlines in the Walmart, and had been unable to get through to the police. 911 had him on hold for three minutes before he gave up.

Phin wondered how big this gang operation actually was.

He looked at the four men again, not liking his odds. With two guys, he could maybe snipe them from a distance. Or shoot one and run the other over. With three, he maybe even had a chance of sneaking up and plugging them. Or perhaps he could start the truck on fire, send it down the hill, and pick them off when they came to investigate.

But with four guys, someone would get a shot off. Phin had already been on the receiving end of machine gun fire earlier that day, and his entire body throbbed. He didn't care to repeat the experience.

He tried to look past them, but the woods were thick. There was a chance he could go around, perhaps make his way through the forest without getting lost in the trees, but that would take time. Time Jack might not have. Phin needed to get to his wife, fast.

The question was how to do that without getting killed.

Phineas Troutt hadn't served in the armed forces, so any tactics applicable to this situation were unknown to him. He wasn't a particularly good shot—Jack was the marksperson in the family. Jack was also the martial artist, with her taekwondo black belt. Phin could brawl if forced to, but his greatest skill was the ability to withstand a punch, and while that came in handy sometimes, being able to take a beating didn't win fights.

But he did have some street sense, and that made him recognize what needed to be done in this situation.

Phin had four extra bulletproof vests he'd taken from the men he'd killed at the Walmart. He wedged one between his left side and the door. Another, he hung on his headrest so it draped across his seat behind him. He opened the window and positioned the third one over it, with space to poke his Scorpion barrel through. The fourth, he put on the dashboard, covering most of the window, the arm hole allowing him to see the road. In the seat next to him, he had another loaded Scorpion, five full mags, and the SIG. Then he pulled back onto the road, picking up speed as he coasted down the hill.

Phin wasn't a military strategist, and he hadn't read the Art of War. But he doubted Sun Tzu ever wrote about how to conduct a successful drive-by shooting.

The gangbangers took notice of Phin's vehicle as soon as he came into view. But they didn't raise their weapons. No doubt they recognized the vehicle, and thought one of their own was returning.

By the time they noticed the Kevlar stacked in places it wouldn't normally be, Phin had already begun firing. He hit the first guy in the legs, tapped the brakes to slow down, and plugged the next man in the head as he ducked for cover. The other two got behind the Mustang and returned fire as Phin cruised past. The back windshield exploded, and Phin felt bullets punch into the back of his seat, protected by the vest.

Rather than turn the car around, Phin came to a stop and then hit reverse, flooring it. He switched his empty Scorpion with a loaded one, then jerked the wheel left and hit the brakes, stopped alongside the Mustang, where the other two were crouching.

They unloaded, and the bulletproof vest Phin had wedged against the window fell inward. Phin ducked beneath it, covering his head, and the rounds drilling into the Kevlar felt like hiding under a blanket while someone pounded the shit out of you.

Then the shooting stopped. That was the problem with machine guns; they emptied really fast.

As the gangbangers reloaded, Phin pushed away the vest and took careful aim. Being only a few feet away, he stitched one guy across the neck, and emptied the rest of the mag into the other guy's pelvis. Then Phin grabbed the SIG and crawled out the passenger door, squatting behind the front tire.

He counted to ten, waiting for someone to make a move.

Then he counted to ten again.

Peeking under the truck, Phin saw the two men he'd just shot lying on the ground, not moving. He kept low, moving to the front of the truck, and saw the third dead man—the head shot.

The fourth was gone.

Phin ran in a crouch up to the Toyota and saw the blood trail on the asphalt. Walking in a wide arc, aiming the SIG, Phin saw the fourth gangbanger crawling on his elbows, dragging his bleeding legs behind him, heading for the tree line.

Phin took a quick look around, didn't see any other threats, and approached the man slowly. When he got to him, Phin stepped on the guy's ankle. He cried out and flipped around, and Phin jammed the SIG into his neck.

"Be still," Phin said. "I'm very, very nervous right now."

Phin patted the kid down. And he was, indeed, a kid. No more than eighteen. Phin found a switchblade, a wallet, and a wooden dugout.

"How many at the house?" Phin asked.

"I ain't telling you shit. Go ahead and kill me, asshole."

Phin stood up and shoved the SIG in his vest. "I already did. You got hit in the femoral artery."

The kid didn't seem to understand.

"You're bleeding to death," Phin said.

"I'm... dying?"

"Yeah."

"No shit?"

"No shit."

"How about a tourniquet or something?"

"Too high up." Phin bent over, took the boy's hand, and pressed it hard against the wound on his groin. "Hold here. Maybe it'll give you a few extra minutes."

The realization on the kid's face was an awful thing to see. From hardcore criminal to scared little boy in just a few seconds.

"I don't want to die, man."

"You should have made better life choices."

"I got a baby."

"How many men are at the house?"

The kid began to cry. Phin fiddled with the dugout, packed the metal one-hitter with a big dab of marijuana. He gave the kid a nudge with his foot, and held up the grass.

"Is this good shit?" Phin asked.

The kid nodded.

Phin crouched, put it to the kid's lips, and blazed it with his Zippo. The kid took a big hit.

"I have a baby, too," Phin said. "How many men are there?"

The kid blinked. The weed must have been damn good, because he actually smiled.

"One-twenty."

"A hundred and twenty guys?"

A nod.

Phin had gotten twelve. That left 108.

Those odds were impossible.

"You should run, man. Save yourself. T-Nail just wants the cop."

"Cop is my wife. Mother of my child."

"She's dead, man. Ain't no way they're letting her go. Hit me again."

Phin flicked his Zippo once more. The kid inhaled deep, blew the sweet smoke out slow.

"My moms told me thug life would kill me," he said.

"Who owns the Toyota?"

"Dave."

"Which guy is Dave?"

"White dude. Beard."

Phin turned to look for Dave, and the kid called to him. "Hey, man. Another light?"

Phin tossed the kid the lighter, then went to Dave and patted down his corpse until he found the car keys. He walked back to the Toyota.

The kid was dead. Eyes wide open. A wisp of smoke trailing up from his parted lips.

Phin took his lighter back, got into the Toyota, and wondered how the hell he was going to save his wife.

JACK

Back in the control room, I stared at the security monitors and hoped to hell my husband was safe. I reasoned that no news was good news. If they knew I was here, they knew about Phin. If they had him, they'd use him as leverage. Not seeing him was a good thing.

But the problem was, I understood how Phin ticked. He was one fiercely loyal son of a bitch. If he knew about this siege, he'd come back for me.

Best case scenario, he'd come with reinforcements. That would be the practical thing to do.

Phin wasn't the practical type.

I pushed it from my mind, focusing on the control panel. The hot water sprinklers were a smart touch. But they would only be an effective deterrent for as long as the water was hot. Harry had equipped his safe house well, but hot water needed a water heater, and water heaters took time to heat water. T-Nail would figure that out, sooner or later, and then commence his attack.

I leaned back in the desk chair and noticed a Kindle Fire plugged into the wall. I opened it up and it immediately came to life.

Harry had a lot of porn on his Kindle. When did clown porn become a thing? For scientific curiosity's sake I pressed a video file and let a few seconds play.

So much groaning. So much honking. When they began doing X-rated things with balloon animals, I switched it off. Besides the adult entertainment, he also had the *Marriage Saver App* he'd told me and Phin about, and a large number of games, with titles like *Balloon Bop Big Top Circus* and *Cookie Factory Crumble Ninjas.* I clicked on something colorful involving a lollipop factory, spent thirty seconds popping virtual bubble wrap to earn silver stars to buy pixie dust, and then exited the app, deeply troubled about how the Western world chose its leisure activities. Give me a good book any day of the week.

I clicked on his device library.

All fairytale erotica. What sort of warped mind would make Alice in Wonderland a porn adventure? And there was no WiFi or 3G, so I couldn't download any new books.

I put the Kindle down, and went back to the schematics, my eyes again finding the word *balistraria.*

What did that mean? It was listed on the house blueprints, several walls labeled with the word.

I used my cell to take a pic of the blueprint, then left the control room to find one of the balistraria spots. In the living room, behind the flat screen TV, there was supposed to be one. All I saw was a bad oil painting that bore a faint resemblance to Michelangelo's sculpture, David. With two exceptions. First, it was McGlade's face, instead of David's. Second, the penis was grossly out of proportion with the rest of the body. If McGlade was that large in real life, his sex partners needed to be concerned about having their lungs punctured during the dirty deed. I highly doubted that was the case.

Much as I didn't want to touch the bad art, I removed the painting and set it down facing the sofa. On the back of the painting was a copy of the exact same painting. As in real life, Harry refused to be ignored.

I turned my attention to the wall, and found...

A wall.

Plain old wood paneling. I rapped it with my knuckles, looking for hollow spots, but it sounded solid wherever I touched it.

Odd.

I went back to the control room, saw the gangbangers were keeping off the property, and then went in search of a dictionary.

It didn't surprise me that Harry had no library. Or bookcases.

But he did have an extensive collection of board games, including Scrabble. On a hunch, I took the Scrabble box off the shelf, opened it, and found a thesaurus inside.

I looked up *balistraria*, and it had a single word synonym: *embrasure.*

Some help. I looked up *embrasure.*

Crenel.

I looked up *crenel*, and was rewarded by an entire sentence.

Any open space between the merlons.

"You gotta be kidding me," I said to myself.

Without hoping for much, I searched for *merlon.*

The solid upright section of a battlement.

Then memories of high school history class kicked in, and I remembered what a balistraria was.

I went back to the wall, studying the wood paneling again. This time I pushed on the seams between panels, and was rewarded by a board that pressed in, then swung out on a hidden hinge.

And there was the balistraria. The crenel between the merlons.

I checked the pic on my phone. There were eight of these spots around the house.

"Nice."

I went back to the control room, to see if McGlade had any other defenses I'd missed, and caught movement on the cameras.

Smoke. And fire.

And at least thirty sprinting men armed with lit Molotov cocktails. Before I could react, they launched them at the house.

The roof, the outside walls, the garage door; they were all soon ablaze. Almost every camera was flickering with orange flames.

I hit the sprinklers. The men retreated, yelling and cursing and trying to protect themselves from the scalding water. But I was less concerned with getting them away from the house and more concerned about burning alive.

Luckily, McGlade had anticipated that kind of attack. Several of the sprinkler jets were aimed at the house, and had already begun extinguishing some of the flames.

Several of them. But not all. And it wasn't a fast process. I guessed the house was fire retardant, but there were spots that continued to burn.

And the longer they burned, the longer I had to leave the sprinklers on.

The longer I left the sprinklers on, the more hot water I used up.

I checked the blueprints, trying to find information about the water heater and how big it was. Harry hadn't spared any expense when it came to this safe house. But every place ran out of hot water eventually.

I watched the monitors and held my breath.

DEL RAY

"Fire's goin' out."

Del Ray looked at one of his soldiers. Older dude, Hispanic, had a triangle soul patch on his chin that was thick as a carpet. He didn't know the man's name; there were a lot of guys on this run, many from affiliates. Del glanced at the patch on his vest, noted he was one of the Hermanos Locos from Milwaukee. Cool. It meant word was spreading, more troops were joining the party.

"And the cop is wasting all her hot water, putting it out."

The man's face scrunched up in obvious thought, then he grinned, showing a gold tooth. "Smart, homes."

He walked off, and Del Ray turned back to the house. He'd anticipated difficulties, but not this extreme. With a hundred-plus men, he could take over a ten story apartment building. But one old cop in the backwoods of Wisconsin was proving a challenge.

He heard the whirring of an electric motor, but didn't turn to face T-Nail as the man rode up. Even though Del had drunk a cup of sizzurp and smoked half a blunt, his hand still throbbed from the nail gun. T-Nail had missed the bones, but the injury still hurt enough that Del Ray couldn't make a fist. He didn't hate his War Chief for the corporal punishment; up in the higher levels, shit got real and brothers had to know their place. But Del was disappointed with how the man conducted himself. He'd been hearing stories about the great T-Nail since Del Ray was a shorty. Epic tales of ass kicking and hardcore drama. So far, T-Nail hadn't lived up to expectations.

It was goddamn disappointing.

"You got a way in?" T-Nail said. His voice had an edge to it, like a car engine getting ready to backfire.

"Working on it."

"You need to do more than just work on it."

"Bitch is smart, G. You know this." Del Ray didn't remind T-Nail that this Jack cop got the drop on him, and that's why he did two dimes. No need to diss on top of injury. "But I got my back-up coming. We'll smoke her ass out, or flatten her crib trying."

"I want her alive. You got a brother on our team that's flakin'?"

Flakin'? Now that was old school. Had anyone used that term since NWA released *Straight Outta Compton* in '88?

"Got one or two."

"How about we put one or two in some cars, run up into that shit, see if we can't knock a damn door down."

Del Ray nodded. "I'll get on that."

It would be a waste of a vehicle, Del Ray knew. But it would buy some time until the real deal got there.

"You think this is just another bum rush, don't you, dog?"

Del Ray looked at his War Chief. "What you mean?"

"This ain't about revenge," T-Nail said. "We ain't wasting all this capital on some personal grudge."

Then why the hell are we all here? Del thought.

T-Nail stared at some point in the distance. "This is an intentional show of force. It's all about power. A little girl cop puts you away, she be in control. You put her in the ground, you be in control. Ain't no gang without control. You know your roots, man? You know where you come from?"

"Born and raised Chi-Raq, homes." That wasn't the truth, but Del had never told anyone the real story.

"I'm Kakwa. My father came from a small village in East Africa. He fought with Idi Amin. You know of Amin?"

Del Ray nodded. Idi Amin was a soldier in Uganda in the 1970s. He overthrew the government and ruled the country as dictator. Legend was he cannibalized his enemies.

"Amin knew what power was," T-Nail said. "He understood control. He showed no mercy. Those who dared rise against him were killed. Amin tortured and killed more than three hundred thousand of his enemies. This is what a great man does. How a true leader acts. His official title was *His Excellency, President for Life, Field Marshal Al Hadji Doctor Idi Amin Dada, VC, DSO, MC, Lord of All the Beasts of the Earth and Fishes of the Seas and Conqueror of the British Empire in Africa in General and Uganda in Particular.*"

That was some hardcore shit. The way T-Nail talked, he obviously idolized the man. "And your pops fought alongside him?"

"My father was with his State Research Bureau. He and Amin were great friends. My father castrated more than a thousand prisoners in Nakasero for his Excellency. But in 1977, the year I was born, my father offended Amin. He was in a bar, and told a joke about Amin's weight. The President for Life forced my father to castrate himself. Then he had him nailed to a concrete wall and skinned alive. I know this, because he made my mother watch."

T-Nail turned and looked at Del Ray. "My mother brought me to Chicago when I was a baby. I grew up hearing how terrible Amin was. She didn't see the purity and logic of his regime. True power, true control, does not ever compromise. A true leader eliminates all obstacles."

Del hadn't known that about T-Nail's father. But it was well-known that T-Nail killed his moms when he was twelve. Pushed her off the fifth floor balcony at the Robert Taylor Homes, before they'd installed the security fences.

Apparently, she'd been an obstacle.

T-Nail pushed the joystick on the Gyro, and began to roll away. "Jacqueline Daniels dies today," he called behind him. "I won't tolerate failure."

And I won't tolerate threats, Del thought. And he was getting damn sick of T-Nail's. The OG was all about power and control, but that door swung both ways. T-Nail was either too stupid, or too cocky, to understand that he was also an obstacle.

Del Ray put it out of his mind for the moment, and looked down at his vest. More than twenty scalps hung from it. A far cry from the thousand that T-Nail's father had castrated.

He smiled to himself. What a fucked-up vest that would make. Can you imagine it?

Del Ray had never seen anyone get castrated.

He wondered what it was like.

HERB

HOMEBOY!" squawked Homeboy.

Herb stared at the bird, and much to his embarrassment, his stomach grumbled. It didn't matter that the parrot was the most obnoxious animal Herb had ever encountered. With its plucked body, it looked like a roasting chicken. And chicken made Herb hungry.

"You give him a nut?" Harry McGlade yelled from the driver's seat of the Crimebago.

Herb looked at his knuckles, which were still bleeding. "Yeah. Awesome pet, McGlade."

"I know he's a little rough around the edges, but I think we're bonding. Check this out."

McGlade switched on the stereo, which was slightly louder than a 737 taking off. Herb forced his hands over his ears as gansta rap shook the entire vehicle, the bass so strong it made Herb's mustache vibrate.

Homeboy opened his mouth in what Herb guessed was a scream—he couldn't hear it over the hip-hop—and then fell off his perch and began to twitch on the floor of his newspaper-lined cage.

"Is he dancing?" McGlade asked. He was holding a CB handset to his mouth, which he'd apparently connected to the speakers.

"I think he's having a seizure," Herb said.

"He loves rap," Harry said, oblivious. "That's him doing the chest pop. Check out those funky fresh moves."

What Harry thought were dance moves looked more like convulsions. Homeboy's whole body twitched and jerked, his naked wings flopping about, his eyes seeming to roll up into his tiny head.

McGlade shut the music off, and Homeboy immediately recovered, climbing back up to his perch by using his beak on the cage bars.

"You okay?" Herb asked the bird.

"METH! METH!"

"You and me both," Herb sighed.

Herb peeked out one of the tinted windows, trying to spot a street sign or landmark to tell him where they were. They'd been driving for half an hour, and by Herb's best estimate they were somewhere near O'Hare airport. He tried Jack on his cell again, got no answer, and then tried the Spoonward PD. It rang and rang and no one picked up. So he used his phone to look up the Wisconsin State Patrol Sawyer Post, and dialed Lieutenant Josh Bickford.

"Bickford." He had a low, scratchy voice, like he routinely gargled coffee grounds.

"Sergeant Herb Benedict, Chicago PD. I've got a cop up in a home in Spoonward, and can't reach her. There's a high chance some bad guys are involved. Can't reach the locals there. No one picks up."

"Shit, Benedict, no one can get ahold of anyone. The fire."

"Fire?"

"You don't know? We're dealing with the biggest forest fire Burnett County has ever seen. Got every man on it. Chief Schuyler is probably busy evacuating civilians. I bet he's got the town phone set up to forward to his cell, but the fire has knocked out some cell towers."

"Is the fire near Lake Niboowin?"

"I got thirteen thousand five hundred square miles in my county, and half are burning down. If your cop buddy had any sense, he got the hell out of Dodge already. I gotta go."

"Lieutenant—"

Herb was speaking to a dial tone.

The Crimebago came to an abrupt stop, and Homeboy screamed, "AAAAAARRRRRRGH!"

"Where are we, McGlade?"

McGlade climbed out of the cockpit and walked past Herb. "One of my storage lockers. Get out and help. I don't know what kind of shape it'll be in. If it's in as bad a shape as you, we're in trouble."

Herb narrowed his eyes. "Can you just go five minutes without being a dick?"

"I dunno. Can you go five minutes without being a fat ass?" McGlade turned to Homeboy and spoke in a baby voice. "Did the lumpy man try to eat you? He looked at you like you were a chicken, didn't he?"

Herb considered shooting him. It wasn't the first time he'd considered it. He'd even picked out a spot where he'd bury the body. But McGlade knew where Jack was at, so any homicides would have to wait until they'd found her.

Still, it was nice to fantasize.

Herb found the door handle and climbed out of the RV, staring at ranks and files of outdoor storage units, all with bright green garage doors. McGlade followed him out. Homeboy was perched on his right shoulder, pirate-style. Herb couldn't resist.

"Maybe you need to replace your prosthetic hand with a hook, Long John Stupid."

"Maybe you should go on the Jenny Craig diet. I'll warn Jenny that you'll try to eat her."

McGlade tugged the garage door open and turned on the light. Most of the entire locker was occupied by some huge vehicle, draped in tarps.

"What the hell is that? A tank?"

"Actually…"

McGlade pulled on one of the tarps and tugged it off, revealing—

A tank.

Herb whistled. "Crowd control, huh?"

"Works for the military. Should work for us. We need to hook this up to the trailer hitch."

"Is it full?"

"Yeah. Ten tons worth." McGlade continued to yank off tarpaulins, and then frowned. "Shit. Tires are low. Need air."

"Where did you even get this thing?"

"I bought it used. I collect weird vehicles, among other things. Did you know I've got one of the original Wisconsin Ducks?" McGlade kicked a tire. "I've got a compressor in the Crimebago Deux. Be right back. And don't touch my dildo collection."

Harry pointed to several large cardboard boxes stacked in the corner of the garage, DILDO COLLECTION written in black marker on the sides.

"I'll try to restrain myself," Herb said.

He checked his phone, searching for *Wisconsin fire*, and got over five hundred hits from the last half hour. The governor had declared a state of emergency. So far, there were no reported deaths, but the fire was out of control with no end in sight. The cause was unknown. Herb found an update on areas that were burning, and was relieved to see that, so far, Lake Niboowin was out of harm's way.

His relief was short-lived.

Most cops were cynical and suspicious, and Herb Benedict was no exception. This fire could have been a coincidence. Or it could have been set purposely, as a distraction. A gang of a hundred-plus, coming into town, would draw attention to itself. Unless something bigger was happening nearby.

Herb recalled Terrence Wycleaf Johnson's trial. Jack had been allowed to testify undercover, but he'd never seen her so scared. The scene at the Robert Taylor homes had affected her, badly, and it took a few months for his partner to get her mojo back. She ceased practically all undercover work after that. Her insomnia, which she'd always had issues with, became worse. She'd even told Herb she wanted to quit the Job, and he'd managed to talk her out of it over a late night beer drinking session.

Herb understood her fear. They arrested bad people, and bad people had a habit of holding grudges. But Herb had assured Jack her anonymity would protect her. She'd be safe.

Now, two decades later, there was a very real possibility that Herb had been wrong.

And that frightened the shit out of Herb. He absently touched the scar tissue under his eyes—physical evidence of an old case that had come back to haunt him—and knew that even with Harry's secret weapon they didn't stand a chance against a gang.

"HOMEBOY! HOMEBOY! METH!"

Harry had returned, pulling along a small air compressor on a hand truck. Homeboy was perched on top, his featherless wings outstretched. Maybe he was pretending to be flying.

"You said you've got reinforcements," Herb said. "Who?"

"Tom Mankowski is supposed to call me back."

"Anyone else?"

"Yeah."

"Who?"

"If I told you who it is, she'd probably kill you."

"Seriously, McGlade. Who else is coming?"

"I'm being serious," Harry said. "I have some friends in low places, and I sent word out to one of them. A specialist. The less you know, the better."

Herb didn't like that. Not a bit.

"So we got me, you, Tom, and your mystery lowlife friend."

"Tom hasn't committed. He's got some other stuff going on."

"So we got me, you, and your mystery lowlife friend."

"And Homeboy."

"HOMEBOY!" said Homeboy.

"Against a hundred," Herb said.

"When you put it like that, it sounds suicidal. And actually, I haven't heard back from my mystery lowlife friend."

"So two against a hundred."

"Plus Homeboy."

"HOMEBOY!" said Homeboy.

"So three against a hundred."

"But there is a potential for five. We can handle this. Remember *The Magnificent Seven*? Phin and I just watched that again. They went up against over a hundred."

Herb ticked off fingers. "The villagers helped them. And they had seven. And none of them was a naked parrot. And they had seven. And most of them died. And they had seven. And that was just a movie."

"Thank you, Negative Nancy. You know there's a diner nearby that has the best cheese blintzes. Maybe that will cheer your lard-ass up."

Herb didn't say anything, but the idea of cheese blintzes did, indeed, cheer him up.

Which was a check in the plus column. But he still wasn't keen on McGlade's plan. Granted, Herb didn't have a better one, but he didn't like their chances. T-Nail had a well-trained, well-equipped army. They had a heavily armed recreational vehicle, a secondhand riot control device, an idiot with a robotic hand, his bald bird, two cops, and some shady underworld figure that might not even show up.

Still, blintzes. He planned on ordering two plates; one for now, and one for the road.

If Herb was destined to die that day, at least he'd die with a full belly.

CODENAME: HAMMETT

Years ago, she assassinated people for the government.

Now she just did it when she felt like it.

She'd been taking it easy as of late. Relaxing with her dogs. Taking occasional lovers. Plotting the end of humanity. It had been weeks since she'd killed anyone, when she got the email alert that someone had Tweeted her a message.

Only a few people knew her Twitter account, and Hammett was just bored enough to check it out.

Long distance work. ASAP. IATA: HYR. Lake Niboowin. 100+ OGs. BYOG.

It was from @TheRealHarryMcGlade.

McGlade.

An idiot. But an amusing one.

Out of boredom, she looked up the Sawyer County Airport, and its distance to Lake Niboowin. A little over five hundred miles as the crow flew. In her Beechcraft Baron 58, allowing for traffic to the airport, she could make it to Spoonward in about four hours.

Add another hour to prep, and another to kennel her pack, and she'd be able to get there before sundown.

Bring Your Own Gun wasn't a problem. Hammett had many to choose from.

But a hundred plus gangbangers was just plain crazy.

She logged on Twitter as @NeoMastiffLvr17 and replied to Harry.

Fee?

It took less than a minute for @TheRealHarryMcGlade to respond.

No fee. Rescue Op. But I'll tap that sweet ass. :D

His next tweet was latitude and longitude coordinates, and a vulgar comment involving oral sex that probably violated Twitter's Terms of Service.

Yeah. He was an idiot, all right.

Hammett typed in HELL NO, sent it, and then called her dogs. She was quickly surrounded by five Mastiffs and a mutt named Kirk.

"You puppies want to go for a walk?"

Over a thousand pounds of dog began to howl. It was a rhetorical question.

Hammett logged off of TOR, stretched out her long legs, got up from her computer, and padded into the foyer, surrounded by animals. As Hammett attached leashes to collars, she idly wondered what McGlade was doing in northern Wisconsin, and whom he was trying to save from gangbangers.

She quickly put the thought out of her head, because Hammett just didn't give a shit.

PHIN

Just like The Magnificent Seven, he thought.

In a movie filled with great scenes, the one that stood out for Phin was when Chico walked into the enemy's camp, disguised as a bandit. By hiding in plain sight, Chico was able to eavesdrop on their plans. Because there were so many, no one recognized him.

Which was how Phin, dressed in gang colors, walked up to Harry's property without anyone giving him a second glance.

But when he got into the thick of it, he realized Chico was a just a made-up character in a movie, because this was the stupidest damn thing Phin had ever done.

He was surrounded—literally surrounded—by gangbangers. They were four deep, every direction he turned. Phin stopped counting at eighty guys. All armed. All focused on the house Jack was hiding inside.

Phin couldn't think of any way to get to her without getting killed.

And there was no way she was getting out.

Not alive.

He mulled it over, dead leaves crunching underfoot. Even if Jack saw him on the outdoor surveillance cameras, and he was able to signal her somehow, what next? Run for the house, she swings open the door, then locks it before anyone else gets in or guns them both down? If, by a miracle, that worked, then what?

Then we're both trapped.

The fact that the bangers hadn't gotten in yet meant something. Harry's little hideaway was apparently a tough nut to crack.

So now what? Stick around, waiting for the gang to get smart enough to find away in? Or try to get help?

Phin thought about what had happened at Walmart. There had been no police. No help. And someone must have hit the alarm to alert the authorities.

No cops, no phone service; this was intentional. All part of the same grand plan. Maybe Phin could make it to the nearest town, convince some cops to come with him. But how many? What good would even twenty armed men do against this army? And would they get back in time?

What Phin needed was the National Guard. Or an airstrike.

He spied the house through a gap in the trees from twenty meters away; for some reason the gang had formed a perimeter at that distance. The front door looked like it had been chewed up. There were scorch marks on the outside wall, and the roof. They'd tried to shoot their way in, and burn their way in, and had apparently failed both times.

Nicely done, McGlade.

But how much abuse could the house actually take? These guys were serious, and seriously well-equipped. Eventually, they would figure out how to get inside.

He saw the Mitsubishi Outlander they'd driven up there in. Well, what was left of it. How disappointing. At the very least, they should have stolen it. Setting it on fire was just a waste.

Phin sniffed the air, smelled traces of smoke. Then he looked beyond the house, into the unnaturally overcast sky. Was that clouds? Or smoke?

This whole situation was seriously fucked-up.

He began to meander through the sea of soldiers, watching and listening. Many of the gangbangers had damp clothes, and some were being bandaged for various burns. Phin found a kid who, based on his colors, was a member of the Six Corner Hustlers. Or maybe he ran with the Vicegods. There were so many sets and subsets, Phin got them mixed up. The banger had blisters on his neck and was wincing as he applied salve from a tube.

"Just got here. What went down?"

Kid made a face, showing a gold grill. Apparently that was still a thing. "Cop bitch turned on the sprinklers, burned us. Fuckin' hurts, man."

"Goddamn," Phin said, finding it difficult to keep his face neutral. Go Jack. "I smell smoke."

"We tried to torch the place. Sprinklers put it out. I say we just wait, let her roast alive when the big flames get here. Her sprinklers won't put that shit out."

"Big flames?"

"You dunno?" He grinned. "We set half of Wisconsin on fire, man. While the pigs deal with that, we can do our thing here. But it's just a matter of time before the fire reaches us. Before we killed the radio, I heard the wind was shifting. The big burn is thirty miles away, but it's coming."

Of course it was. Because things weren't already bad enough.

"What's the plan?" Phin asked. "Just camp here until we all roast?"

"Hell if I know. Ask Del Ray."

"Where he at?"

"I dunno, man. Just look for the bad muthafucka with the scalps on his colors."

Phin had no idea what that meant, but he didn't let on. He continued to weave through the crowd, stopping once to stare at what looked like a James Cameron villain; a huge black dude strapped to some sort of electric rolling machine. Even though the dirt ground was uneven and littered with detritus, his funky oval wheels turned like drill screws and glided over top, propelling the man forward, backward, and even sideways.

Phin averted his stare before the man looked his way, but he caught the symbols on his leather vest. The man was War Chief; the leader of the Eternal Black C-Notes. C-Notes were one of the worst gangs in Chicago.

Jack had apparently pissed off some very heavy people.

Phin didn't notice anything like scalps on the giant, so he walked past and kept looking. Finally, near an older model Chrysler van, he spotted a skinny kid with a big fro and a furry vest. The guy watched him approach. He had rat eyes. Round. Black. Unblinking. As Phin neared, he understood the scalp comment. The man's gang vest was stitched with the scalps of the dead.

What the hell was wrong with kids these days? Weren't YouTube and Xbox enough to keep them busy?

"General," Phin said, seeing the tattoo on the back of his hand. "'Sup?"

It was a gamble questioning a higher-up, but Phin figured he ranked enough to give it a shot.

"You just get in?" Del asked.

Phin nodded.

"How's the action in Joliet?"

Phin looked away, into the woods, and spat. "Aurora."

"Aurora. Right. Crazy Ks."

Phin stared at the kid, hard. "Crazy Js." He'd taken the jacket from a Crazy J lieutenant, picked because it was one set he knew the symbols for. "You playin' me, General? Or is this some kind of bullshit test?"

Del Ray blew out a breath and said, "Shee-it," drawing it out into two syllables. "S'your name, cat?"

Phin thought fast. "Mick."

"Mick what?"

"Glade."

"You got steel balls, Mick Glade. Thought I heard them clanging together when you walked up. Need a man with steel balls."

"What's the play?"

"We're gonna hit the garage door, kamikaze style." Del Ray held up one steady hand, then slapped the other into it. "Boom! Bitch is ours."

"In this?" Phin kicked the tire on the Town & County van.

"You down?"

Phin said, "Shee-it." He rubbed his nose and exaggerated a sniffle.

"Ride ain't just for glory, Mick. You crack that door, we can set you up with ice."

"How much?"

"How much can you snort, homes?"

"A lot."

"Then the answer is a lot."

Phin grinned. "Always up for a drive in the country. Bucket got airbags?"

"'Course."

"When?"

"Ain't no time like the present."

Phin considered it. This might be a way to get close to Jack. With enough of a head start, he might be able to get her into the car and take off before anyone knew what was happening.

Assuming Jack was watching the monitors.

Assuming Jack would recognize him in gang colors, and see him through the windshield.

Assuming Jack wouldn't turn on the scalding sprinklers, or otherwise try to stop him.

Lots of assumptions, there.

And if he made it inside, then what? What if they couldn't escape? Rather than only Jack being trapped, they'd both be trapped. Stuck there, sitting ducks, waiting to be slaughtered by gangbangers or burned alive by the approaching forest fire.

If they were both killed, that would leave Sam without any parents. Phin didn't want to think about what would happen to his little girl if she had to be raised by Harry McGlade.

The better bet was for Phin get the hell out of there, try to find help. That's what Jack would want him to do. Even if Phin did get to her, she'd no doubt be pissed off he took the risk.

"So you down?" Del Ray asked.

Was he down with seeing his wife for maybe the last time, even if it wound up becoming a huge fight with her screaming at him before both of them were killed?

Phin looked toward the house, pictured Jack's face, and said to himself, "Hell yeah."

JACK

I stared at the monitors, listening to ambient sounds through the console speakers.

It was like watching a natural disaster unfold live on CNN.

I was afraid, of course. For me. For Phin. For Sam, because if we died I really didn't want her being raised by Harry McGlade. She'd go to my mother first, of course. But Mom was old, and there was a convoluted relationship between my mother and Harry that could potentially lead to Samantha and Harry Junior becoming step-siblings, which was almost as frightening as the three ring circus outside.

But underneath the fear and dread, my current situation was the stuff of black comedy. I'd spent two years, locked up in my house afraid that a lone serial killer named Luther Kite might show up, and the moment I leave I'm surrounded by a hundred killers who were not Luther Kite. Cue Alanis Morissette and her *Ironic* song.

There had been no more attacks since the fire, which Harry's sprinklers had finally extinguished. The temperature gauge registered 122°, and it had only risen a single degree since I'd shut off the water. I didn't know if that was hot enough to repel them.

Escape seemed impossible. They'd torched our SUV. The house was surrounded. The lack of any cell signal told me they'd secured their perimeter.

Eventually someone would come looking for me. Phin. Harry. Val. The local authorities. In theory, my chances would improve the longer I was able to hold out. Unless T-Nail's plan banked on someone trying to save me.

I recalled several times in my past when I was faced with hostage situations. None of the memories were pleasant.

What if they had Phin, and began cutting off his toes one at a time until I let them in?

I couldn't handle that.

There was movement on the monitor. I watched, jaw clenched, as a van approached the house and began to drive in circles on the lawn, slowly picking up speed.

I guessed the game plan, and frowned.

Harry's front door held up to gunfire and a grenade, but I didn't think it could withstand a three ton head-on collision.

The van began to honk. The driver was no doubt trying to psyche himself up. As a cop, I'd seen more than a few car accident aftermaths. Airbags only did so much. The moron who was driving either had a death wish, or was ignorant of the dangers involved. I didn't know whether to blame his parents, society, or the bad example set by television shows, which showed people walking away from crashes that would almost always prove fatal in real life.

I stopped dwelling on his motivation and began to dwell on mine. Was I going to just sit there while someone rammed his way inside?

No.

I jogged into the living room, over to the balistraria.

Balistraria. Embrasure. Crenel.

The open space between the merlons. Every good castle had one, and Harry's house was no exception.

I swung the plate back, exposing the cross-shaped hole in the wall, and peeked outside. It was a window, of sorts, only three inches wide and two feet high, shaped like a lower case letter *t*. In medieval times, archers shot their arrows through the balistraria from safely inside the castle, the tiny opening large enough to aim accurately through but practically impenetrable to enemy forces.

I didn't have a bow and arrow. But I did have a Bushmaster Predator with a drum of 5.56 NATO rounds.

I shouldered the weapon, thumbed off the lever safety, and aimed through the balistraria at the approaching van.

PHIN

Keeping his foot steady on the accelerator, Phin drove in another circle, his free hand tapping on the horn.

BEEP BEEP BEEEEEEP... BEEP BEEP BEEP BEEEEEEEEP!

He swung past the tree line, catching a brief glimpse of Del Ray.

BEEP BEEP BEEEEEEP... BEEP BEEP BEEP BEEEEEEEEP!

Back toward the house again. Was Jack even watching?

More important, was she listening?

BEEP BEEP BEEEEEEP... BEEP BEEP BEEP BEEEEEEEEP!

Once more around. Del Ray was beginning to look agitated. Maybe he thought Phin was chickening out. That was fine. Better he thought Phin was a coward, than trying to signal his wife.

BEEP BEEP BEEEEEEP... BEEP BEEP BEEP BEEEEEEEEP!

Come on, Jack. I know it's a monotone, but you know this.

Just listen, Jack.

Listen.

JACK

I couldn't make out the driver in my scope. He blurred past, too fast to see, and too fast to track.

I narrowed my choices down to two. I could spray the van, hoping to hit the tires or engine block to stop it. Or I could target the driver.

Shooting somebody, even in an obvious self-defense situation, didn't appeal to me. But I didn't see any other way to stop the van. Even if I blew out the tires and killed the motor, momentum could still carry it into the house. Then I'd be forced to shoot everyone who came in.

But if I shot the driver, it would not only prevent a breech, it would also give the rest of the gang something to think about. The woods they hid in weren't as defendable as the house. If they knew I had a rifle, and the ability to use it, they'd be less inclined to continue their siege.

So by killing this one joker, I might actually be saving the lives of dozens.

I didn't like the idea. Murder disgusted me. Self-defense or not, I had no desire to take another person's life. But I didn't see any other choice.

Plus, that rhythmic horn tapping was getting on my nerves.

PHIN

He did another lap, and paused honking for long enough to lower the driver side window. He couldn't call to her, because then the gang would know. But maybe Jack would see him. That was the first part of Phin's plan.

The second part, Phin was vague on. If Jack saw him, maybe Phin could get her into the vehicle and they could drive off. They'd be chased, of course, but at least it was a chance at escape.

BEEP BEEP BEEEEEEP... BEEP BEEP BEEP BEEEEEEEEP!

"Come on, Jack," Phin whispered to himself. "Pay attention."

DEL RAY

Something was wrong.

This Mick dude was driving around honking like some sort of circus clown. At first, Del thought he was gathering speed. Then, he assumed Mick was having second thoughts. But now, Del had no idea what was happening.

He could tell the man had a coke habit—the dried blood around his nostrils was a dead-giveaway. Had Mick snorted away his mind? Was he so stoned right now he had no idea what he was doing?

And why was he honking that same beat, over and over?

Unless…

Unless that man wasn't really a Crazy J.

When realization came to Del Ray, it came fast. He whipped out his cell phone, checked the text messages his surveillance team had sent earlier, and the attached pictures. Pictures of the cop's house in the suburbs. Pictures of Jack.

And one blurry shot of Phineas Troutt.

Del stared at the photo and felt his ears burn. The General of the Eternal Black C-Notes had just given van keys to his target's goddamn husband.

JACK

Rather than try to lead the moving van, I pointed the rifle at a static spot on the property. As the van did a loop, I adjusted my aim. For some reason, the driver had opened his window.

Which made it easier for me. The next time he circled, I'd take the shot.

BEEP BEEP BEEEEEEP... BEEP BEEP BEEP BEEEEEEEEP!

Jesus, that was irritating. And it was the same tune, over and over. As if he was purposely trying to annoy me. Like Phin did when he sang *You and Me Against the World*.

The van came back around. I breathed out and put steady pressure on the trigger, beginning to squeeze...

PHIN

He saw Del Ray pull his gun and shout, but Phin couldn't hear him over the horn.

"Goddammit, Jack!" Phin growled. "Why can't you recognize—"

JACK

"You and me against the world," I said, finally getting it.

That was the tune the van was honking.

Phin's behind the wheel.

I pulled my aim just before I fired, shooting into the woods.

The woods shot back.

But instead of attacking the house, the gunfire was focused on the van. Phin skidded in the dirt, his two rear tires blowing out, correcting his angle and heading for the garage as his windows splintered and his side panels were chewed up by bullets.

I had to beat him there.

I ran, barreling around the corner, beelining for the door, flinging it open and frantically searching for the garage opener.

There. On the wall.

I pressed the button, then jammed the rifle stock tight into my shoulder, taking aim as the heavy, steel door slowly raised up on pneumatic pistons.

The garage door opened to a battlefield. The sound was unworldly. Even on the busiest shooting range I'd never heard so many guns fire at once; like a single, continuous gunpowder explosion without any pause between shots. The van no longer looked like a van. It looked like a robotic skeleton, disintegrating before my eyes in sparks and wisps of smoke.

It was ten meters away and slowing down.

Phin wasn't going to make it.

Incoming bullets ricocheted off the concrete garage floor, and I slammed my back against the side wall and crouched, returning fire. The van swerved right, left, right. The tires were shredded, the rims throwing up dirt and dead leaves as they bit into the ground. I couldn't see Phin through the spider web cracks in the front windshield, but if he tried to exit out of either door, he'd be ground meat.

Then the windshield bulged, and popped out, and Phin was scrambling out over the hood, using the van as cover, sprinting toward the garage.

I hit the opener again, and the heavy duty garage door began to roll back down as I laid down some suppressing fire.

At five meters away, I began to think that he might actually make it.

Then automatic weapon fire caught him on the right, and he pitched sideways, hitting the ground and skidding on the heels of his hands.

His eyes met mine, and time stopped.

I couldn't hear the gunfire.

I couldn't see the bullets kicking up dirt all around him.

Phin's face became my whole universe, and I committed it to memory. The determination there. The resignation. The pain. The sadness.

But most of all, the look in his eyes. The look that had never left, since we'd first been together. No matter what we'd gone through. No matter how hard things got.

The look that told me, more than words ever could, more than actions ever could, how much he loved me.

In super-slow motion, more bullets stitched across his back, but his gaze didn't falter, his eyes locking on mine until the garage door closed.

PHIN

He couldn't draw a breath in, and the bullets kept raining down. He wondered if, beneath the vest, he had any ribs that weren't broken.

But he didn't feel any pain.

Phin's lame rescue attempt had failed miserably. Save for one thing.

He'd gotten to see Jack one last time.

And, strangely, that was worth it. As the gang closed in around him, Phin smiled.

"Bye-bye, Jack. Ya'aburnee."

Then the garage door began to open once again.

JACK

As soon as the garage door was two feet up I hit *stop* and scooted underneath it, going sideways so the tank on my back didn't get caught. Then I crawled across the open ground as bullets kicked up dirt on either side of me.

Phin was two meters away.

He shook his head at me, his mouth curled in a grin. I lip-read him as he said, "You idiot."

I got up on one knee. According to the manual, it was point and shoot.

I pointed at the woods and squeezed the trigger, spitting out fifteen meters of flame. I sprayed a wide arc, the X15 hissing like a dragon clearing its throat. Gangbangers scattered. The gunfire ceased. General panic erupted everywhere I aimed.

I guess they'd never seen a flamethrower before.

Phin had a stupid-ass smile on his face, and he reached out his hand for me.

I grabbed it.

The touch was electric.

I continued to spit fire as I dragged Phin, inch by inch, back to the garage.

A shot blew past my scalp, so close I felt the wind.

Another creased my thigh.

Two hit my vest, punching the air from my lungs.

I reached the garage door.

Killed the flame.

Squeezed underneath.

Pulled Phin in after me.

And then, with my final reserves of strength, I slapped my palm against the opener and the garage door sealed itself shut.

For a moment, we both lay there on the concrete. Not moving. Not talking. Then Phin began to make a noise. A croaking, barking kind of noise. I knew what a death rattle was.

The last sound a man made before his heart stopped.

This wasn't a death rattle.

My husband was laughing.

"I can't believe you did that," he said between chuckles.

"Me? You were driving in circles like some kind of moron."

"I was trying to save you."

Now it was my turn to laugh. "Yeah, way to go with that."

My hand found his, and we squeezed so hard we practically fused our flesh together.

"You hit?" he asked.

"In the vest. You?"

"Once or twice."

"Can you walk?"

"Won't know until I try."

I managed to take a knee, then pull myself up to stand. I braced against the wall for Phin to climb me, noting the smears of blood he'd left on the concrete floor. I took the back sling off my shoulders, setting the X15 on the floor. Then we stumbled back inside, limping to the infirmary. I flipped on the overhead light, bathing my man in bright neon.

He looked like he'd crawled through hell. His face, neck, and hands were scraped and pock-marked from windshield glass. His shirt shredded.

"Jesus, Phin."

"Tough day at the office."

I carefully helped him out of his Kevlar, and stopped counting slugs caught in the weave after two dozen.

His chest was purple, like he'd been spray painted.

"Oh... baby."

I was almost afraid to touch him, but I reached a tentative hand out and traced my finger down his right arm.

"Did any penetrate?" I asked.

"I don't know. But I like it when you say *penetrate*."

I reached for his belt buckle, gently tugging down his fly, surprised by his reaction.

"You're kidding," I said, gripping him in my hand.

"You with that flamethrower. It was the sexiest thing I've ever seen."

"We can't," I said, and as I said it I realized how badly I wanted him. "You're one big bruise."

"I'm not bruised there."

"Phin..."

"Are you hit?"

He ran his fingers down my arms, tearing the Velcro from my vest. Then his hands were inside my shirt, cupping my breasts.

"Those are fine," I said. It came out softer than I'd meant.

"They sure are."

"This is stupid."

"So let's be stupid."

He moved closer, his cheek against mine, his lips next to my ear. His hands moved down the small of my back and pulled me close.

"I've missed you so much," he whispered.

And that was all she wrote. Whatever dam had been inside me for the last few months finally burst into a billion pieces. I didn't just love this man. I wanted him. I wanted him so badly it made my whole body throb. I wanted to devour him. I wanted to possess him. The entire world could have been blowing up around us—and for all I knew it was—and all I cared about was sex.

Then my pants were down—whether he did it or I did it I had no idea—and he lifted me up on the examination bench, and my knees were hooked around his shoulders, my hands in his hair, pulling his face between my legs and wondering why the hell I'd been avoiding this for so long. What an idiot I'd been. How could he have put up with me? Then my panties were off, and his lips and tongue found me, and it was too intense and too fast and too hot and I yelled at him to stop because I didn't want to come this way, I wanted him inside me, but he didn't listen and my orgasm shook me so violently I screamed until my throat burned.

Somehow he got up on the bench, entering me hard, driving into me, and I knew he wasn't going to last long and I didn't want him to and the thought of him coming was the most arousing thing ever.

Phin lasted twenty seconds.

It only took me ten.

We cried out together, my face buried in his shoulder, his arm cradling my head, my ankles locked around his back. I continued to grind against him as he slowed and eventually stopped.

"So," I said, staring into my husband's eyes. "You liked the flamethrower?"

Phin laughed, then grimaced in pain. The grimace softened, his eyes becoming moist.

"You okay?" I asked. I meant it in a whole lot of different ways.

"I'm so sorry, Jack. I shouldn't have left."

"You deserve a medal for putting up with me. I've been awful."

"We've both been awful."

"You've been patient. I've been a bitch. You were right, Phin. It's you and me against the world. I don't know how I forgot that. But I won't, ever again. I promise."

He shifted his weight, the grimace returning.

"We need to tape your ribs. Are any broken?"

He nodded.

"How many?"

"How many are there?"

I switched out of slut goddess mode and into nurture mode, slipping out from beneath him, going through McGlade's first aid drawers. I found a rack of vials and picked out some morphine sulfate, then searched for a syringe.

"What is that?"

"Morphine."

Phin shook his head. "I don't want that."

"It will take away the pain."

"It will also dull my senses."

"Phin, you look like one of the California Raisins."

"It's just pain."

"Do you have any coke left?"

He raised an eyebrow. "I threw it away before I came home."

"Well, that was stupid."

"It was a conscious choice. You over drugs."

"And now you've got fifteen broken ribs—"

"Probably closer to twenty."

"—and I don't know what to do."

"Advil. And check if Harry has Demerol."

I went back to look for pain meds, and felt Phin's hand on my thigh. I flinched when he found a wound.

"You were shot."

"It's a scratch," I said.

"It's bleeding."

Phin got up off the bench and stood next to me. He found some Quikclot combat gauze, and tried to wind it around my bare thigh.

"Open your legs," he told me.

I did. And then his fingers were rubbing something that definitely *was not* my bullet wound.

"Phin. I'm trying to find the Demerol."

"Give me a break. It's been a long time."

I stopped what I was doing and turned, searching his face. "How long has it been?"

"About four minutes."

He did something that made me press against his hand. "How long before that?" I breathed.

"The last time was with you, Jack."

"You never cheated?"

"Of course not."

"Really?"

"Jack, you're my wife, and the mother of my child. If I had to wait for you forever, I would have."

I went doe-eyed, my heart went mushy, and I couldn't get him in my mouth fast enough.

This time, he lasted longer than twenty seconds.

Once again, I did not.

T-NAIL

A flamethrower.

When he saw Jacqueline Daniels run outside, spraying fire, T-Nail started to laugh.

It wasn't a joyful laugh; Terrence Wycleaf Johnson hadn't found humor in anything since he was a child. His laugh was the evolutionary result of pent-up stress, so it was more like an involuntary scream than an expression of mirth.

He sounded like a Rottweiler barking. And probably resembled one as well. No smile, no crinkled eyes. Just curled lips and bared teeth.

The laugh only lasted a few seconds, and then he stared, expressionless, as the cop pulled what was obviously her husband back inside the garage.

Had this happened on C-Note turf, he would have executed Del Ray on the spot. Nailed him to a wall and peeled off his face while his soldiers watched. But that would have to wait. Del Ray was insubordinate, and unreliable, but he was still their best chance at getting into that goddamn fortress. Earlier, he'd mentioned a plan.

It was time to find out what that plan was.

T-Nail powered the Gyro over uneven terrain, and caught Del Ray sitting on the hood of a Lexus, staring off into the woods.

"Dynamite is coming," Del said. "Four cases. On its way from Minneapolis-St. Paul."

"When does it get here?"

"Tough to guess. We're jamming radio frequencies so I can't call, and I don't know how far the wildfire has spread. Their direct route may be blocked."

"Guess," said T-Nail.

"Could be two hours. Could be ten hours. But it will get here."

"And will it be enough to get inside?"

"It'll be enough to blow the whole damn house up. We'll either get in, or bring the roof down on top of her."

"I want her alive. I want them both alive."

Del Ray met T-Nail's gaze. T-Nail didn't see any fear there, which was a bad sign. He knew Del Ray was tough. He knew Del Ray was violent. But for the first time, T-Nail wondered if Del Ray was insane.

T-Nail had known some crazies. On the streets, and in the slam. They were the ones you had to be afraid of. They couldn't be bargained with. They weren't predictable. Only sure way to deal with a crazy was to put them down at first opportunity.

But before T-Nail could do that, he needed the dynamite.

"Ramming the house with a truck, that was your idea?"

Del Ray nodded.

"Try it again," T-Nail said. "Use the bus."

He waited for Del to protest. To say something about the cost, or the fact that if the bus was cooked, they couldn't get home. But the dude just nodded again. Playing it cool.

"When this shit is over," T-Nail told him, "the Chi-Town Mavericks are looking for a War Chief. Big set. Eight thousand strong. You the man for the job. You down?"

Del didn't hesitate. "Hells yeah, I'm down."

T-Nail held up his hand, and they shook on it.

"Let's kill this cop and get home." T-Nail turned the Gyro around, motoring away.

Maybe that would keep the crazy in check until the cop was dead.

HERB

After hitching Harry's secret weapon to the Crimebago, Herb was surprised when they got on the expressway and headed in the wrong direction, back toward Chicago.

"I'm pretty sure Wisconsin is north."

"It still is. But we need to pick up Tom Mankowski. I just got a text. He changed his mind and is coming with us."

"Great. So now we're three against a hundred."

"You keep forgetting Homeboy."

"HOMEBOY!" squawked Homeboy.

"How, exactly, is Homeboy going to help?"

"Oh, I'm sure he will," Harry said.

(Author spoiler alert: Homeboy doesn't help at all.)

"What about those amazing cheese blintzes you promised?" Herb asked.

"No time. Jack could be getting gangbanged by gangbangers right now. You want to be the one to tell her she was assaulted for an extra half an hour just so you could stuff your food-hole with tasty, lactose-filled crepes?"

Herb didn't want to be the one to tell Jack that. But he really did crave those tasty, lactose-filled crepes.

As Harry cranked up the music, Herb scooted next to the refrigerator to see what consumables McGlade had stocked. The answer was; almost none. It was packed with about fifty airline-sized bottles of Jagermeister, and half a jar of grape jam.

"Don't eat the jam," McGlade said. "I use that to entertain female guests."

Herb shut the fridge.

He tried Jack's cell phone again.

No answer.

He texted his wife, giving her a vague idea of where he was headed, downplaying the fact that it was probably a suicide mission. Then he picked up the bag of peanuts. When Homeboy saw the bag, he started bobbing his head up and down, screaming like he'd been lit on fire.

Herb put the peanuts back.

In the driver's seat, McGlade was butchering the words to some rock song about keeping your car shiny shiny. His singing ability, like everything else about Harry, was lacking.

"This band is pretty good," Herb said. "Be nice to hear them without your attempt at a duet."

"It's *The Rainmakers*. They rock."

"They still around?"

"I saw them in Kansas City last year. Lead singer is amazing. Listen to that dulcet voice."

"I'd like to. You're preventing that."

"I can't remember his name. Bob Something. Bob Walkenstick. Bob Liverwurst. Bob Rockinghorse. I'll think of it."

"Well, it would be nice to hear him, and not you."

Harry stopped singing.

He lasted a whole two minutes.

Herb thought about Jack. If they did wind up saving her life, she was going to owe him. Big time.

"There's nothing worth fighting for any way you cut it," McGlade sang.

Herb hoped that wasn't true. Then he sighed the sigh of a trapped, unhappy man, and tried to settle in for the long trip ahead.

PHIN

The bulletproof vest hurt so much to put on, Phin almost told his wife to forget it.

But seeing her again had made him more determined than ever to live through this ordeal. So he clenched his teeth and let Jack strap it on him, with only four ibuprofen and a few ace bandages to help with the pain.

"You're an idiot for coming back for me," Jack said, helping him into a shoulder holster.

"I was waiting for you to say that."

After the sex, they'd caught each other up on recent events. Phin didn't mention how many people he'd dispatched, and Jack hadn't asked outright. She had an empathy gene that Phin lacked, and tales of killing—even heroic killing in self-defense—tended to turn her off.

"You could have gone for help," she said.

"If there was a cop in town, he would have shown up at the Walmart. And the nearest town is hours away. The fire is keeping the authorities busy. Even if I did manage to find help, I might not have gotten back in time. I went with my gut."

"And now we're both trapped. And Samantha…"

Phin hugged her, even though it hurt like hell. "We're going to defend ourselves. We can't win, but we can make the price so high that they give up. And if the fire does reach us, I'd rather be in here than out there."

Jack pulled away. "I don't see a happy ending here, Phin. Even if we make it through this. We're always going to be targets. The Folk Nation is huge."

"We're not fighting the Folk Nation. We're fighting one old gang member with a grudge. We get rid of him, the problem should go away."

"Get rid of him?" She narrowed her eyes. "You mean murder him."

"This is a war, Jack. It isn't murder."

"I could make a good argument that all war is murder."

"If you'd capped him twenty years ago, we wouldn't be in this situation."

"I don't murder people, Phin."

Phin considered bringing up someone else from Jack's past, but kept quiet. We all learned to live with the things we've done, and Jack was no exception.

But if Phin had a shot at T-Nail, he was going to take it.

Hell, if Phin had a chance to wipe them all out, he wouldn't even blink. There wasn't much he wouldn't do to protect his family.

"So, while I was valiantly rushing in here—"

"Stupidly rushing in here," Jack interrupted.

"—to save your life and have great sex—"

"The sex was pretty great."

"—did you come up with any sort of plan?"

"I did." Jack winked. "It's all about the balistraria."

"You're kidding. This place has balistraria?"

"You know what balistraria are?"

"Doesn't everyone? Merlons, right? Arrowslits."

She frowned. "Maybe I just went to the wrong schools."

"How many does the house have?"

"Eight."

"So we can kill them through the holes."

"No, not kill. Wound."

Phin's turn to frown. "Jack, we're fighting for our lives, here."

"I know. But you kill one man, you take him out of the fight. But if you wound a man..."

"You take two people out," Phin said, getting it and nodding. "Him, and the one helping him."

"So instead of killing a hundred, we can wound fifty. Not only can we save ourselves, but we can still sleep at night."

He shrugged. "I sleep fine. You're the one with sleeping problems."

Jack placed her hands on Phin's shoulders. "Promise me you're not going to start killing kids."

"Give a kid a gun and he isn't a kid anymore."

"Phin." Jack used the same voice when chiding Sam.

"I'll try my best. We're not all expert shots."

"Just be careful."

Phin put his hands on Jack's hips, drawing her close. She tilted her chin up to be kissed.

Such a natural position for married couples. But Jack had been keeping Phin at arms' length for so long, it almost took him by surprise. He touched his lips to hers, lightly, tenderly, and then her tongue was in his mouth.

Phin pulled away, grinning. "Where have you been?"

"I think I've been so worried about losing you, that I pushed you away. But when I was really confronted with losing you it kicked my ass."

"Or maybe you just needed to get laid."

Jack's grin matched his. "Can't argue with that. Let's get you a gun."

In Harry's armory, Phin chose an Armalite AR-10 with a twenty inch barrel and a twenty-five round magazine. Jack selected a Vortex scope, attached it to the rail, and then Phin followed her to one of the balistrarias. He watched as she shot a tree and spent about thirty seconds futzing with the optics to zero out the weapon.

"You're good to go," she said, handing him the rifle.

Phin gave it a once-over, familiarizing himself with the position of the safety, the mag release, the charging handle, and then he adjusted the stock for a comfortable hold. He sighted the rifle through the balistraria and aimed at a knot on a big pine tree. Phin never learned how to accurately judge distance through a scope, but he'd passed that tree while walking among the gang and estimated it to be about sixty meters away. He pressed the butt of the rifle tight into his shoulder, exhaled slowly through his mouth, and before he took his next breath he slowly squeezed the trigger.

His round took a big chunk out of the knot.

"Nice," Jack said. She'd been standing over his shoulder, peering through the balistraria with binoculars. "You're pretty good, lover."

Phin allowed himself a small grin. In a warped way, Jack's compliment was even more intimate than the sex they'd just had. Maybe Phin's earlier diagnosis had been correct; Jack was an adrenaline junkie who hadn't had a fix in years. She'd never admit it, but Jack missed the excitement.

If they got out of this, Phin promised he'd take her skydiving. Or swimming with sharks. Or maybe he'd take her into the city, and they could rob a few drug dealers. Anything to keep the spark lit.

Phin squinted through the scope and swept to the right, balancing the gun on the cross T bar of the balistraria, pivoting only a centimeter because the focus was so long. He stopped on a familiar sight.

The General.

Not the big guy strapped to the Segway. This was the younger dude, with all the scalps on his vest.

Phin aimed at the man's head. Even though Jack insisted on wounding, Phin wasn't planning on missing this kill shot.

DEL RAY

There was gunfire. A single shot. Del didn't know where it came from, but random shooting had become commonplace since they'd arrived. Some cats just couldn't help themselves from shooting prematurely.

He ignored it, and focused on the task presented to him. T-Nail wanted to wreck the bus. Apparently, during his time in the joint, the OG had forgotten the value of money. This operation was already costing a fortune, and trashing the bus would add on forty K. All he had to do was wait for the dynamite to arrive, and they'd be in, and still have a ride home.

But Del knew this wasn't really about money. Or time.

It was a crazy-ass Idi Amin-style abuse of power. T-Nail was doing it, just because he could.

The next obvious step was for T-Nail to try and eliminate him. Del knew that offer of War Chief was wack. As soon as they killed the cop, T-Nail would come gunning.

Del Ray had to pre-empt that shit.

Another shot. Sounded like a long gun.

Really? Brothers can't keep it holstered?

He walked through the woods until he hunted down a gangsta named Spread. Dude was always up for action. And though Del didn't think his men were expendable like T-Nail did, he knew that Spread was skimming off his street take.

"Yo, gangsta, wassup?" Spread held out his hand for the C-Notes shake.

"T-Nail getting restless. We gotta get in there, dog."

"Place is like Fort Knox, homes. We need a nuke or something."

"We need someone to crash the joint."

"In what? A tank?"

Del Ray held up the keys. "The bus. And you my huckleberry."

"Me? Shit, Del. I'm not up for that."

"You up for a rum runner?"

Spread's eyes got wide.

"I know you're withholding, Spread. You think you can play me like that?"

Spread apparently didn't know better when it came to stealing, but he knew enough not to lie. "Del, man, I'll pay the money back. I—"

Del Ray held up one finger, silencing the man. "Boys are all agitated. Riled up. They'd love to get you in a beat down right about now. Don't know if you'd even live through it, dog. So what's it gonna be? You up for hitting the house? Or we gonna form a circle and blood out?"

"Out?"

"How can I trust you anymore, Spread? You stealin'. C-Notes are all about family and honor. You don't do this, you out."

"And if I do it?"

"Clean slate. We cool. Still gotta take your corner away. But you stay in."

"And no beat down?"

"No beat down."

Spread nodded and took the keys. "Thanks, General."

Del Ray watched him walk off, heading for the bus. T-Nail was wrong about power. True power wasn't people fearing you. It was all about give and take. A good leader knew what his people needed. Spread would bust his ass trying to show Del he was worthy to stay in the C-Notes.

That was the kind of allegiance Del Ray wanted.

He was feeling pretty pleased with himself, and that was when the bullet hit his head.

HERB

I thought Tom had an apartment in Portage Park," Herb said.

He was peering out one of the Crimebago's porthole windows in the rear portion of the recreational vehicle. They were not in Portage Park. They weren't even in Chicago.

"Just making a quick stop first," Harry said.

Herb pushed down his bubbling anger. Getting into a pissing contest with McGlade produced ample heat, but no light. They still had a long trip ahead of them, and civility was essential if Herb wanted to avoid a homicide conviction.

"Jack needs us." Herb kept his voice even, channeling his inner Buddhist monk.

"I'm aware of that, El Gordo. I'm the one who told you about it, remember? Or have the fat cells clogged your brain?"

Monks were serene. Zen. Nothing bothered them. "Why didn't you run your errands before you picked me up?" Herb said, at one with universal calm.

"Yeah, that was one of the options. But then we would have missed out on all this fun we're having."

"Where are we, Harry?"

"We're in the Crimebago, stupid. Watch Homeboy, I'll be right back."

McGlade had parked in front of what looked like an expensive apartment building, or maybe it was a condo. Herb blew out a stiff breath. He checked the GPS on his phone, and saw they were in Skokie.

Could a monk hate somebody? Or did that violate some inner-peace rule?

"I hate him," Herb said to Homeboy.

Homeboy didn't reply. He was sitting on his perch, one eye closed, the other staring blankly into space.

"You asleep?"

No response. His featherless chest was moving, so he wasn't dead.

"Want some meth?" Herb whispered.

Homeboy's other eye immediately opened and he screeched, flapping his naked wings like crazy.

"METH! METH! AAAAAAAAAAAAARG! METH! METH!"

Herb shushed him, using soothing tones. When that didn't shut him up, Herb tried holding up the peanut bag and shaking it seductively. The bird kept on flapping and screaming, its eyes bugging out, shifting weight from one foot to the other in some sort of junkie dance.

The poor thing really wanted some meth. Herb was worried it would give itself a little birdie heart attack. And, knowing McGlade, this stupid exotic animal probably cost thousands of dollars. Herb had taken a staycation because money was tight. He couldn't afford to buy Harry a new parrot.

"METH! AAAAAAAAAAAAAAAAAARG! METH!"

In an effort to get it to settle down, Herb tossed a handful of peanuts at the animal. This seemed to agitate Homeboy even more. Homeboy stopping screaming "METH!" and just screamed, like he was being torn apart by dogs.

Apparently throwing things at birds didn't have a soothing effect.

Desperate, Herb opened the cage and reached inside. Maybe petting or holding the animal would calm it down. It was either that, or Herb would have to hit the streets and try to score some meth.

Rather than shy away, Homeboy leapt onto Herb's arm. Herb hadn't expected that, and was startled enough to take several steps back, taking Homeboy with him as the parrot continued to scream. Herb fell onto the floor, and Homeboy jumped onto his face, his talons latching on to Herb's nose. It perched there, its wings outstretched, squawking so loud Herb could feel it in his whole body.

That's when the cabin door opened. Both Herb and Homeboy stopped panicking and looked in the direction of the sound. Harry McGlade stood there, holding a toddler on his hip.

"I knew it. I'm gone for two minutes and you try to eat my bird."

Herb found himself peeking up at Homeboy's plucked ass. Not a good position to be in.

"Get this thing off me, McGlade."

Harry made no move to help. Instead, he took his cell out and began taking pictures.

"Harry..." Herb warned.

"You asked why I picked you up before running errands? Because: this. Say something funny for YouTube."

"Harry, if this bird shits on me..."

"That would totally go viral. See the birdie, Harry Junior?"

Harry Jr. said, "Plab!"

Herb reached up and gently grabbed Homeboy. It reminded him of the one unpleasant time he petted a Chinese Crested puppy; a hairless bag of bones with loose, warm skin. Incredibly, Homeboy allowed himself to be held without fighting back, and Herb returned him to his cage.

"That was anti-climactic," Harry said, putting his phone away.

Herb waited a few seconds, allowing his blood pressure to settle, before asking, "Why is your son here?"

"Because: sex. Have you met Junior's baby mama? She's a hot yoga instructor. Great body, but dealing with her is like licking your finger and sticking it into a light bulb socket."

"Why is Junior here in the RV, McGlade?"

"Because it's Daddy's court-appointed visitation time. Don't worry, we're dropping him off with a babysitter. Don't tell the court." Harry set the diapered child on the floor, where he flopped onto his face. "Watch him while I drive. Don't let Junior touch Homeboy. Birds have all kinds of nasty diseases."

Herb frowned. This adventure just kept getting better and better.

Harry Junior managed to get up on all fours, and crawled past Herb and toward the kitchenette.

"Is this vehicle baby-proofed?" Herb asked Harry, watching Junior attempt to open up a cabinet. "Are there child locks on things?"

McGlade didn't answer, instead turning on the music.

Harry Junior was able to get the cabinet open—answering Herb's question about child locks—and reached inside. He yanked out a plastic tray, filled with knives.

Herb scooped the child up, getting a whiff of a full diaper.

"Your child needs to be changed!" Herb yelled over the tunes.

"Try changing him into a stripper. That would be awesome. Or a case of beer. Try Grain Belt. I haven't had that beer in years."

"METH!" screeched Homeboy.

Herb stared at Junior. "I don't want to be the bearer of bad news, kid. But you're probably going to be in counselling for the rest of your life."

Junior's lower lip began to quiver, and then tears suddenly appeared and he was bawling.

The kid was even louder than Homeboy. Which Homeboy must have taken as a personal challenge, because his squawking went up several decibels.

McGlade dealt with it by turning up the music. He began singing something about the howling of dogs and wailing of babies and being miserable.

Herb could relate.

JACK

You were aiming at that guy's head," I said to Phin, putting down the binoculars and giving him the stink eye.

"Wind must have taken it," Phin said, completely deadpan.

"The trees shield against the wind. You took the headshot."

"Well, I missed."

"You shot his ear off."

"Wounding him. Which is what you wanted."

I wasn't sure how to make Phin understand, because I didn't know if I fully understood myself.

"Hon," I said, using his pet word for me. The one he hadn't used in months. "The only thing that separates the good guys from the bad guys is the choices we make."

"The dude wears a vest made of scalps. Human scalps."

"That's horrible. But it proves my point. We can't be like that."

"They're trying to kill us, Jack. They're the enemy."

"And we have to be better than the enemy. We have a daughter together. A beautiful, wonderful daughter filled with unlimited potential. Is this the example you want to set for Sam? Kill or be killed?"

"If we don't live through this, we won't be able to set any kind of example."

"Well, it's the example I want to be. What if Sam came up to you one day and asked about the bad things you've done. Would you tell her?"

"Yes."

"You'd tell her about everything? The drugs? The robberies? The deaths?"

Phin didn't answer. But his expression softened a bit.

"Phin, you think our daughter wants to know those things about you? I don't even want to know those things about you. Did you notice I didn't ask how many people died at the Walmart?"

"I did notice that. I made a judgment call."

"This is a judgment call, too. And we're choosing to wound, not kill. Okay?"

Phin closed his eyes. Then he nodded. "Okay."

"Arms and legs."

"Okay."

"You promise?"

He looked at me. Really looked at me. I saw acceptance there. And determination. And most of all, love.

I hoped he saw the same things in my face.

"I promise," my husband said.

"Kiss on it."

Phin gave me a soft kiss on the lips. He cared enough to listen to me, even if I wound up being wrong.

I really didn't want to be wrong.

"We're going to live through this," I said. "But I want to be able to live with myself, and with you, when it's over."

"I will shoot to wound, Lieutenant. You have my word."

He went back to the balistraria. I picked up my Bushmaster and took the merlon next to him.

The gang was in panic mode, running this way and that way. Many were trying to take cover behind trees that weren't wide enough.

There were arms and legs aplenty.

Long distance shooting required many of the same skills as my specialty, which was handguns. Steady hands were important, but so was concentration and patience. I'd seen men no more than a few meters away unload an entire magazine and miss every shot because they'd been too excited or emotional. The calmer you were, the better your aim.

I sighted an exposed shoulder, roughly a hundred and fifty meters away. I relaxed, letting the rifle become an extension of my body. Pointing a gun was like pointing a finger.

To my left, Phin fired.

"Hit," he said.

I kept focus, pulling the trigger so gently I felt the exact moment of the breakpoint. The firing pin snapped home, the bullet went where it was supposed to. I watched the man spin and fall, clutching his new wound.

"Got two," Phin said.

"It isn't a contest. These are human beings."

Phin shot again. "Three."

I found a target, in full retreat sprint. Led him. Squeezed. His knee blew out, and he ate the ground.

Phin fired again. Didn't say anything.

"Missed?" I asked.

"What counts as wounded?"

"Taking the man down."

"Well, he's down."

"Phin…"

"He could live. Maybe. With immediate medical attention. And a heart transplant."

I looked at him. "This isn't a joke."

"I'm doing my best."

"Do better."

"Yes, ma'am."

I located another poor sap who didn't know the tree he hid behind was too narrow. He was two hundred meters away, which probably seemed like far enough.

It wasn't. I shot him in the hip.

This went on for ten minutes. They continued to run away. We continued to shoot arms and legs.

"They're at three hundred meters," I told Phin. "Remember how to read mil dots?"

"No."

"Aim one and a half dots below center, allow for bullet drop."

If you fired a bullet straight at shoulder height, and dropped a bullet at shoulder height, they'd hit the ground at the same time. Gravity exerted its dominance over mass no matter how fast the mass was travelling forward. The work-around was the parabola. When you threw a ball, you didn't throw it straight. You also threw it up, so it arced. It was the same with bullets. Raising the barrel meant the bullet went up before it went down. The round lost a little speed, but could go farther.

"Let's check the sides," Phin said.

We went to opposite balistrarias, across from each other in the living room. Here, the gangbangers hadn't retreated as far, and I was able to pick off three in short order. Phin got one.

We switched again, and plugged five more.

By this time, they'd all gotten the point, and had either ran out of range, or had taken adequate cover. I went back to my original balistraria, and only saw men I'd already hit.

"Give them time to grab the wounded," I said, resting my stock on the floor.

"You're being too kind here, Jack."

"And when they come to get the wounded," I continued, "shoot them."

He glanced at me, grinning. "I love you."

I wasn't proud of the fact that we were bonding over this. But, truth was, I hadn't felt this alive in months. Or years.

Shit. Maybe I was one of the bad guys after all.

I went into my duffle bag, reloading my magazine, and then Phin starting shooting as fast as he could pull the trigger. I hurried over to him.

"What's happening?"

"We're in trouble."

I looked through the binocs.

Heading straight for the house, two hundred meters away and picking up speed, was a bus. I couldn't see the driver; he'd stacked bulletproof vests on the dashboard.

I let the binocs fall, bringing up my gun. "Aim for the engine block," I told Phin.

But Phin was gone.

DEL RAY

Del Ray pressed a clotting cloth to the remains of his right ear. In all his years of banging, he'd never been shot before.

It hurt. A lot.

They'd taken out a dozen of his men, but there were no fatalities. Either the cop and her husband were poor shots, or they weren't playing for keeps.

Interesting.

It was also interesting how they'd done the shooting. Apparently, there were some sort of slits in the walls where windows should have been.

Del wondered who the hell owned this place.

Could it be somebody connected?

That would be bad.

Except for a few occasional and temporary alliances, the C-Notes avoided the mafia. Wiseguys kept their action to the ritzy parts of town, Folks kept it to the hood, and they stayed out of each other's way.

What if the cop was protected? Had they just started a war with the mob?

It was a winnable war. The bangers had more men, and more guns, than the wiseguys. But there would be huge costs.

How many brothers was T-Nail willing to lose just to have his revenge? These were Del Ray's homies. He'd known a lot of them since he was a shorty. Some of them weren't even born when T-Nail went to jail. They shouldn't be forced to die for him.

He watched Spread fire up the bus, and then he called one of his lieutenants, LeBron, over.

"Take five guys to Walmart in town. I need you to do some shopping."

PHIN

The punt gun was over three meters long, and when Phin went to grab it his ribs wailed at him. The weapon weighed damn near a hundred pounds.

Phin hefted it onto his shoulder, the pain squeezing tears out of his eyes, and then stared down at the box of shells, each over four centimeters wide and the length of three D cell batteries. To grab them, he had to do an awkward squat, and he couldn't lift the box. He was able to palm two of them, and barely got back into a standing position.

Gunshots echoed throughout the house. Jack, firing at the bus.

Phin went sideways through the doorway, and then carried the gun—step by agonizing step—into the living room.

"Help me," he called to his wife.

She fired once more, and turned to him. Her eyes went wide. "Seriously?"

But Jack immediately came over, helping Phin wrestle the gigantic barrel up into the balistraria, where it barely fit.

"A hundred meters and closing," Jack said, checking outside.

Phin hurried back to the butt of the gun. He knelt down, his broken ribs grinding against each other, and stared at the hammer and the trigger assembly. He had no clue how to load the weapon.

"Open the breach," Jack said. "There should be a lever or a button."

There wasn't anything. Phin could make out a seam, and a hinge, but he couldn't figure out how to unlock it.

"Eighty meters. Load it, Phin."

"Working on it."

Phin ran his hands along the underside of the stock, touching the trigger guard. It wiggled. He pulled on it, and the gun snapped open.

"Seventy meters and picking up speed."

Phin slid one of the giant cartridges inside, closed the breach, and lifted up the weapon to his shoulder as he knelt there.

"Fifty meters. Don't shoulder it! You'll break your collarbone."

He adjusted his grip so the stock was under his armpit and the recoil wouldn't hit him.

"To the right!"

Phin shuffled on his knees.

"More... more... stop! Fire!"

Phin pulled the trigger.

Nothing happened. He'd forgotten to cock the hammer.

"Thirty meters! Shoot!"

Hammer back. Trigger squeeze.

Nothing.

"Bad round!" Jack yelled at him.

Phin opened the breach again, tugged out the dud shell, rammed a new one in, and closed the weapon. He drew the hammer back.

"Ten m—"

He pulled the trigger and the punt gun went off with the force of a cannon, tearing itself out of Phin's hands, skidding backwards across the wooden floor.

A moment later, the house shook. Phin couldn't hear the impact because he'd been deafened by the punt gun. But the bus must have hit them. Jack helped him up, and they jogged into the control room to gape at the monitors.

What was left of the bus—the punt gun shredded the whole front of it—had narrowly missed the garage door, instead slamming into the side of the house. They watched a man stagger out of the missing side door, then half-run/half-stumble back into the woods.

Jack said something, but Phin couldn't hear her above the ringing. Guns were loud. Rock concert loud. But that punt gun was preternatural. It was like holding a firecracker next to your ear. He squinted at Jack, trying to read her lips, and her hands were on his arm, trailing down to his finger.

Which didn't look like a finger at all. Because fingers weren't supposed to be jutting out at that angle. And facing the wrong way.

When the punt gun recoiled, it had dislocated and broken his index finger, which now curled around like a stretched-out Slinky.

Phin had a moment of sickly realization; the injury had been so quick, and his adrenaline pumping so hard, that his body didn't know yet that it had sustained an injury. But the pain was going to hit, and hit hard.

Which it did. Even harder than he ever could have guessed.

On the plus-side, it made him completely forget about his broken ribs.

On the minus side, he felt his knees give out, and the room got spinny, and as he fell onto his ass he hoped he didn't throw up because he didn't want to look weak in front of Jack.

So instead, he did something even worse.

He passed out.

HERB

Homicide Detective Tom Mankowski didn't dress well enough to be called a *metrosexual*, but his long, reddish blonde hair was tied back in a bun, and his two-day growth of beard was man-scaped just enough to call him a *hipster*. Which Herb didn't do. But he did think of the word while shaking Tom's hand. He also thought about how much this cop looked like a young Thomas Jefferson, straight off the nickel.

"Welcome to the Crimebago, Tom," Harry said from the driver's seat as he pulled back into traffic. "That's Harry Junior, and Homeboy. Harry Junior is the one wearing the diaper and napping next to Herb. Homeboy is the one in the cage. Herb is the land whale. Help yourself to whatever is in the fridge, and if the ride gets boring you and Herb can play some chess, assuming Herb knows how. Board is in the cabinet with Junior's toys, next to the dishwasher."

Tom took a seat across from Herb and said, "Why is the parrot named Homeboy?"

"Former owners. I don't know whether to blame their parents, or society in general. Something went wrong somewhere."

"Why is it naked?"

"He's addicted to methamphetamine, so he plucked out all his feathers."

Tom nodded, as if that answer made perfect sense. "So, how have you been, Sarge? Haven't ran into you in a while."

"I spent all morning with McGlade, that's how I've been. You?"

"Not that bad. But close."

Tom talked about The Snipper case; a serial killer targeting webcam models. Things weren't going well.

"I've been following that one," Harry interrupted. "Seems like a real nutjob. Herb and I have run into a few of those."

More than a few. There was a period of a few weeks, after the Michigan incident, that Herb had been unable to sleep because he'd been afraid to close his eyes.

"Herb had his eyes sewn shut by a psycho," Harry said.

Hence being afraid. Herb would never forget that pain, that fear. And Harry had endured even worse.

"I had it even worse," Harry said.

Harry had been electroshocked by the same killer.

"I was electroshocked by the same guy," Harry said.

Herb wondered, for a brief moment, if Harry was somehow reading his mind. But he dismissed the thought; it was impossible to read someone else's mind when you didn't have one of your own.

"One guy kidnapped me, broke my arm, and kept twisting it to lure Jack to him," Herb said. "That one was bad."

"Dude, electroshock is worse than a tiny little fracture," Harry said.

"He was grinding bone on bone."

"Bone on bone is like foreplay. I still don't have full control over my bladder."

"Did you ever?" Herb asked.

"When I laugh too hard, I spurt like a sprinkler. Got kicked out of Amy Schumer's last movie, because some kid tripped on the puddle I made in the aisle. In hindsight, shouldn't have ordered the five liter pop at the concession stand."

"That's not an electroshock problem, McGlade. That's a prostate problem."

"You're a prostate problem."

"That doesn't even make sense."

"Sure it does. You're a pain in the ass."

McGlade began to laugh at his own joke. Then he said, "Ah, dammit. Cleanup in aisle pants."

"I was tied up and branded by a guy," Tom offered.

"How much branding are we talking here?" Harry asked. He was stuffing fast food napkins into his open fly.

"Enough that I passed out. And then the killer licked the burn."

"Sounds like a fairy princess tickle party compared to my hand." Harry waved his prosthetic limb. "Fingers cut off, one at a time, stumps cauterized with a blowtorch. Doctors couldn't save anything, had to amputate. Remember that one, Herb?"

"Yes. I got a chest full of roofing nails."

"Yeah! Right! I remember making a joke about you getting nailed. You missed it because you were in the ER, under sedation. Also, I didn't go visit you. What else you got, Tom?"

"I was just bitten by a guy."

"Bitten, huh? Well, it's not a contest. Because if it was, you'd lose. But you're young yet. Plenty of time for more maniacs to torture you before your career is over."

"Fingers crossed," Tom said.

Harry turned the music back on and sang off-key about stupid ways to die.

"So how's the personal life?" Herb asked Tom. Tom's pained expression was all Herb needed as an answer. "Question withdrawn. You play chess?"

"A little."

Herb bent over and opened the cabinet. It contained two very dirty stuffed animals, a Fisher-Price See n' Say, an open box of wood screws, three chewed-up He-Man dolls, a dirty diaper that seemed to have petrified into stone, half a box of twelve gauge shotgun shells, and the aforementioned chess set.

Herb placed the box on a pull-out table and removed the contents: Five pawns, a checker, and a pewter race car from an old *Monopoly* game. Plus a cheese curl.

There wasn't a board.

"Well, looks like it's gonna be *Zombie Sugar Jackers*," Tom said, pulling out his cell phone.

"What's *Zombie Sugar Jackers*?" Herb asked. The cheese curl had a dark smudge on it, but it was still looking pretty good.

"It's like a cross between *Candy Crush* and *Angry Birds*, with some *Fruit Ninja* and *Clash of Clans* mixed in. But with zombies."

"I don't know those other games. But I like zombies. It's fun?"

"It's like electronic crack. I had to remove the app from my phone when my girlfriend was visiting, or else I would have been playing it the whole time she was here."

You couldn't get a better endorsement than that. Herb took out his cell and went to the app store. He found *Zombie Sugar Jackers* in the Top 10 bestseller category.

"Huh. And it's even free."

Tom chuckled. Herb downloaded the game and settled in to play.

The tutorial was convoluted. Some silly backstory about the Queen of Sugarland having to defend her kingdom from candy-loving zombies known as the Munch Bunch. She did this, naturally, by arranging three of the same kind of chocolate candy in a row on a large grid. Herb began matching candies, and soon figured out the game was a lot deeper than he'd guessed. Getting three in a row often involved several moves. If you failed, you had to redo the level. All the while, the Munch Bunch zombies were getting closer. If they got too close, they'd surround you with a Snack Pack Attack, and it was game over.

Herb found the app to be a worthwhile distraction. There was a good mix of dexterity, intuition, and timing. Within ten minutes he was fully invested.

"How do you blow up the Gloomer Glum Rocks?" Herb asked Tom when he got to level 8.

"Peppermint mines."

"Where do you get peppermint mines?"

"You buy them with sweet beets."

"Where do you get—"

Tom paused his game and glanced at Herb. "Have you planted your sugar garden yet?"

"What is—"

"Lower left-hand corner. Blinking icon."

Herb clicked the icon, and watched a quick tutorial of how to grow sweet beets and candy canes. It led to a mini-game where you had to throw coconuts at the Munch Bunch to keep them from devouring your garden before it grew to maturity. Herb was doing quite well until some giant gooey monster came by and devoured seven rounds worth of growth.

"What the hell just ate my sugar garden?" Herb said, staring at his barren field.

"The Honeybeast."

"How do I stop the Honeybeast from eating my sweet beets and candy canes?"

"You have to join a sugar clan for protection."

In hindsight, obvious.

"Are you in a sugar clan?" Herb asked.

"Yeah."

"Can I join yours?"

"I'll send you an invite, but you have to be approved by the clan leader. What's your gamer name?"

"HBenedict1966."

A moment later, a pop-up banner appeared on Herb's screen from RnRSpiderCopTurbo, which Herb had to admit was a much cooler gamer name than HBenedict1966. Herb accepted the invitation.

"I put in a good word for you with the clan leader, KickAximus Scrote. He's got a Rank 58 Garden. One of the top players in the country."

Herb read the latest pop-up. "KickAximus just messaged me, asking if I'm willing to die for my clan. What do I say?"

"Say you pledge your chocolate shield to his sugary cause, and give him ten candy bars in tribute."

"Where do I get candy bars?"

"Upper right of screen."

Herb clicked on an icon and saw they were 99 cents each.

"That's ten bucks," he said, frowning.

"If you don't want to pay, you can earn the candy bars in the game."

"How?"

"By trading in fifty sweet beets."

"But the Honeybeast keeps eating them."

"Better make up your mind quickly. KickAximus will be going to bed soon."

Herb looked at his wrist, remembered he stopped wearing a watch when he got the smart phone, and then checked the time. "It's only a little past noon."

"He lives in the United Arab Emirates, ten hours ahead."

"He's in bed by ten?"

"He's eight years old."

Herb didn't want to spend the money. After all, the reason he was on a staycation was because his financial portfolio was less than stellar. Technically, he didn't even have a financial portfolio. He had a 401k that he never put enough into, and Bernice had a coffee can filled with Kennedy silver dollars under the bed. His wife had dreams of travelling when he retired, and Herb wanted her dreams to come true. That meant pinching pennies.

But seeing as these ninety-nine cent candy bars were for a little kid, Herb made peace with the purchase and clicked *Buy Now*. Two minutes and ten dollars later he was the newest member of the BigguPooPoo Clan.

"Our clan name is vaguely offensive," Herb said.

"Eight-year-old kid. Not many things funnier than potty humor. Our co-leader is PeePeeMonkeyBooger."

"His younger brother?"

"His dad. I think they're oil sheiks."

"Oil sheiks?"

"Richer than kings. Blame it on our inexhaustible appetite for fossil fuels. Have you seen KickAximus Scrote's garden? Kid must have put ten grand into the game. Instead of upgrading by playing, he just pays for it."

"So why did he need my ten candy bars?"

"You can always start your own candy clan. Then members would pay you tribute."

"Can I do that?"

"Not with your crummy little Rank 7 Garden."

Herb made a face. "This game really doesn't seem to be fair to the people who want to play for free."

"Welcome to the wonderful world of casual gaming."

"And to think I used to waste my time reading fiction."

"I know. Look what you've been missing. Okay... you're in the clan, so I can give you a Nose Bopper Gun. That should keep the Honeybeast away so you can grow your sweet beets and candy canes."

"Thanks, Tom. What level are you at?"

"Got a Rank 32 Garden, and I'm on Level 116."

Herb wished he had a Rank 32 Garden and had reached Level 116. He went back to gardening. After defending several rounds against the Munch Bunch, he bopped the Honeybeast and had his first successful harvest. Then he was able to buy peppermint mines with the sweet beets to blow up the Gloomer Glum Rocks.

Which was when the Munch Bunch finally closed in and devoured him.

Herb tried to restart, but the app locked him out.

"My game isn't working."

"Did you lose?"

"Yeah. That Munch Bunch doesn't play around."

"You ran out of nectar fuel?"

"The Curly Whirl keeps drinking it."

"Wait ten minutes. Your reserves will automatically refill."

"Wait ten minutes? Doing what?"

"I check CNN."

"The answer is on CNN?"

Tom paused his game again. "*Zombie Sugar Jackers* is freeware. But they make money via in-app purchases. One of the things you can purchase is more playtime, in case you lose. Or else you can wait ten minutes, and you can play again for free."

"That's insidious."

Herb wished he'd thought of it. That was an even better scam than being an oil sheik. One day, the Middle East would run out of oil. It was virtually impossible to run out of sweet beets and peppermint mines.

Tom nodded. "Yeah. They're raking it in. You can also buy cheats to make the game easier."

"What's the fun in that?"

"Well, let's say you can't get past level 58 because the Carmel Donut Dragon keeps burning up your sweet beets. You can buy a Bubblegum Bomb to gum up the dragon's wings so you can pass the level."

"Can't I get a Bubblegun Bomb some other way?"

"They pop up randomly in your garden, but you have to harvest them before they disappear. It's basically impossible."

Herb still had nine minutes and forty-six seconds on his Sugar Timer before he could play again, so he switched to CNN. The Wisconsin wildfire was the top story. Hundreds of acres had been destroyed, and evacuations were in full effect.

In other news, one of the Kardashians did something, and North Korea was still acting like North Korea.

Herb went back to *Zombie Sugar Jackers*, watching the seconds tick slowly by. Still seven more minutes before he could play again.

"This waiting thing is stupid," Herb said. "Why don't I just go play another game?"

"Stronger men have tried, Sergeant. If you figure out how, let me know."

To kill some time, Herb checked out the Sugar Store within the app. It sold more than just candy bars and bubblegum bombs.

Players could buy a plethora of things to improve the game. More land. Better seeds. Fertilizer. Magic spells. Powerful weapons. Defensive walls. Troops to help guard the garden. Extra chances to collect three candy bars in a row. Faster clocks to speed up waiting time. And the purchases were so cheap, just 99 cents here and $1.99 there, Herb didn't feel too guilty about buying a few. This was pocket change. And defending your Rank 7 Garden wall from the Honeybeast was more important than pocket change.

"Tom, who's attacking our candy clan?"

"Rival clan. The PooBanger DeathCloud. They're tough."

"For a bunch of kids from the Middle East, you mean."

"No, these guys are the graduate physics professors at MIT. Put all your sweet beets into fence defense, or they'll steal your super soil. You won't be able to grow anything for a week."

"A week?" That alarmed Herb. And he became alarmed again when he realized that it alarmed him.

The PooBanger DeathCloud came closer, casting a shadow over the BigguPooPoo Clan.

"Uh-oh, they know our defense strategy," Tom said. "Our Kangaroo Kittypults have no effect."

"They're stealing my fence, Tom. It took me a hundred sweet beets to build that fence. What do I do?"

"Put up your shield."

"Where is—"

"In the Treasure Menu. Find the shield spell."

"It cost six chocolate bars. I don't want to pay six chocolate bars."

"Then we might as well both quit the game. The PooBanger Death Cloud will wipe out our clan. And then my clan leader will banish you, and then me for recommending you. Without clan protection, we'll be easy prey for the BBQ Chickenwing Buzzards, who want to peck the meat off our bones."

"This game got dark."

"You buying the shield, or quitting?"

Herb bought the shield.

They fended off the attack, and as a reward each received a Gummy Blizzard Spell to protect them from the Munchasaurus Rex. Tom and Herb high-fived.

"So, how much money have you spent on this app?" Herb asked.

"A few bucks. Did you just get some Marshmallow Loogies?"

"Yeah. Bonus for beating the Jelly Unicorn."

"Want to trade some for Silly Berries?"

"Hell yeah."

They gamed on.

Ten minutes later, as Herb was tending his garden, he had a small revelation.

"Have you ever noticed," he said to Tom, "how much of life is getting through the mundane stuff to get to the good stuff?"

"What do you mean?"

"Well, John Lennon said that life is what happens to you while you're busy making other plans. But I think life is what happens in between getting to the things you really want."

"You mean like tending sweet beets because you need to buy peppermint mines to blow up the Gloomer Glum Rocks to get to the next level."

"Yeah. Well, no. I mean on a wider scale. Waiting in traffic, to get to your destination. Sitting through commercials, before your show comes back on."

"Reading a pointless chapter in a book, so you can find out what happens to the characters."

"Exactly."

Tom paused his game. "I hear what you're saying. So that's a bad thing?"

"Actually, the opposite."

"Explain."

"We're in this RV, going to help our mutual friend, Jack. So it seems like our point for being here, our purpose, is so we can do something later on. But what if our purpose is actually to do what we're doing right now? Every second you're alive, that's your reason for living."

"So we should live in the moment," Tom said.

"Exactly. And make each of those moments count."

"What about putting off some things so you can do others?"

"If everything counts," Herb said, "then you should be able to prioritize what is most important. That's what you should be doing."

Tom took a moment, then nodded. "I like your philosophy."

"Maybe you shouldn't. I think I'm just trying to justify why I bought the Nougat Gnome."

"You didn't already have one? Man, everyone needs a Nougat Gnome."

Herb smiled. "Then it was $4.99 well spent."

JACK

When my husband blacked out, I immediately reached down and gave his mangled finger a hard tug, trying to twist it back into position. When I got it looking more-or-less straight, I leaned over and threw up in a waste paper can.

My throwing up woke Phin up, and he took the can from me and threw up.

"Did you fix it?" he asked. "I'm afraid to look."

"*Fix* isn't the right word."

"How'd you do?"

"I'm afraid to look."

"Okay, we both look on three. One... two... three."

We both looked.

Then we fought over the garbage can.

Phin and I leaned back against the wall. I had no idea how we managed not to puke on each other.

"Big gun," he said.

"Think McGlade is overcompensating for something?"

"Definitely."

I nestled next to Phin, and he put his arm around me.

"Am I hurting your ribs?"

"All I feel right now is my finger. Harry doesn't have any Demerol?"

"I can go check again."

I moved to get up, but his arm stayed around me. "Just a sec."

"What?"

"I haven't held you in a long time. I just want another minute or two."

I snuggled up against him, body armor to body armor, listening to him breathe.

"I should have played pool with you," I said. "Earlier."

His arm tightened around me. "It's okay."

But it wasn't okay. "I should have played pool with you. And I should have sparred with you, the other day in the garage."

"You don't have to do this, Jack."

"But I do. I do have to do this." My shoulders began to shake. "I actually thought I didn't love you anymore."

"And how do you feel now?"

I looked at him. His eyes were as glassy as mine. "It's me, Phin. I'm the one I don't love. Maybe it's hormones. Maybe it's the baby. Maybe it's what happened in Michigan." I sniffled, and let out a sound somewhere between a snort and a sob. "Maybe it's menopause. But I hate me. And I took it out on you. Because if I could get you to hate me, it would reaffirm my own feelings about myself. And now I hate me even more."

"Shh." Phin leaned over, even though it probably hurt like hell, and put his cheek against mine. "Stop it. You're saying mean things about the woman I love."

"Why?"

"Why do I love you?"

I nodded. I felt weak asking, lesser somehow, but I really wanted to know.

"Because you're extraordinary, Jack. Most people are average. Or less than. A few people are exceptional. But you're... you're just a whole different class. Smart. Strong. Brave. Successful. You put killers behind bars. You have a black belt. You've won shooting competitions. You're a great mother. Great in bed. Fun to be around. Hell, if you didn't exist, I would have to invent you somehow."

"So why don't I like me?"

"Because you're an idiot."

I laughed at that.

"I'm serious," Phin said. "For someone so extraordinary, you're really not self-aware. You have no concept of your impact on the world. On other people. You magnify your own faults in your head, and don't accept or appreciate your accomplishments."

"So how do I fix that?"

"Counselling. Or Prozac. Or both. You won't change, but you can learn to live with it without being crippled by it."

I kissed him on the cheek. "Thanks. You're extraordinary, too."

He smiled, but it was a wistful smile. "No, I'm not. See, I do have a little bit of self-awareness. You're the hero in this family, Jack. I'm just a tough guy who got really lucky."

Phin kissed me on the nose.

"I love you, Phineas Troutt."

"I love you, Jacqueline Daniels. Now help me find some Demerol, or I'm going to ruin my tough guy rep and start bawling."

T-NAIL

When he'd motored far enough into the woods for some privacy, T-Nail undid his pants and pressed on his bladder, pissing into the woods. After he zipped up, he noticed the forest around him.

It was quiet.

T-Nail had known quiet before. There was the desperate quiet of his toddler years, left all alone while his mom hustled on the streets. There was the frightening quiet, walking alone at night, knowing someone was watching and waiting to jack you. There was the angry quiet, being punished in solitary confinement for committing some stupid prison infraction.

This quiet was different. It held no threats. It caused no pain.

T-Nail wasn't big on introspection. In the joint, counselors constantly spouted crap about using the time to think and reflect. T-Nail never bothered to look at how he became who he became. Why should he? Did a wolf wonder why it hunted? And even if the wolf had the capacity to consider all of the creatures it had killed to feed itself, would that convince the wolf to give up meat?

Hell no. A wolf is a wolf.

Just like T-Nail was what he was. Born to lose, but too mean to accept it.

It sure was quiet, though.

Maybe this was what it felt like to be at peace.

Peace was something T-Nail had never known. He wasn't even sure if he understood what it meant. Ever since he could walk, he'd been angry. Upset with the world. Upset with his place in it. Life was an ongoing struggle. Sex and drugs could make you forget about life for a short time, but forgetting wasn't the same as being at peace.

Being alone with nature, T-Nail wondered if this was how other men found peace. Not in the northern Wisconsin woods like some redneck, but in the motherland. How would it feel to stand on the banks of the River Nile in Uganda, looking out over the East African Plateau? To see Mount Kadam across the savanna? To have the sun shine down on your face in a land where you weren't a minority, misplaced and despised, brought in against your will?

For a moment, T-Nail could almost picture it.

A noise, nearby, ruined the moment, making him flinch because it sounded like a machine gun.

It wasn't a gun. It was a bird. Pecking, rapid-fire, on the side of a tree.

T-Nail had never seen a live woodpecker before.

He watched. The bird went about its work. Pecking and pecking. Wood chips flying everywhere. Searching for food or making a home or whatever it was woodpeckers did.

"Just doing your thing, huh bird? I got a thing I do, too."

T-Nail drew his nail gun and fired, shooting the woodpecker through the head, pinning its dead body to the bark.

Then he steered the Gyro back toward the house. There was more killing to do. And T-Nail had to do it.

He didn't know anything else.

HERB

The Crimebago stopped at a gas station next to a roadside eatery called Charlie's Cheese Chalet. The three men exited the vehicle, McGlade fueling it up while Tom and Herb stared at their phones, finishing up the latest levels.

"Meet you guys inside," Harry said as he attended to the gas. "Order me a burger."

Tom tucked his phone into his pocket, stretched, and then stared at the RV, paying special attention to the large object hooked to the trailer hitch.

"Remind me again why we're towing a tank," he said.

Herb kept his eyes on his screen. He was only thirty seconds away from his sweet beet harvest. "Crowd control, McGlade said."

"We're going to clean up Jack's mess," Harry said, grinning like the idiot he was.

"Funny guy." Tom began walking toward the restaurant. Herb followed.

"You know it's going to be delicious," Tom said, "because how else could they afford a giant plastic mouse sitting on a giant plastic hunk of cheese?"

Herb looked up from his harvest long enough to eye the obligatory anthropomorphic roadside attraction, which stood alongside the building facing the highway. The towering, smiling *objet d'art* was missing an eye, and the paint was peeling on the cheese making it look more gray than orange. It was meant to lure in travelers, but this close it was downright scary.

"We should have stopped at the place with the giant lumberjack," Herb said. "Or the one with the dinosaur."

"That was a waterslide park."

"Waterslide parks have food," Herb said.

"Sure. Some of the finest culinary establishments in the world are attached to water parks. I heard *Seb'on* in Paris just put in a wave pool."

Herb completed gathering his sweet beets and put his cell away. "There used to be this indoor waterpark in Roselle. Not much of a park, actually. Just two slides and a hot tub with so much chlorine it bleached your skin."

"Sounds nice."

"The snack bar had something called the *Humungawich*. Half a loaf of French bread stuffed with two quarter pound beef patties, six strips of bacon, two fried eggs, chicken strips, popcorn shrimp, fish sticks, onion rings, topped with mac and cheese. You could swim right up to the snack bar, eat it in the water."

"Sanitary."

"It was a hot zone. Place closed after an E. coli outbreak. But I miss the *Humungawich*."

"I miss it, too, and I never even had it."

They entered Charlie's Cheese Chalet, and Herb perked up. Rather than the crumbling dive the giant mouse suggested, the inside was clean and tidy. Along the near wall were rows of glass coolers, sporting dozens—maybe hundreds—of cheese varieties. The center of the shop was strewn with shelves and racks of souvenirs and knick-knacks. Off to the right was the eating area, tables and chairs set up to receive diners.

Herb went straight for the counter and smiled at the clerk, who was a chesty woman wearing an apron with a silk-screened picture of the giant mouse on it.

"You probably don't hear this much, but you've got a lot of cheese."

She nodded, but didn't smile. Odd. Usually Wisconsinites were a lot friendlier than their Illinoisan counterparts.

Tom tapped Herb's shoulder, and looked to the right. Herb followed Tom's eyes, and then understood why the cashier wasn't smiling.

Taking up the rear corner table of Charlie's Cheese Chalet were youths of obvious gang persuasion. Herb whispered, "Eternal Black C-Notes. Folk outfit from Bronzeville."

"Black C-Notes? There's also a white guy and a Hispanic."

Herb shrugged. "Maybe it's affirmative action. Or quotas. Or maybe kids just don't care about race anymore."

"Think they're here for Jack?"

"Unless they came all the way from Chicago for some cranberry cheddar. Actually, that sounds pretty good." Herb turned to the cashier. "I need half a pound of cranberry cheddar. And can you show me your selection of muensters?"

The worried-looking lady let Herb try a sample slice of hickory nut muenster.

Herb shivered as the cheese melted in his mouth. "Oh my god. My tongue just had an orgasm."

Tom gave him a nudge. "Shouldn't we do something?"

"I am. I'm sampling cheese."

"I mean about the United Gangs of Benetton."

"Doesn't matter. Whatever we do, when McGlade comes in he'll mess it up. Best thing is to wait for him to make his scene, then play clean-up." He turned back to the cashier. "Can I try some of the garlic dill muenster?"

As the marvelous flavors of dill and garlic danced on his taste buds, the door opened and McGlade came in. Junior was under his arm. Homeboy was on his shoulder.

"Be ready to shoot your way out," Herb told Tom.

McGlade walked up to the duo. "The Crimebago is going to take about ten minutes to fill. You guys order food?"

"I'm sampling."

"Jesus," Harry said, looking at all the cheese. "We may be here for weeks. Hey, sexy counter lady, do you have burgers?"

"We have sandwiches."

"Got any Velveeta?" Harry asked.

The clerk stared at him.

"I'm just messing with you. Give me a Panini, extra provolone and onions. Want anything, Junior?"

"Blablaba."

"He'll have the same. But blend it and put it in a bottle for him."

McGlade then turned and walked up to the gang. Herb unbuckled the strap keeping his SIG Sauer in his shoulder holster, then leaned back on the counter to watch the show.

"You got a problem, old man?" one of the black kids said.

"I do. I found myself a little esurient, and was trying to decide between the Norwegian Jarlsberger and the Venezuelan Beaver Cheese. So I thought I'd come over here and see what you fromage gourmands prefer."

"What you say?" said the white kid. He was flicking a Zippo lighter on and off.

"Kids today don't watch Monty Python? Okay. What are you guys eating?"

"We didn't order yet. Just chillin'. You got a problem with that?"

McGlade shrugged. "It's a free county. Says it right there in the Bill of Rights. First Amendment. Freedom to chill."

"What's that thing?" asked the Hispanic kid, pointing.

"That's my son, Harry Junior. Junior, say hello to these nice inner city youths."

"Plab," Junior said.

"Not the punk, that thing on your shoulder."

"That's Homeboy."

The gangbanger sneered. "I ain't your homeboy, old man."

"His name is Homeboy."

"What the fuck is it?"

"He's my service animal. He's a seeing-eye parrot."

"A what?"

"You heard of seeing eye dogs? Same thing, but in bird shape."

The kid seemed genuinely perplexed. "But... you can see."

"I'm color blind. Homeboy helps me distinguish between green and red."

"Why he naked?"

"Homeboy is from Europe. He got used to all the nude beaches there, and refuses to conform to uptight conservative American values. I think he does it for attention."

The second black guy spoke up. "You fuckin' with us."

"Yes, I am. So what are you children doing in a cheese shop in Wisconsin? I know your colors. Folk, right?"

"You a cop?"

"Naw. Cops have a badge. And rules. I'm just a concerned citizen. But those guys over there?" Harry pointed to Tom and Herb. "They're cops. You tell by their eyes. See how they look like they've given up on life? How they seem to be itching to violate the rights of underprivileged urban youth? Those are pigs, Homeboy."

"I said I ain't your homeboy."

"I was talking to my assist animal. Say, you guys got any meth on you?"

"METH!" screeched Homeboy, making all four gangbangers startle up out of their chairs.

It made Herb and Tom jump, too.

"Look, man, we ain't looking for trouble."

Harry smiled wide. "But I am."

For a moment, no one said anything. Herb stopped chewing and stepped away from the counter. He couldn't tell if any of the youths were carrying, but maybe if McGlade pushed them far enough he'd have probable cause to search them.

"What you want?" the white kid asked.

"You know if you keep playing with that lighter, you're going to set yourself on fire."

"My boy said what you want, cracker."

"You do know that your boy there is also a cracker, right?"

The white guy made a face. "Shit, Hackqueem, racism hurts both ways. Not cool."

Their apparent leader shot the kid a glance. "Shut it, Jet Row." Then he turned back to McGlade. "What you want?"

"You guys happen to know anything about a party up north. Pig hunting party?"

They all returned blank stares.

"The name Jack Daniels mean anything to you?"

"Man, I prefer Patron."

That was apparently clever enough to warrant group giggling and high-fives.

"Here," McGlade said, setting Junior on their table. "Hold my son for a second while I get my gun."

McGlade tugged out a Smith & Wesson snub nosed .44. All thc gangbangers went wide-eyed.

"You guys see Dirty Harry? This is like his gun, but a smaller barrel. Long barrels are for accuracy. I only use this to kill people up close. Now I'll ask slower, in case the first time was too fast. Do. You. Guys. Know. About. Some. Shit. Up. North?"

There were a whole bunch of head shakes.

"Word on the street is the Folk Nation declared war on a cop. Is that where you're headed?"

"No, man. We're just out joyridin'."

The guy pointed out the storefront window at a car.

"You're out joyriding in a Prius?" Harry said.

"It's economical, plus better for the environment," said the Hispanic kid.

McGlade glanced over at Herb. Herb shrugged.

Hackqueem seemed to grow his spine back. "Man, why you messin' with us? This is just some bullshit racial profiling."

"No it isn't," Harry said, pointing. "He's a cracker."

"We out, man."

Hackqueem stood up and stormed past McGlade, his posse right behind him. Tom went to follow, but Herb held him back.

"You think they were telling the truth?" Tom asked.

"Seems like they were. But it doesn't matter. We can't waste time with them. We have to get to Jack." Herb turned to the cashier. "We need a cheese and sausage tray to go. How much for a three pounder?"

The woman smiled for the first time since they'd walked in. "It's on the house, officer."

"No, we'll pay. And that gang kid was right. Racism hurts. Just because someone looks different, or dresses different, doesn't mean you should be afraid of them."

"The fat man is correctomundo," Harry said, sidling up with Junior on his hip. "You should treat all customers equally."

Herb waited for the punch line.

"Unless they're wearing a turban," Harry said, in a stage whisper. "Because then they're probably a suicide bomber."

Tom sighed. "Haven't you heard, McGlade? It's the twenty-first century. Racism isn't funny."

"Actually, Tom, anything can be funny. Ask Mel Brooks. But don't confuse my humorous reference to the omnipresent Islamophobia inherent in this country with racism. It's satire, used to make fun of the ignorant boys and girls who actually are racists. And calling me a racist because I made a joke you didn't fully understand means you're the one who needs to practice a little tolerance. We've all become so politically correct that no one can say anything without some pinhead crying bigotry. Chill out, brother."

Harry paid for his Panini, tipped the cashier with the change from a fifty dollar bill, and walked out.

"And that was the Harry McGlade Show," Herb said.

"Why hasn't someone killed him yet?"

"Kill him? They keep making TV movies about him."

"You're kidding."

"Latest was *Deadly Patrimony*. One of the Baldwins played Harry."

"Which Baldwin?"

"Not the popular one."

Tom clucked his tongue. "Deadly Patrimony. What does that even mean?"

"It means we can no longer have any faith in media entertainment." Herb headed for the exit. "Cheese plate is on you. I spent all my money on *Zombie Sugar Jackers*. Thanks for that."

"My pleasure," Tom called after him.

But it didn't sound like it was his pleasure at all.

DEL RAY

His team came back from the Walmart with all the supplies Del Ray had wanted, and some bad news he didn't want.

"All dead, General. Killed them like rats."

Del had been holding out hope that the soldiers he'd sent after the husband were maybe lost, or getting stoned somewhere.

Instead, they'd been killed. And Del Ray had been the man who sent them to their deaths.

Eyes were on him, so he didn't show any weakness. He played it cool and squelched the scream building inside him.

"Those were our brothers. When this is over, we'll get them and take them back home. Make sure their kids and baby mamas are taken care of."

His men nodded, but Del saw uncertainty there.

"I got a plan," he said. "No more dead homies. We gonna take that house, and that cop and her husband, and they're gonna pay. Then we'll get the hell out of here."

"Fire is getting' closer, too," said LeBron, his lieutenant. "Sky is gettin' real smoky."

"We're going to end this before it reaches us," Del assured him.

He directed seven men to put on the stolen camouflage hunting clothing, and then instructed them on what to do with the cans of aerosol insulation and duct tape. Waders, rain coats, and motorcycle helmets were distributed to four others.

Then he began to read the instruction manual for the power tools they'd taken.

Things were about to get real.

PHIN

They didn't find any Demerol, but McGlade did have some bottles of procaine, which was the generic of Novocain. Phin's finger had swollen to almost twice its regular width, and had turned an angry shade of red. The pain was in the Top Three of the worst Phin had ever experienced, and it throbbed and peaked with every heartbeat.

They were in the living room, and Phin was reclining in an easy chair in case he passed out again. Jack was kneeling alongside him, her hands in latex gloves.

"Bad?" Jack asked.

"Ya'aburnee." He grimaced, then translated in case she'd forgotten. "I want you to bury me."

Jack wrinkled her nose. "I still don't understand that."

"Right now it means I'm in so much pain I want to die. But when it's about love, it means I want to die before you, because I couldn't stand to live without you."

"That's stupid. It doesn't make sense."

"It does to me," Phin said.

"Okay. Well, I'm not going to bury you right now, much as you want me to. You ready for this?"

"Yeah."

Jack opened up a syringe package—one with the hypodermic needle already attached—then drew two cubic centimeters of procaine out of the bottle. Phin had his elbow on the armrest, his broken finger facing Jack. In his other hand was a wooden spoon.

Jack's face was as pale as he'd ever seen it.

"Where do I..." her voice trailed off.

"In the finger. At the base. Right where my palm ends."

"It's going to hurt."

"It already hurts."

"But jamming in a needle is going to make it hurt worse. I could do the wrist, then move down until your whole hand is numb."

"This is my shooting hand. I need to be able to feel my other fingers to return fire."

She nodded, bringing the needle to rest on his palm.

Phin placed the handle of the spoon in his mouth, his molars clenching the wood.

He closed his eyes.

"Okay... here it goes..."

When the needle went in, he screamed and bit the spoon in half. Jack finished the injection. Phin spat out the two pieces of wood and leaned forward in the chair, fighting nausea.

"Is that going to be enough?" Jack asked, looking terribly unsure.

"I don't know. It's going to take a little while to kick in."

"That was awful."

"Yeah."

"I think it hurt me more than it hurt you," Jack said.

Phin snorted. "I doubt that. But thanks."

She put her hand on his knee. "I don't like seeing you hurt."

"I know."

"I'd rather endure the pain myself."

He tried on a weak smile. "See? Maybe you understand ya'aburnee better than you thought."

"No. That's still pretty stupid. Is your finger getting numb?"

The procaine took its time, but it eventually worked its magic and blocked the nerves. As it did, Phin once again became aware of his broken ribs. They ached, but it was a welcome trade-off.

"I need to splint it," Jack said.

"Just make sure I can still hold a gun."

Jack touched his elbow, softly, as if he would break. "Can you stand up?"

"It's my finger, Jack. Not my knees."

"We should do this in the control room. I want to see what they're doing outside."

Phin nodded, and allowed himself to be helped out of the chair. He put his arm around Jack's shoulders as they walked, letting her take just a little of his weight because her body felt so nice next to his. His whole hand was getting numb. Too numb, in fact. Phin didn't feel a thing when he accidentally bumped the wall and jammed his bad finger.

"Phin! Oh... god."

His index finger was now bent completely backwards, and his bone had broken through the skin.

"That's going to be tough to splint," he said.

He stared at the injury, watching the blood spurt out with his pulse, and Jack turned away and threw up again.

HERB

So how much have you spent on the game so far?" Tom asked.

They'd stopped in Lake Loyal, Wisconsin, so Harry could drop his spawn off with Val Ryker, a friend of Jack's. Val was the town's former police chief, and she apparently owed McGlade a favor. Or maybe he had some sort of blackmail leverage over her.

"A few bucks," Herb said.

Herb had spent one hundred and twenty-six dollars on *Zombie Sugar Jackers*. But his Rank 24 Garden was totally pimped out. He had a Fuzzy Cloud of Wondergrowth raining on his crops so they grew 25% faster, and his Venus Taffytrap could stop the lower-level Munch Bunch zombies from attacking when Herb took a break.

Assuming that, eventually, Herb would take a break.

A banner came up. Kickaximus Scrote was asking for ten more candy bars in tribute.

"Hey, what's up with that UAE kid asking for more candy?" Herb asked.

"He can do that whenever he wants. He's clan leader."

"I thought the little shit had to go to bed."

"I forgot it was the weekend. No school tomorrow."

"So what do I do?"

"Pay him."

"But it's ten bucks."

"You have to. You pledged your chocolate shield to his sugary cause."

"And what if I don't?"

"He'll kick you out. But first he'll send the Root Beer Locusts and wipe out your garden."

"But I gave him a refill on Nose Bopper Syrup just ten minutes ago."

"Kickaximus Scrote rules the BigguPooPoo Clan with an iron fist."

"Screw this kid," Herb said. "I'm giving him one candy bar, and messaging him to say that's all he's getting."

"Good luck with that."

A few seconds after he sent the text, Herb got a response.

"He called me a wanker, and told me to suck my own dick," Herb said, frowning at his phone. "This kid is only eight?"

"Probably closer to nine."

"He's an asshole."

"You'd better give him the other nine candy bars," Tom said.

Herb didn't do that. Instead, he messaged KickAximus Scrote and told him it was past his bedtime and he should let the adults play for a while.

Then the Root Beer Locusts wiped out Herb's garden.

"Seriously?" Herb said.

As Herb was trying to figure out what just happened, his phone flashed a message.

You've been kicked out of the clan, sucka!

"I see you were kicked out of the clan," Tom said.

"What the hell? Now I'm being attacked by a Dinosaur Storm."

"You don't have a clan to protect you."

Herb tried tapping the screen in random places, but there was nothing he could do. "The Dinosaur Storm just killed my Venus Taffytrap. Is that permanent?"

"You can buy another one when you join a new clan."

"How do I join a new clan?"

"Go into world chat. Maybe someone will send you an invite. It's usually about twenty candy bars."

"Twenty candy bars!? What the hell kind of game is this!?"

"I told you. Electronic crack." Tom's face got really serious. "Crack isn't good, man. You should've just said no."

Harry entered the Crimebago, without Junior.

"What's electronic crack?" he asked, starting up the RV. "Is it Combville? I used to be really addicted to Combville."

"*Zombie Sugar Jackers*," Tom said.

McGlade nodded. "I rule that game. My clan is ranked number twelve worldwide."

Tom called bullshit.

"Check it," Harry said.

Herb checked the global rankings. The number twelve clan was named Harry's Enormous Balls.

"You see my enormous balls?" Harry asked.

Herb rubbed his eyes with his thumb and forefinger. He really didn't want to check out McGlade's stats. Herb had shown a staggering lack of willpower during the last few hours, and was sick with himself. He needed to exercise a little self-control.

"Holy shit!" Tom said.

Herb waylaid self-control and checked Harry's stats. "You have a Rank 61 Garden," he said, flatly.

"Yeah. The limit used to be 60, but the developers raised it because: rich guys."

That made it official. Life truly wasn't fair.

Herb's envy of McGlade's garden was interrupted by a Murder Cyclone, which sucked up all of his Wonder Dirt. Now Herb couldn't grow anymore sweet beets or candy canes. As Herb lamented the loss, the cyclone returned, wiping out his Fuzzy Cloud of Wondergrowth.

"Let me join your clan, McGlade," he said.

"Seriously?"

"I don't have a clan, and a Murder Cyclone just hit me."

"Murder Cyclone's suck," Tom said. "But the worst is the Hate Volcano. It sends you back ten levels."

"Ten levels? You're making that up."

A new message flashed on Herb's screen.

A Hate Volcano has erupted. You are now back at Level 63.

"C'mon, Harry." Herb swallowed the tiny bit of pride he still had and said, "Please."

"On one condition, oh jiggly one."

"What?"

"Tell me you love Harry's Enormous Balls."

"Jesus, Harry. That's so—"

"I love Harry's Enormous Balls!" Tom blurted out.

"Let me have your gamer name, Tom. I'll send you an invite."

Tom told Harry his name. Herb got another message.

The Death Plague has descended upon you. Your garden is now half size.

"I love Harry's Enormous Balls," Herb muttered.

"What was that? I couldn't quite hear it."

"I love Harry's Enormous Balls!" Herb yelled.

"HOMEBOY!" squawked Homeboy.

"See? Was that so hard? What's your name?"

"HBenedict1966."

"Naw, I don't like that. Change it to TubbyTubbyDoubleChin."

"No." Herb folded his arms over his chest. "I'm drawing the line there."

"You should do it before you're hit by a Havoc Quake," Tom said.

"What's a Havoc Quake?"

"You lose everything and have to start over at the beginning."

"What was that name again?" Herb asked.

And that's how TubbyTubbyDoubleChin embraced Harry's Enormous Balls.

"Welcome to the clan, guys," McGlade said, pulling back onto the road. "I wish you much luck with your candy jacking, and I'm sure we're going to have hours of fun, gaming together. Also, you each owe me twenty candy bars in tribute or I'm kicking you out."

JACK

I wasn't cut out to be a doctor.

I managed to straighten out Phin's finger bones best that I could, did a sloppy Frankenstein horrorshow job of stitching him up, and then made a splint out of a tongue depressor and some medical tape.

"Think they left?" Phin asked.

He was staring at the monitors. We hadn't seen, or heard, anyone on the property for over half an hour.

"I'd love to think so, but I wouldn't put money on it. T-Nail won't give up."

"What's that guy's deal?"

I considered it. "I honestly don't know. I've met my fair share of crazies. People who liked to kill. People who were compelled to kill. People who did it for money. People who did it for a cause. But T-Nail... he's different. When you look him in the eyes, there's not a person there. It's just blank. You can't reason with him. There's no empathy. No emotion at all. It's like looking into a void."

"Born that way? Abused? Bad environment?"

"I have no idea. I've never known another killer like T-Nail. He once nailed a man to the floor and peeled off all of his skin. All of it, scalp to toes. One strip at a time. The Medical Examiner estimated it took him two days to die. The victim's brother—the one who testified against T-Nail at the trial—was forced to watch. He said T-Nail had the television on the whole time, and kept stopping the torture to change channels."

"That's not an image I needed in my head."

"This isn't someone who kills for fun. It's more like..." I looked for the right words. "It's more like natural selection. T-Nail is asserting his dominance in the food chain."

And at the moment, he was right at the top of that food chain. The wolf waiting for the bunnies to leave the burrow.

"What about the witness?" Phin asked. "Will T-Nail go after him?"

"He died of a heroin overdose three months after the trial."

The overdose had been intentional. Poor kid left a note that read, *I can't make the screaming stop.*

"What the hell?" Phin pressed a button on the control panel. One of the monitors had gone dark. "Electrical problem? Or did they cut it?"

Jack squinted at the board. "The panel says the camera is still live. And Harry thought of everything. I don't think he would have forgotten to bury the cable."

"Oh, hell." Phin pointed at another monitor. A kid in a hunting mask was sticking duct tape over the lens. A moment later five others were doing the same thing on other cameras.

I hit the sprinklers. We only had one working camera left, and we watched a guy in a green and brown outfit sprint off into the woods.

"They're wearing camouflage," Phin said. "Son of a bitch. We didn't see them sneaking up."

I pushed away from the console. "This is bad."

"It's about to get worse."

A man wearing rain gear and a motorcycle helmet walked into frame. Right through the streams of scalding water.

"What's he holding?" I asked.

But I knew what it was when he pulled the cord and the engine fired up, the unmistakable buzzing sound coming through the console speakers.

It was a chainsaw.

I stood and hurried into the living room, Phin half a step behind me. After grabbing my rifle, I headed for the nearest balistraria and pressed the hidden panel.

It didn't open.

Phin took his folding knife out, and began prying at the seam in the wood. He managed to get it unstuck, and he put his good hand in the crack and yanked outward, breaking the thin veneer, revealing the opening.

The balistraria had been sealed up with some sort of yellow gunk. I touched it with my finger, and it was slightly moist and gave in a little bit.

"Foam insulation," Phin said. "You spray it on, and it expands to fill the space and gets rock hard."

There was a knocking sound, just beyond the balistraria, on the outside of the house. Phin began to carve away at the stiff foam with his knife, and then met resistance. He leaned on his blade, but couldn't push any farther.

"They're nailing boards over the foam."

From bad to worse to impossible. "Can we cut through it? A saw? A drill?"

"We can't see them on the cameras so we don't know where they are. If we cut through, they'll notice. They could be standing right there with shotguns."

I cast a frantic glance around the room. "Maybe they missed one."

Phin and I quickly checked the other seven balistrarias, rushing from one to the next.

All of them were sealed.

"I doubt they all have raingear," Phin said. "The hot water from the sprinklers will keep the majority away."

"The hot water will run out, Phin. I don't know how big Harry's tanks are, but they can't last forever."

We went back to the control room just in time to see some kid tape over the last outdoor camera, rendering us blind to the gang's activities. The microphone still worked, and the sounds of revving chainsaws blared through the speakers.

They were cutting into the walls.

Phin turned the volume knob, killing the sound. I looked at him, and saw something in his eyes I'd never seen before.

Defeat.

"We can survive this," I said.

He stayed silent, and stared at an empty patch of wall.

"We pick a room, seal ourselves in with food and weapons. Even if they get inside we still have a chance."

"Okay."

"We can still fight back. It's not over yet."

"Okay."

I folded my arms across my chest. "You don't think we're going to make it."

He didn't reply.

"Phin. Please answer me."

"I think we can make a last stand. But that's what it will be. A last stand."

We'd been in desperate situations before. But I'd never seen Phin act like this.

"Maybe help will come," I said. "Harry. Herb. Val."

"Maybe."

I slapped the console with my palm. "Dammit, Phin. We need to do *something*."

He didn't seem to be listening.

"Phin…"

My husband closed his eyes. When he spoke, his voice cracked. "I can't…"

"You can't? You can't what? Talk about this? Make a plan?"

"I can't watch that guy skin you alive for two days."

I knew what he was leading up to. It wasn't where I wanted to go. We still had some options left.

"We're not there yet," I said.

"We need to discuss it. And we need to discuss it now."

"No, we don't."

"If they get in, we might not have time."

"You're talking about suicide."

No answer.

"If they get in, you think we should... kill ourselves." Those words left an ugly taste in my mouth, and an even uglier image in my head.

Phin's eyes slowly opened. He looked at me, and his gaze was so sad that something inside me broke. I knew exactly what he was thinking.

"You're going to shoot me," I whispered. "And then yourself."

He didn't reply. He didn't nod. But it was all there, in his eyes.

"No," I said, shaking my head. "We're not through yet. And we're not dying like that. That's not how we go out. We're not cowards."

"Jack, you don't know the meaning of the word *coward*. You're the hero. You'll fight to your last breath. I know that."

"You're no coward, either."

"But I'm not brave like you. I'm not hero material. I'm a tough guy. I can take more abuse than most." He raised his voice. "But I am *not* watching you get skinned alive. And if it comes to that, I *will* take the coward's way out."

Out of all the conversations I never wanted to have, this was at the top.

"We have a child together. And you'd blow my head off?"

Phin clenched his jaw, so hard I saw his cheek muscles bunch out. "Only because I know you'd never do the same for me."

What he said hurt. But he was right. I couldn't ever take Phin's life. No more than I could take my own. This whole stupid macho war ethic was alien to me. Kill or be killed? That was insane. Women weren't wired that way.

I reached out, held his good hand. "That's not ya-aburnee, Phin. What happened to you wanting to die first because you couldn't stand to see me go?"

Phin pulled away from me. "Are you telling me not to do it?"

"Phin…"

"If we're trapped, and can't get away, you want to become that psycho's captive? We've both been in that situation before, Jack."

He was right. We'd been at the mercy of lunatics.

"And we lived through it," I said. "We can live through this, too."

"But what if we can't?"

"There's always hope."

He let go of my hand. "What if there is no hope? What do you want me to do?"

I doubled down. I didn't want to even consider this course of action. Not now. Not ever. "We'll figure that out when it happens."

"There might not be time. I need you to tell me, if all hope is gone, what you want me to do."

My eyes teared up. I shook my head.

"Tell me what you want, Jack."

"We can live through this."

"And what if we can't?" he yelled. "Tell me what to do!"

"You want to take the coward's way out!"

"Ending our lives on our terms isn't cowardly. Would you rather be tortured to death? Watch me be tortured to death? If they get in here, that's going to happen. And they're going to get in here. There's no doubt. So what the hell do you want to do about it!?"

My whole body shook and I screamed, a scream of rage and hate and anguish and despair. "Fine! You win! Kill me! I want you to kill me, then kill yourself!"

My lower lip was trembling uncontrollably, tears soaking my face. Phin threw his arms around me, and I held him as tight as I could, and my lips found his and I kissed him, kissed him harder than I ever had before, kissed him like it was the very last time.

Because we both knew it probably was.

DEL RAY

A brilliant plan, flawlessly executed.

They'd blinded the cameras, and boarded up the sniper holes. The cop and her husband were trapped like blind cats in a cage, defanged and declawed, waiting for death. Del Ray had some brothers testing the walls with chainsaws, looking for ways in.

Maybe they wouldn't need to wait for the dynamite. And the best part? Not a single soldier hurt or killed.

That's how generals were supposed to roll.

He heard the distinctive whir of the Gyro engine get louder, but Del Ray didn't want to deal with T-Nail's shit at that moment. So he walked the opposite way, heading south around the house, just beyond the reach of the hot water sprinklers. He thought about blazing a blunt, but instead took a pull from the sizzurp bottle in his back pocket to take the edge off the pain in his hand and ear. Del could think better on codeine than on weed, and something was hanging on the outside corner of his mind, trying to climb its way inside. Something about the outdoor cameras. Something he was missing.

He noticed the sprinklers had stopped steaming, and drew closer to check. Del stuck a bare hand into the drizzle.

Warm, but not boiling.

Without putting on a raincoat, he walked across the damp property toward the house. He got wet, but not burned, and his curiosity compelled him forward. Del touched the house, running his hand over the stacked logs, then giving it a thump with his knuckles. Solid. This place really was a fortress.

He walked along the perimeter, staring up at the roof overhang, searching for the closest surveillance camera. Del found it, the lens taped over. It was high quality, with night-vision, but an older model; perhaps ten years out of date, judging by its size. Continuing along the wall, he walked over to one of his men wielding a chainsaw. Del gave him a tap on the shoulder to get his attention.

"Walls are thick," the soldier said. "And there's something behind them."

Del leaned over, peeking into one of the slits the man had cut. He used the flashlight app on his cell to see inside.

Concrete. And it had cured alongside the wood.

There was no way they were getting in with saws.

Del was about to tell the soldier to quit when he heard the Gyro approaching fast. He waited for T-Nail, who easily navigated the wet ground on his Mecanum wheels. The pitch of the gearbox was lower than normal, and Del knew it was going to need a battery change soon.

"Why are you stopping?" T-Nail called out, his voice arriving a few seconds before he did.

The gangsta cast a panicked look at Del.

"Saws can't cut through," Del answered for him. "Cement behind the wood."

"It was a shit plan anyway."

T-Nail's shirt was soaked with water, which had blended with blood from his shoulder wound, staining it pink. Damn good thing Del had waterproofed the electronics on the Gyro. But maybe T-Nail should have asked him to make sure, before he tried taking a $30k electronic wheelchair through a field of sprinklers.

"I was thinkin'," Del said.

"'bout damn time."

Del ignored the jab. "This place is pretty tight. All kinds of crazy security. What if it's mafia?"

"You think the outfit owns this place?"

"Who else would? Goddamn castle out here in bumblefuck, no other house for miles. You know if the cop is protected?"

"I been in the slam for twenty goddamn years and only found out 'bout her a few days ago. You're the one should know this shit."

"I dug into it. She don't seem dirty. But this place, man..."

"I want to talk to her."

"The cop?"

"No. Yo mama." T-Nail scowled. "Yeah, the goddamn cop. Can we write some shit down, hold it up to the camera?"

That thought trying to get into Del's head finally popped in, fully formed.

"There might be a better way," he said. "Security on the place is dope. Cameras got motion detectors and night vision. Seems like they thought of everything." He lowered his voice. "But they deaf."

"What?" T-Nail barked.

"They deaf," Del said, louder.

If T-Nail noticed the deliberate diss, he ignored it. "What you sayin'?"

"Why would they spend all of this money on being able to see, without being able to hear? I bet one of these cameras has a microphone. Probably the one by the front door."

T-Nail motored the Gyro past Del, forcing the smaller man to hop out of the way so his feet weren't run over. He ordered his soldier to tell the others to quit with the saws, then followed T-Nail to the front of the house.

There, under the awning, embedded in the wall next to the taped-over camera, was a round metal audio grill. Del stood on his tip toes to try to pull the duct tape off the lens, and couldn't reach it.

"Out the damn way." T-Nail extended himself to a standing position and removed the tape. Then he said, "Can you hear me in there?" He looked back at Del Ray. "Can they hear?"

"Depends. Mic could be off. Or broken. Or they might not be near it."

"Can they answer back?"

Del squinted at the microphone. "Could be an intercom, goin' both ways. But I dunno if it's wired or not."

"What's the difference?"

"If it's wireless, it won't work. We're jamming the radio signals."

T-Nail turned his attention back to the camera. "If you hear my voice, let me know. You hear me, Jacqueline? Answer me, or I'm gonna kill a cop."

PHIN

A monitor on the console flickered, and Phin noticed the duct tape had been removed from an outdoor camera. T-Nail and his general, Del Ray, stared into the lens. Phin gave Jack a nudge and they turned up the volume.

"...gonna kill a cop."

T-Nail yelled, *"Bring her here!"* over his shoulder.

"I don't hear the saws anymore," Jack said.

Phin didn't know if that was a good thing or not. Maybe they couldn't get in with chainsaws. But it looked like they were about to do something worse.

It took a long minute, but two of the thugs brought a handcuffed woman over. She was about Jack's age. Caucasian, dirty blonde hair, thin, wearing jeans, a flannel shirt, and a softshell jacket.

"Tell them who you are."

"I'm Officer Barbara Knowles, Spoonward PD."

"Officer, let me tell you what's going to happen," T-Nail said. *"There are two people inside this house. I'm going to count to five. If they don't open the door, I'm going to cut your lips off."*

Jack stood up, but Phin caught her wrist.

"Phin, we can't let this happen."

"We can't open the door."

"One..." T-Nail began.

"We have to do something."

"What?"

"I need men over here!" Del Ray yelled over his shoulder.

"Right now there are only four of them out front," Jack said. "Maybe we can open the door, save her."

"Do we shoot to kill?" Phin asked. "Or are you still on your *wound only* kick?"

"Two..."

"Head shots," Jack said.

It was about time. But as Phin stood up he saw six more gang-bangers converge around the front door, Scorpions at the ready.

"Too many now," Phin said. "We can't risk it."

"We can't let them do this, Phin. What if it was me out there?"

"That's the point. You're in here. And you're staying in here."

"Three..."

"Is there some sort of way to talk to them?" Jack said, searching the control panel.

Phin had found the button earlier. A button marked FRONT DOOR SPEAKER. It was in an odd place, in the lower corner of the console.

But there was a problem. While Phin and Jack could see and hear, T-Nail and crew couldn't know that for sure. If Jack spoke to them, they would know they had a communicative audience. Which meant things would get even worse.

"Four..."

T-Nail held a short-blade hunting knife to the woman's face.

"Please open the door!" she cried.

Jack was frantic now, her eyes darting everywhere. Phin tried to shift his weight, to block the button from her view, but she caught the movement, pushed him aside, and pressed it.

"Hello, Terrance," she said. "It's me. Lieutenant Daniels."

"Name is T-Nail. And you ain't a cop no more, Jacqueline. How you been likin' your retirement?"

"It's been pretty good up until now. How was prison?"

"Got tired of the food. So I left."

"And this is how you want to spend your newfound freedom? Nursing an old grudge?"

"We're way beyond the nursing stage. We're right in the thick of it."

"That officer has nothing to do with this. Let her go."

"I'll make you a deal. You open up, I'll let this fine cop here go back to her life. I'll even kill you and Phineas quick. You don't open up, you get watch me cut her up into little pieces, and then you get to watch me do the same with Samantha."

Jack immediately put a hand over her mouth. Phin felt his heart become stone.

"That's right. A team in Lake Loyal snatched your daughter. She's on her way here right now."

"It's a bluff," Phin said. It had to be a bluff. If it wasn't, Phin knew he wouldn't be able to go on.

Jack walked away from the console and began to pace the small room. "They know her name. They know she's in Lake Loyal."

"She's with Val and Lund. You think they'd just hand over our daughter?"

"What if they have her, Phin?"

"Even if they do, it'll take hours for them to bring her here. Which gives us hours to figure something out."

Jack went back to the button. "The door won't open. When your men shot it up, they jammed the lock."

Phin had no idea if that was true, but kudos to Jack for thinking on her feet.

T-Nail sneered into the camera. *"Then open the goddamn back door."*

"Only one door," Jack said.

Del Ray stepped closer to the camera. *"So you sayin' you built this castle without an escape route?"*

"I didn't build it."

"Who did?"

Phin and Jack traded a glance. "A powerful friend," Jack said. "One who is going to be pissed off at what you've done to his house."

"Fuck your powerful friend," T-Nail said. *"You got five minutes to figure out how to let us in. And four minutes are already up."*

JACK

How could we buy more time?

"The punt gun," Phin said.

I shook my head. "We'll hit the hostage."

"She's dead anyway. This would be quicker than what T-Nail has in mind."

"I'm not killing an innocent woman, Phin."

"So instead you're going to watch T-Nail cut her lips off?"

"Thirty seconds..."

I looked around the room, searching for an idea, and my eyes locked onto the Kindle Fire. I snatched it up and powered it on, hitting the app I wanted.

"That's your idea?" Phin asked. "Reading an ebook?"

"Fifteen seconds..."

I turned up the sound on the Kindle and held it to the microphone. It spoke.

"Ooo, you like that don't you, you sexy muthafucka."

DEL RAY

The soldier on Del's right asked, "Was that Samuel L. Jackson?"

"I am Samuel L. Jackson, and I'm gonna fuck you so hard the coroner gonna have to pull the sheets outta your dead ass."

Everyone except Del, T-Nail, and the officer burst out laughing.

"Get to work, bitch. This thang ain't gonna suck itself."

More laughter. The men doubled over and began slapping their own thighs like the cats from *Fat Albert*.

"What is that?" T-Nail demanded, turning to Del. "A TV?"

"It's an app," Del said. "Called *Marriage Saver*."

"What the hell does that even mean?"

"It's a program for tablet computers. It shows uncanny valley animations of celebrity faces saying sexual things. You're supposed to put it over your partner's face when you're getting busy, so you can pretend you're banging Beyoncé. It got a lot of media attention because it was using celebrity likenesses without permission."

"That's the dumbest thing ever."

Del thought, *I bet you coulda used that in prison.* But he kept it to himself. Instead he said, "Lots of apps are stupid. Like *Meer Kat Simulator.* Or *Pandapult.*"

"Panda-what?"

"You launch pandas into the air and they explode like fireworks," said the guy on T-Nail's left. "I'm on level 263."

"How many times do I have to tell you to wiggle that finger ya got up my ass? Wiggle, bitch, wiggle!"

"I'm done with this shit." T-Nail grabbed the screaming cop by the hair and pulled her close. As she thrashed, he brought his knife to her face, slicing her cheeks.

Del was unsure what to do. Cop killing, even this far away from home turf, was bad business. He'd given instructions to his men that the local authorities were to be detained, not harmed. But this wasn't the time to make a stand against T-Nail. That had to be done in private.

"Yo, T-Nail, I got an idea."

T-Nail pointed the knife at Del. "You gettin' weak on me, Del? Boys told me you didn't want to kill these cracker cops."

"Ain't got nothing against wastin' pigs. But there's a time and a place."

"And that time and place is now. You got all them scalps on your vest. Don't see no cracker bitches on there. Why don't you show us how it's done, son?"

Earlier, Del Ray had imagined putting a white woman's scalp on his vest. But this wasn't how he did this thing. And now the crew was staring at Del, waiting for him to make a move.

"Please don't do this," the cop begged. Tears and blood mingled on her face.

"Gimme the knife," Del Ray said.

T-Nail handed it to him. It was heavier than Del expected.

"No no no no no..." the woman sobbed.

"Hey, cop in the house!" Del Ray called out, keeping his eyes on the deputy. "You better do somethin' fast. Or you gonna see me scalp a ho."

PHIN

He knew what he had to do. Clenching his jaw, Phin hit the speaker button.

"You're the problem," he said to Jack.

"What?"

"They're here because of you. They're killing that woman because of you."

Jack looked confused. "So you want to let them in?"

"I don't want to die because yet another psycho from your past wants revenge."

"What the hell are you saying?"

Phin picked up his 1911, easing his middle finger onto the trigger.

"I'm saying they don't want me. They want you. And if you were dead, they'd go away."

Jack's face blossomed with realization. "Phin... put the gun down. You're scaring me."

"If my option is to die with you, or live alone, it's no contest."

"Phin, don't!"

"Sorry, Jack."

He fired three times.

T-NAIL

When the shots came through the speakers, the deputy pulled free and went running off into the woods. T-Nail was fully focused on the camera, trying to figure out what just happened.

"Did you just kill her?" he said to no one in particular.

"Oh my god," the dude said. *"What-did-I-do-what-did-I-do-what-did-I-do? Oh, Jack. I'm sorry. I'm so, so sorry..."*

"He's foolin'?" T-Nail asked. "Right?"

Del Ray shrugged.

"Go find the deputy," T-Nail told his men. They took off. He turned to Del again. "If that asshole killed her..."

Del Ray got in close, whispering. "If she's dead, we need to cut out, G. That cop gets away, we gonna have 5-0 all up in our business."

T-Nail pushed him away. "How we know she's dead?" he yelled at the speaker.

No answer.

T-Nail remembered a long ago Christmas. One of his mama's johns wanted to be more than a paying customer, and he bought T-Nail his first—and only—bike to try to win her affection. But mama didn't have no affection in her. A week after he gave it to T-Nail, he came and took it back. That was the last time T-Nail ever cried about anything.

Having Jack taken away from him felt a lot like that bike.

"Prove to me she's dead," he ordered Phineas.

"How? You're jamming my phone. I can't send a picture."

T-Nail looked at Del Ray. Del shook his head and leaned in to whisper, "If he's lying and we turn off the radio jammers, he could get a message out."

Again he shoved Del away. "Just open the goddamn door!"

"Hold on a minute. I got an idea."

They waited. One of the soldiers came back, said they couldn't find the Deputy.

"You should have cut that bitch's face off like I told you," T-Nail snarled.

Del Ray put his hand on his belt. "You're the one who let her go," he said, his voice low and steady.

"You questioning my authority, punk?"

"No, sir. But I ain't the one. She pulled out of your grip, not mine."

T-Nail drew his nail gun, placing it against Del Ray's head. The kid didn't flinch.

"That all you got to say?"

"Naw. I got something else." Del cleared his throat and began to recite. "And if I bleed and die today, never over my grave pray, I lived true and I lived free, I lived and died to serve the C."

The C were the C-Notes. It was the last line of the Creed; the oath every C-Note had to memorize. Was Del trying to play on T-Nail's sense of brotherhood?

If so, it was a waste of time. The gang didn't mean shit to T-Nail. He was the alpha predator. The dominant lion of the pride. He didn't care which click he ruled over. If it wasn't the C-Notes, it could be two dozen other gangs.

T-Nail wasn't in this for brotherhood. The C-Notes weren't his family. T-Nail didn't have a family.

And he wasn't in it for the cash, or the drugs, or the hoes.

He was a banger because the world sucked. But it was better to be the one giving the orders than the one taking them.

Seemed like Del Ray felt the same, because he refused to back down, even with a nail gun to his head. The moment stretched as the two men stared bullets at each other.

"Okay, I've got a picture. I'm going to try sliding it under the door."

T-Nail scowled, then holstered his weapon. A few seconds later, something small and white appeared under the steel door. T-Nail instructed the nearest soldier to grab it.

It was a Polaroid snapshot. Blurry, and scratched-up from being pulled through the tight gap. But even with its imperfections, the pic showed Jacqueline Daniels. She was sprawled out on her back, head tilted to the side, one eye open. Blood covered her face and ran out of her gaping mouth, and gory brains were tangled in her hair and splattered across the floor behind her.

"Looks pretty dead to me," the soldier said.

T-Nail crushed the picture in his hand and threw it to the ground. Then he steered the Gyro into the forest, trying to figure out his next move.

JACK

I stared down at the chunks of brains in my hand, and inappropriately thought of a bad pun.

I guess this is what it means to hold a thought.

Phin returned with several rolls of paper towels and helped me wipe the Chef Boyardee out of my hair.

"I smell like a birthday party for three-year-olds," I said.

"Did they buy it?"

"Dunno yet." I tossed more noodles into the trash can. "It was a good idea. But next time we dump the canned goods on your head."

We weren't safe yet. Even if they believed I was dead, T-Nail might still want to come after Phin. The gang didn't seem to be leaving the property, and we were stuck there for as long as they camped out.

Stuck there, worrying about Sam.

At least the officer had gotten away.

"Do I want to know why McGlade has a Polaroid camera?" I asked, trying to take my mind off of my daughter.

"For the exact reason you're thinking. Do you want to see a picture of him naked with a dwarf, a double amputee, and a four hundred pound Hispanic woman dressed like She-Hulk?"

"Yes," I said.

Phin chuckled. It was kind of forced, but it was nice to hear him laugh.

"I suppose I could hunt through his stack of nude selfies and look for it," Phin said. He was picking me clean of pasta like gorillas groom each other. "Who takes a picture of themselves jerking off? What's the point? Does looking at himself turn him on?"

"This is Harry McGlade we're talking about. So of course it does. Are my teeth still red?" I did a horse impression, smiling with my lips jutting out.

"Yeah."

I spat into a paper towel, my saliva still pink with ketchup. Then I pulled another bit of lasagna out of my hair.

"I guess this is what it means to hold a thought," I said, trying out the joke.

Phin didn't laugh.

"Get it? Because this is supposed to be my brain."

Phin kept a straight face and said, "That's using your noodle."

I didn't laugh at his joke, either. "Maybe this situation just isn't funny."

"How about: you seem to have dinner on your mind."

"Yeah, we should stop."

He reached out his good hand, and I took it.

"Kissing me right now is probably not going to happen, huh?"

"Now that's quite a saucy thing to say."

"Enough with the bad puns. Just kiss me."

Phin moved in for the smooch, and then T-Nail came on the speaker.

"You see this?"

They looked at the monitor and saw it. And Jack realized, with complete certainty, that she and Phin were going to die.

T-NAIL

The dynamite finally came, brought in by a set from Minneapolis-Saint Paul. Four cases, fifty pounds per case. They'd been delayed by the forest fire, which they insisted was heading this way. T-Nail gave the crew props for making the trip, but he wasn't sure what to do with the boom. Part of him wanted to blow up that son of a bitch Phineas for taking Jacqueline away from him. Another part wanted to chug a bottle of cognac and sleep for a week.

T-Nail was tired. Blood loss was a big factor; between the broken leg and the bullet wound to the shoulder, he had to be down a few pints. Though T-Nail didn't believe in spirituality, or the soul, or any of that new age religious bullshit, he knew his weariness went deeper than just his body. His brain, his identity, his sense of self, every little thing that made him who he was, felt like it had been through a rum runner. Beaten up. Bleeding. Nearly dead.

Del Ray assumed T-Nail was last year's model. Out of touch. Obsolete. That was incorrect. Technology may change. Business may change. But people don't change. Human motivation had remained the same for tens of thousands of years.

And one of man's biggest motivators was revenge.

There was a famous quote attributed to Confucius that history got wrong. *Before embarking on a journey of revenge, dig two graves*. The western world took that to mean those seeking vengeance were also killing themselves.

Wrong. The real meaning behind that quote was that revenge was necessary to preserve your honor. It was something T-Nail learned in the pen. Honor was more important than life, so if you die during your of pursuit honor, so be it.

T-Nail didn't really agree with either interpretation. But he came up with one of his own that fit.

Take everything you can, and destroy those who try to take from you.

Jacqueline had taken from him. She'd taken two decades of his life. And T-Nail had missed out on his chance for payback.

It made him feel like a tire with all the air let out.

He wiped a hand across his face, and caught a whiff of some food, which made him realize how hungry he was. T-Nail sniffed again, then noticed the red smear on his fingers. He touched his tongue to it.

Spaghetti sauce.

The only things he'd touched lately were the cop, his knife, and that photograph of Jack.

The realization hit him like the spray of a cold shower.

That wasn't blood. It was a trick.

Jacqueline was alive.

He bellowed for the Minneapolis crew and had them follow him back to the house.

"You see this?" he told the camera.

T-Nail told the gang to set it up next to the front door.

"How much?" they asked.

"All of it."

PHIN

They ran into the cellar because it was the furthest room from the front door. But it didn't matter. You can't hide from high explosives.

Phin looked at his wife and saw fear there. But he saw strength, too. More strength than he ever possessed. It was one of the things he loved most about Jack. She was a fighter. Not a thug, like him. But a seeker of truth. A defender of the weak. A champion in every sense of the word.

"You're the best person I ever met," he said.

Then he pointed his gun at her head. For real this time.

Jack didn't flinch. She met his stare. The moment stretched so long it felt like time had stopped.

But time hadn't actually stopped. The seconds still ticked away, each one bringing death closer.

"This is really the end, isn't it?" his wife said.

"Yeah."

"They're either going to get in, or we're going to be blown up."

"Yeah."

Jack smiled, which was incongruous with the tears in her eyes. "So many things are going through my head right now. I… I know I've been terrible these past few years…"

"A terrible year with you is better than ten great years without you."

"We've had our moments, haven't we?"

The gun was getting really, really heavy. "I wouldn't take a second of it back. Not a second."

Jack sniffled, then wiped her face with her palm. "Before you..." she took a deep breath, "before you do what you have to, I want to say thanks. Thanks for sharing your life with me, Phineas Troutt. Thanks for Sam." She laughed. "Thanks for the great sex we just had. And for all the sex. Thanks for every kiss. Thanks for every smile. Thanks for fighting for me. I'm a better person, because I knew you."

Phin started to choke up. "I don't believe there's anything... after. But I swear, Jack. If there is something, if there is someplace beyond this life, I'll find you. If it takes a thousand years of searching, I'll find you."

"I love you so much."

"I love you, too."

Phin couldn't pull the trigger with his eyes open, so he shut them. Tight. This hurt. This hurt so bad. But there was no other choice. This way, they died on their terms. Not T-Nail's.

Do it.

Just do it.

Shoot her, confirm it, then eat the gun.

Just...

Do...

"Wait!" Jack said.

He looked at her, a question on his face.

"Call me *honey* one last time," Jack said.

"What are you talking about?"

"You used to call me honey. It was your pet name for me. I never noticed it, until you stopped."

"I stopped?"

She nodded. Phin didn't think it was possible to feel more devastated, but that did the trick.

"Aw, Jack. Shit. I'm so sorry. I wasn't even aware of it."

"It's okay. But say it once more before you..."

Phin turned away, staring at a shelf full of canned goods. "I can't."

"You can't call me honey?"

His hand began to shake. "I can't shoot you. I can't do it." Phin lowered the gun. "I don't have the guts."

He adjusted his grip on the pistol and handed it to her, butt-first. "You have to do it."

She shrank away. "No…"

"You're the strong one. Ya-aburnee. Kill me, then yourself."

"Phin…"

"Please, Jack. We're dead either way."

"What about hope?"

"There is no hope."

"I don't believe that," Jack said. "You're probably right. We're going to die. It's going to be horrible. But when I look at you…" Her voice cracked. "It gives me hope."

Phin lowered the gun. "So… what do we do?"

He watched Jack clench her fists. Her face went from sad to determined.

"We fight. We fight until we can't fight anymore. Then we keep fighting. If this son of a bitch wants to kill us, he's going to have to work for it. And it's gonna take a helluva lot more than a box of dynamite."

"The odds are terrible."

"You want to bet the odds?" Jack asked. "Or bet on us?"

There wasn't any time to think it over. And even if he had time, Phin already knew what his answer was. "Okay, we fight," he said. "Being skinned alive may not be that bad."

"Might even be fun."

Phin reached for his wife. "I love you, h—"

Then an explosion rocked the house and the roof collapsed on top of them.

HERB

When they were five miles outside of Spoonward city limits, Herb lost *Zombie Sugar Jackers.*

He didn't lose the game. He lost the Internet signal.

"My phone reception is gone." Herb held his cell up in the air and launched into the universal *wave-it-around-to-find-a-bar* routine.

Tom was doing the same, which made Herb feel slightly less ridiculous.

"No 4G in the boonies?" Tom asked.

"Statie told me the fire took out some cell towers."

"Is it wrong to be irritated because a miraculous technology that sends data through the airwaves to wireless computers we can hold in our hands isn't working due to a state of emergency?"

"Try adjusting the rabbit ears."

"Huh?"

"They were on old TVs."

"Rabbits were on old TVs?"

"That's what the antennas were called. You're probably too young to remember."

"Can we switch to WiFi or Bluetooth?"

Herb shook his head. "I just had a case where a killer hacked a neighbor's WiFi connection to spy on her. It's easier than you think. With normal equipment, WiFi only has a range of about thirty meters. Bluetooth, less than ten. And both need some sort of WAP."

Tom raised an eyebrow. "They need a derogatory term for Italians?"

"W-A-P. Wireless access point. Like a router. We don't have one. No hotspot either. And no ad hoc network. With a hotspot or ad hoc, we could maybe text each other, but we still couldn't connect to the Internet or reach anyone beyond our short range."

"Fascinating," Tom said. He didn't look the least bit fascinated.

"I'm full of useless bits of information."

"Such as?"

"The national game of Argentina is Juego del Pato. It's basically basketball, played on horseback."

"I think there was a scene in *Evita* with Madonna doing that. What's another?"

"Nikola Tesla created a death ray."

"Tesla? The guy who invented alternating current?"

Herb nodded. "He called it a teleforce. It was a charged particle beam weapon. He died before he sold the final plans. Tesla claimed it could bring down ten thousand enemy planes from two hundred miles away."

"What do you do, memorize Wikipedia at night?"

"I tend to remember esoteric stuff. Such as; about a dozen people die each year from shark attacks. But three thousand people a year are killed by hippos."

"So stay away from him, Tom," Harry called from the front seat. "Especially since he hasn't eaten in a while."

"I thought you were still listening to music," Herb said. Several hours ago, they'd forced McGlade to put on headphones after he sang *Long Gone Long* by The Rainmakers seventeen times in a row.

"I was. But we've got a road block situation coming up, and I thought it best to let you cops handle it."

Herb leaned over and peered out the driver's window. He saw the yellow tape and blinking construction horses dead ahead, and a black man with a flag who was standing in the middle of the road and waving to get Harry's attention.

McGlade slowed the Crimebago down, and Herb fished his badge out of his wallet and made his way to the front seat. As Harry hit the brakes, Herb noticed he had a one pound bag of peanut M&Ms in his lap.

"Why didn't you tell me you have candy?"

"Duh. Because I wanted it all for myself. You could have bought your own M&Ms any of the four times we stopped for gas. Or did you spend all your money on *Zombie Sugar Jackers*?"

"Why do you have to be an ass all the time?" Herb asked. He was pretty sure he still had eight dollars and change left in his checking account.

"An ass? That's mean. You should be more considerate of other people's feelings, jumbo."

"Look!" Herb pointed out the window. "Strippers!"

"Where?"

While Harry was looking, Herb took a handful of M&Ms.

"Dick. You're going to pay me back in tribute."

"Roll down your window," Herb said, his mouth filled with chocolatey goodness. "Guy is here."

The construction worker was young enough that the hair on his upper lip couldn't quite be called a moustache. Harry opened the window halfway.

"What?"

"Road is closed."

Herb flashed his badge. "Not for us. Can you show me your license and permit?"

The kid blinked, then said, "Hold on a second."

He walked off.

"They need a license and permit to do construction?" Harry asked.

"Hell if I know. But I'll bet the union doesn't hire high school kids. You think he's a C-Note?"

"I dunno. Let's ask. Hey!" he called out the window. "Are you a gang member pretending to be a construction worker!?"

The kid replied by yanking a gun out the back of his jeans and firing. Which, in Herb's eyes, pretty much indicated a yes answer. Harry attempted to climb over Herb to get away, falling on top of him, pressing against the larger man cheek-to-cheek. McGlade's quick cowardice in the face of danger probably wasn't necessary; the gangbanger was less than five meters away, and not a single slug hit the vehicle.

How bad a shot did you have to be to miss a gigantic Winnebago from spitting distance?

The gunfire stopped. Maybe so the kid could get even closer.

Harry wiggled atop Herb. "It's like being on a waterbed," he said, "but it smells like pork chops. When was the last time you washed your neck?"

"Get off me, you idiot."

"Again with the name calling."

McGlade disentangled himself. Herb pulled his weapon and got up onto his knees, reaching for the passenger side door.

That's when the RV bounced and someone said, "Umph!"

Herb looked in the back of the Crimebago and saw the side door wide open. Tom had the construction worker cum gangbanger face-first on the floor of the vehicle, his gun at the man's head and his knee in his back.

"I didn't bring my cuffs," Tom said.

Herb had his. He secured the guy's hands behind his back, then patted him down. Cell phone. Wallet. Folding knife. Lighter. Box of weed. Rolling papers. Suspicious baggie containing white powder. Eyeglasses. And two Clif Bars, a White Chocolate Macadamia Nut, and a Spiced Pumpkin Pie. He went through the wallet. Thirty eight bucks, a debit card, and a driver's license saying his name was Chester Newton and he lived in Hyde Park.

"Took this off him." Tom held out the filthiest-looking semi-auto Herb had ever seen. "Don't you ever clean your gun? I'm surprised it fired at all."

"Ain't mine," Chester said.

"What do you mean it ain't yours? I took it out of your hand."

"I mean I don't own it. It's a loaner."

"Who lent it to you?"

Chester didn't reply.

"Answer the question," Herb said.

"I got no answers for you."

"Then we have no use for you," Harry said. He took the Magnum from his shoulder holster. "So you don't mind if I just shoot you right now."

"You'll mess up the floor of your luxury vehicle."

"He's right," Harry said. "Let's take him outside to shoot him."

"You cops ain't gonna shoot me."

"Why not?" Tom asked. "You shot us. And I have to tell you, man to man; you can't aim for shit. You should seriously consider another career choice."

"I didn't have my glasses on. Couldn't see you."

"Why did you take them off in the first place?"

"I'm in disguise, man."

"Disguised as a road worker?" Herb asked.

"Yeah."

"And there aren't any road workers with glasses?"

"When you say it like that, it makes me sound stupid."

"How many of your equally intelligent buddies are up in Spoonward?" Herb asked.

"What?"

Herb raised his voice. "How many guys?"

Chester scowled. "I seriously don't know what you're talking about. I was told I got to stand by the road, turn traffic away. They gave me a gun and didn't tell me nothin' else. And why would they? You never heard of plausible deniability? They don't tell me shit, so I can't tell you shit. Man, you cops are stupid. Now I'm not saying nothing else until I talk to my lawyer."

"Maybe we're not going to arrest you," McGlade said. "Maybe we're going to make you blow us one at a time."

He seemed to consider it. "A'ight. But just you and the tall guy here. Not the fat one."

That stung. "Hey! You saying I'm not attractive enough to rape you?"

"That's exactly what I'm sayin', jelly roll. Dunno if I could even find your dick in all that flab."

"I always wondered about that," Harry said. "What do you do, Herb? Lift your stomach out of the way? Or use a hand mirror?"

Herb ignored Harry. He picked up the kid's cell phone. No signal. Herb scrolled through the texts, which featured a lot more smiley emojis than he would have guessed. But nothing about Spoonward or Jack.

Tom motioned for Herb to confer privately. He whispered in the older man's ear. "We don't have jurisdiction, can't call in the locals, and even if we took him to the nearest authorities, they're all probably busy dealing with the fire."

"So we let him go?"

"Or let McGlade shoot him."

"What if we let him shoot McGlade?" Herb suggested.

"Are you guys talking about me?" Harry asked. "I heard my name."

"I have a few more questions," Herb told Tom. Then he leaned over the kid. "Where'd you steal these Clif Bars?"

"What, 'cause I'm black, I got to steal?"

"No. Because you're a gangbanging thug, you got to steal."

"I bought them at Whole Foods Market."

"Bullshit." Herb had been looking for Spice Pumpkin Pie for months. It was his favorite flavor Clif Bar. But no stores carried it. If this kid had a source, Herb wanted to know.

"Read my lips, fat white man: Whole Foods."

"I'm supposed to believe you shop at Whole Foods?"

"What is it with you and stereotypin'? Just 'cause you're a fat cop, you hear me makin' jokes about you lovin' Dunkin' Donuts?"

"I do love Dunkin' Donuts."

"Well, they do not love you, pork belly."

Harry nodded. "You really should watch your blood sugar, Herb."

"I want to know," Herb plowed onward, "about the Clif Bars."

"You got cholesterol clogging your ears? Whole. Foods. Market. I go there all the time. Great organic fruits and vegetables, and I like their selection of low fat deli meats. You should consider it, for both health and aesthetic reasons."

"You say you care about health?" Herb asked. "What about this shit?"

Herb dropped the weed and white powder on the floor next to the banger.

"Cannabis and coca leaves grow wild on God's green earth, and are one hundred percent natural. It's not like I'm doin' meth."

"METH!" Homeboy screeched. They'd put a cover over his cage so the bird could sleep.

"What you got under that sheet? A little man in a cage? What the hell is wrong with you people? You okay in there, little man?"

"HOMEBOY!"

"What up?" Chester replied.

"HOMEBOY!"

"I said what up? You hear me, little man?"

This was wasting everybody's time, and they needed to get to Jack.

"You crazy white people aren't gonna lock me up in a small cage, are you?" Chester said.

Herb sighed. "No. But I'm sure a judge will, sometime soon."

"METH!"

"At least give the poor little guy some meth," Chester said.

"It's my parrot," Harry said, yanking off the cover.

The kid recoiled. "What the hell did you perverts do to that poor bird?" He turned to Herb. "You pluck him so you could eat him?"

"And, we're done here," Herb said. He uncuffed the kid and tossed him his wallet and glasses. Herb kept everything else.

"Take off," he told him.

"You lettin' me go?"

"Only if you promise, from now on, you'll be a law abiding citizen."

"Serious?"

"I actually don't care," Herb said. "Just take off."

Chester didn't move.

Herb sighed. "What's the problem, Chester?"

"You got my keys. Got my phone. Got my stash. Uncool, man."

"Consider it a life lesson. Stop shooting at people."

"What about the gat? Told you it's not mine. I don't give it back, I'm gonna get in trouble."

"Okay," Herb said, "I guess I could take out the bullets and let you have it."

"Really?"

"No! Get the hell out of here!"

Chester got the hell out of there.

"He seemed nice," said Harry. He let Homeboy out of his cage. The parrot hopped onto McGlade's arm, then leapt off and plummeted to the floor with a dull *THUNK*. After a brief recovery, he pounced on the baggie of cocaine and tore it open with his beak.

"No, Homeboy!" Harry said, grabbing his bird. "That's not meth! It's coke!"

Homeboy buried his face in the powder and made snuffling sounds as McGlade grabbed him and pulled him away from the drugs. The parrot looked pretty damn happy.

"COKE! COKE! COKE! COKE!"

"Cool," said Harry. "He learned a new word."

He put the bird back in his cage, and Homeboy hopped onto his perch and swayed back and forth in obvious narcotic euphoria.

Then he began to sing *Long Gone Long* by The Rainmakers. McGlade joined in.

Herb went to the bathroom, mostly to get away from the noise. When he finished, they were on the road again. The duet had ended, with Homeboy pecking at his own body, apparently searching for any feathers he'd missed. Tom was eating a White Chocolate Macadamia Nut Clif Bar.

"Where's the other one?"

Tom jerked his thumb at Harry.

"This really is the road trip from hell," Herb said to himself.

He sat back down and hoped, for the three hundredth time, that Jack was okay.

T-NAIL

When he opened his eyes, T-Nail realized he'd been knocked over. He yelled, but couldn't hear his own voice over the ringing in his ears.

Two hundred pounds of dynamite packed a bigger punch than he'd guessed.

Del Ray had tried to warn him. He wanted to mathematically figure out how many sticks of dynamite to use before proceeding, then went on a rant about directing the explosion toward the house, using sandbags, and making sure everyone was at a safe distance. T-Nail didn't want to waste the time. The forest fire was so close he could see the orange glow coming from the north, like a false dawn. So he had his men drop all the crates in front of Jack's front door, hook up the wires and detonator, and then it was boom time.

T-Nail had been fifty meters away when he turned the key on the handheld detonator box.

Now he had no idea where the box was. It had been blown out of his hands.

He waited for the smoke to clear, half-expecting the house to be erased. Turned out only half of it was. A good part of the roof had also collapsed. It looked like a giant stepped on it, leaving most of a footprint.

Several men rushed to T-Nail, righting him and the Gyro, and as his hearing returned their murmurs became words.

"Are you okay?"

"Does anything hurt?"

"What do you want us to do?"

"Dig them out," T-Nail ordered.

The possibility that the blast had killed Jack and her husband was large. That would be disappointing, but T-Nail felt better knowing he was the one who did it.

Del Ray approached. He didn't say anything to T-Nail. He just examined the Gyro.

"Servos are fine. Kevlar shielded the electronics from the blast. You lost your gun."

T-Nail saw the empty holster. Then he checked the other side and saw he still had the nail gun. He drew it, and fired into the dirt.

"Still works."

"For now. Your battery is almost dead. You need a fresh one."

"I thought the nail gun worked without a battery."

"The battery charges the compressor. Without it, you only have the CO_2 that's still in the tank."

"So change the battery."

"The replacements were on the bus."

"So?"

Del pointed. The bus, which had been abandoned alongside the house, was buried under rubble.

"Get a team on it. How long will my charge last?"

"If you conserve? Forty-five minutes. Maybe an hour."

"Find the batteries, and get some men to push me toward the house. I want to see their bodies when they're uncovered."

"Two hundred pounds of dynamite." Del Ray shrugged. "Might be nothing left but mush."

"Then I want to see the mush. You have your orders. Move your ass."

JACK

First there was light. Then came sound.

"Jack! Talk to me, please!"

I was on my back, squinting at the glare.

"I can't see with your flashlight in my face."

Phin turned the beam away and pulled back the focus so it illuminated the room. Or rather, what was left of it. The storage room had imploded, and the ceiling was now half a meter above my head.

My husband sounded close, but I couldn't see him. "Are you hurt?" he asked

I did a body part inventory, checking for pain and damage. Everything hurt, but not unbearably. And I took the fact that all my nerves were firing as a good sign. Nothing seemed damaged beyond repair.

But for some reason, when I tried to move, I couldn't. And there was an uncomfortable weight on my chest.

"I don't think so. But I'm stuck."

"We're trapped under canned goods."

Phin played the light across my body. I was buried in cans of lasagna, all the way up to the ceiling.

"You're stuck too?"

"Yeah."

"Are you hurt?"

"Let me check." He was quiet for a moment. "Yeah. My ribs are broken. So is my finger."

"Seems like your sense of humor is intact."

"We'll see how long that lasts when T-Nail starts skinning us alive."

"That's my man. A shining beacon of optimism."

"I'm very optimistic," he said. "I'm optimistic we're going to die horribly."

"Thanks for reminding me. I'd forgotten."

"Happy to be of service."

I sniffed the air. "I smell tomato sauce. And hot dogs."

"Apparently McGlade liked Vienna sausage. Obsessively. The good news is, we won't starve to death."

"Maybe if we last long enough, we'll die of coronary artery disease."

"Don't knock it. Chef Boyardee just saved our lives." Phin pointed the flashlight to a spot near our feet. Cases of cans were stacked one on top of another, and they seemed to be the only thing supporting the ceiling. Harry's food horde had protected us from being crushed.

I started to laugh.

"This is funny to you?"

"If it wasn't for those crates of lasagna," I said, "we both would have pasta way."

It took Phin a moment to absorb the pun, and then he laughed along with me.

"It's good that Chef Boyardee still works for them," Phin said. "I heard he got canned."

Maybe we found this so funny because it was the only way we could relieve stress. It was a defense mechanism. Or maybe we were just making the most of the little time we had left.

When the titters died down, he said, "But, seriously, we're fucked. I can't tell if we're sealed in. If so, we'll run out of air and suffocate. That's assuming the roof doesn't finish collapsing and crush us."

"There's that optimism shining through again. You should be a motivational speaker."

Phin's voice turned serious. "Can you reach your guns?"

His question cut through the artificial mirth and put me back in that dark place. The one where we killed ourselves.

"I thought we were going to fight."

"I'm all for that. But unless you want to defend yourself by throwing canned produce, a gun would be nice. I lost mine. I still have my folding knife, a belt knife, and a pen."

"A pen? Good. You can write T-Nail a stern letter."

"It's a tactical pen. Machine steel. Pointy. Can be used as a stabbing weapon or a striking weapon. It also has a glass breaker."

"Perfect. If we're attacked by panes of glass, we're safe."

"Can you reach your guns?"

I wiggled, not wanting to jostle the cans on my chest too much for fear the house of cards would collapse. "I think I can get into my shoulder holster."

"Take it slow and easy."

"I like it when you talk that way. It's sexy."

"Why does it take near-death situations to bring out your playful side?"

I lowered my voice to Kathleen Turner Jessica Rabbit level, "I'm pinned here, Phin. Completely helpless. Why, you could do anything to me." I breathed low and throaty. "Anything at all."

"Just try to reach your damn gun."

I stopped goofing around and tried to reach my damn gun. Navigating my hand through stacked canned goods wasn't easy. My fingers sought out gaps, then I slowly eased through them, moving the cans aside.

"I got to my holster."

I managed to unsnap the leather strap, but when I yanked the butt of the weapon, I could immediately tell by feel that something was wrong.

"Shine the light over here," I said, pulling the revolver free of the cans.

As I suspected, the cylinder was bent.

"It's broken." I turned it over in my hand, pulling and prodding. "Ejector rod won't work. Cylinder won't turn, and the chamber is misaligned."

"Does it cock?"

I tried to thumb back the hammer. "No. Shit, Phin. My mother gave me this gun when I graduated the police academy."

I went from feeling giggly to stifling a sob. Full blown hysteria was peeking around the corner, trying to stare me down.

"I'm sorry about your gun, Jack, but can we save the sentiment for later? How about your ankle holster?"

I wrangled control over my emotional state and tried to shift my body. "No way. I'm pinned. Can't even move my legs."

That's when we heard it. A faint, echoey rumble.

"Is the house settling?" I asked.

"No." Then Phin said what I feared he'd say. "They're digging us out."

DEL RAY

After instructing the men according to T-Nail's orders, Del went back to Lil' K.

Lil' K joined the set on his fourteenth birthday, just a week ago. There had been no blood in/blood out. No rum runner. None of that old school bullshit. Just a gathering of homies. Lil' K recited the memorized oath with a bit of coaching from Del, and then they got their party on.

Seemed like yesterday.

At present, Lil' K was standing up against the trunk of a big pine tree. He was struggling to breathe, because he had a length of copper pipe sticking through him. The projectile had hit him when the house exploded, and pinned him to the tree with so much force that three brothers couldn't pull it out. Lil' K finally begged them to stop because it hurt so bad, and they did.

He didn't have much time left.

"You hangin' in there, homes?" Del Ray said as he approached. "You get it? Hangin'?"

Lil' K offered a weak smile. His teeth were red. "Hurts real bad, General."

"You a C-Note, dog. We eat pain and dish out payback. You know the creed."

"I know. Eat pain and dish out payback, then tag the pussy on the way back."

"Hells yeah, C." Del Ray did not high five. He was afraid to touch him.

"This past week... been the best of my life."

That was sad as hell. This kid hadn't even begun to live.

Del thought of all the things he'd never get to see. Never get to do.

It wasn't supposed to happen this way. Bangin' was dangerous. Hustlin' always had risks. Streets were mean. But this wasn't the streets. This was the woods. Far from home.

"Wish I had a cold forty right now," K said.

"You an' me both, cuz. But you know you're underage. That shit is bad for you."

Another weak smile. The smile faded as quick as it came. "I'm not gonna make it, am I?"

Del didn't sugar coat. "No."

"That's okay." He cleared his throat, spat blood. "And if I bleed and die today, never over my grave pray, I lived true and I lived free, I lived and died to serve the C."

Del Ray gently touched his shoulder. "You're family. C-Note through and through."

Some birds began to sing. Something you didn't hear much in the city.

"Never had a family before," K said. "It was nice."

Del felt some tears well up, and he wanted to turn away. But he didn't. You never turned away from your own.

"You know, I didn't grow up on the streets," Del said.

"For real?"

"Suburbs. Straight-up middle class. We had a big lawn. Little swing set in back, with a plastic slide. A two car garage." Del had never told anyone this before. "When I was ten years old, we lost it all. Dad loved riverboat gambling more than he loved us. Had to move in with my cousins in Englewood. Scared the shit out of me. I faked being street so I didn't get my ass whupped. Made up all these stories about myself. About how bad-ass I was. How my grandma was full-blooded Sioux Indian. I don't have any Sioux blood in me. My real name isn't Del Ray. It's Paul. Paul Michael Palmer. But I left all that behind. Joined the C-Notes at fourteen, just like you. Haven't seen my mom or dad since. Never looked back. The C's are my family now. Remember the Creed?"

Lil' K gave a weak nod.

"Being a C-Note ain't just about turf, and scrappin', and hustlin'. It's about pride. Honor. Responsibility. Community. Equality." Del began to recite. "We are strong because we all are one. Brothers and sisters united—"

"—to make a better world for every daughter and son," Lil' K said, finishing the line.

"I'm proud of you, my man. Your life has meaning. And I won't ever forget you."

Lil' K didn't respond. He passed before Del finished talking.

Del Ray wiped off his cheeks, and closed Lil' K's eyes.

Then he took out his straight razor.

JACK

They're getting close," I said, listening to the excavation sounds grow stronger.

"Take this," Phin said. He was holding the flashlight in his bad hand, and waving his folder in the other. "You ready?"

"Yeah."

"On three. One... two... three!"

It was a bad throw. I stretched for it, and the knife handle bounced off my fingertips, landing on the floor somewhere in between us.

"I can't reach it," I said, extending my arm as far as I could go.

Phin couldn't either.

"What's plan B?" I asked. The team working to dig us out seemed very close.

"My belt knife."

"What are you going to use?"

"I've still got the tactical pen."

"Give me the pen," I told him.

"You made fun of the pen."

"Have you trained with one?"

"No. But I haven't trained with a knife, either. Unless stabbing someone is considered training."

"I've trained with batons before. There's a mini version of a baton called a *Koga*. A short impact weapon. I know how to use it."

"Yeah. You stab whoever is nearby."

"Just throw me the damn pen."

A light hit my face. Not Phin's.

"I see them!" someone yelled.

Phin tossed the pen. I snatched it out of the air and quickly shoved it down my shirt, into the elastic of my bra.

"I love you," I told my husband.

"I love you, too."

Then they pushed their way in and swarmed on us.

HERB

"Welcome to beautiful downtown Spoonward, Wisconsin," McGlade said. "Don't blink or you'll miss it."

Herb couldn't recall ever being in a town of five hundred residents, but the main street was as he imagined it would look like. Post office. Tiny library. A few shops. And the police station. It was the only building that had lights on.

"Let's be quick about this," Herb said. "We run in, tell whoever's there what's happening, and go get Jack. How far away is your place, Harry?"

"About ten more miles."

Herb had argued against stopping in Spoonward to inform the authorities. The longer he spent in the RV, the more anxious he became. That gang kid, Chester, had given Herb a speck of hope. If the C-Notes had him guarding the road, they hadn't finished with Jack yet. There was a chance she and Phin were still alive.

But with every passing second, the odds got worse.

Tom had talked Herb out of going directly to Jack. A liaison with the locals, if it worked, would be incredibly helpful. They could provide more manpower, more guns, and the necessary stamp of approval. If things went sour, this could become a bureaucratic and media nightmare. Harry hadn't been a cop for decades, and Herb and Tom were a long way from their jurisdiction. Going into a different state, guns blazing, would cause more than just disciplinary action. They could all wind up in prison.

McGlade pulled up next to the police station.

"Just let me out here," Tom said. "I'll talk to them."

"We can all go in."

"We don't know how long it will take. You and Harry need to go find Jack."

"You sure?" Herb wasn't keen on this idea. Splitting up seemed to never work out well. "What if there isn't anyone there?"

"I see people through their window. Someone is home. You got a paper map, McGlade?"

Their GPS had died at the same time their cell service had.

"Yeah. In the good old glove box."

Harry opened the glove compartment, and half a dozen Clif Bars spilled out. Herb decided to kill him. After they rescued Jack.

McGlade fished out a map, then wasted thirty seconds finding his hideaway and circling it in pen. He handed it over.

Tom offered Herb his hand. "Be careful. I'll be right behind you guys. If the Chief doesn't give me a ride, I'll steal his squad car."

"Good luck," Herb told him.

"Who needs luck when I have natural charm?" Tom asked.

"Ned Beatty had natural charm, too," Harry said. "Things didn't work out well for him in *Deliverance*."

Tom opened the side door, and then smiled. "They're cops like us. What's the worst that can happen?"

T-NAIL

They dragged Jacqueline and her husband into what used to be the living room. The roof was gone, and the stars had come out. The men had set several bonfires to light up the area, but there was also ambient light from the forest fire, creeping toward them in the distance. They'd also stripped the couple of their body armor and frisked them, taking a knife and a flashlight from the man, and a knife and gun from Jack's ankle holsters.

Now it was just a question of which one to hurt first.

"I've been waiting for this moment for a very long time," T-Nail said, raising his voice so all of the men gathered around could hear. Every eye was fixed on him. The flickering flames, and the half-destroyed house, made the setting look surreal. Almost tribal. This wasn't Uganda. And T-Nail wasn't Idi Amin. But this might be the closest he ever got to either.

"The Eternal Black C-Notes are all about honor," he continued. "And a man's honor is more important than his life. This woman," he pointed at Jacqueline, being pinned to the floor by four of his soldiers, "tried to take my honor." He filled his lungs and bellowed, "No one takes a C-Notes honor and lives!"

He expected whooping and applause, but there was only silence.

Did they fear him so much they were afraid to cheer? That had to be the reason.

T-Nail pushed his joystick forward, and the Gyro moved slower than normal. They still hadn't found his spare batteries, but that didn't matter. This moment was his, and he was going to relish it.

So what would be the best way to punish Jacqueline?

He stared into her eyes. Saw defiance.

T-Nail knew that look. He'd seen it many times in his enemies.

It never lasted, no matter how strong they were. He would have her begging within the hour.

"The man," he ordered. "Hold him down and stretch out his arms and legs."

The soldiers followed orders, and cleared a path for T-Nail as he rolled up.

"You are going to die badly, Jacqueline Daniels," T-Nail told her. "But before you do, I'm going to show you what's going to happen to you. On him."

T-Nail pulled the nail gun out of his holster.

It only took eight nails to pin Jacqueline's husband to the wood floor.

PHIN

He couldn't move.

But then, that was probably the point of being nailed to the floor.

Phin was face-down, arms and legs stretched out. T-Nail had shot him with his nail gun through the soles of each foot, the muscle of each calf, through the meat of the triceps, and through his palms.

Surprisingly, it didn't hurt very much. Maybe it was because the nails pierced him so quickly, his nerves didn't have time to react. The pain was nothing compared to his broken finger. Or even his cracked ribs. While Phin wouldn't recommend his current predicament as a fun way to kill a Saturday night, he'd been through a lot worse.

Then he looked at Jack. At the horror in her eyes. The pity. The sadness. The hopelessness.

And Phineas Troutt's heart ached worse than any physical pain he'd ever endured.

JACK

I finally understood.

Watching the man I love get hurt like that, made me finally understand what ya-aburnee meant.

I hope you bury me.

It was the truest, purest thing ever said by anyone.

I couldn't watch him die. Not Phin. Not the man I loved so much.

As scared as I was for myself, I didn't want to outlive him. I wanted to die clinging to the hope that maybe, just maybe, Phin would make it.

I wanted to die first.

I had to die first.

"I get it," I said, keeping my voice strong. "I get it, Phin. I know it's too late to matter, but I understand. I understand ya-aburnee."

"It's about damn time," Phin said.

"Hey! Terrance!"

T-Nail looked at me.

"Do you want to know the real reason you were in jail for twenty years?" I said. "It's because I was better than you. That's why you spent two decades behind bars. That's why you can't walk. Because I'm strong, and you're weak. And you're afraid to show how weak you really are, in front of your gang. So you need their help to kill me."

I raised my voice.

"You talk about honor," I continued. "Where's your honor? I took your life, and I took your legs. Why don't you face me, man to woman? Or are you a coward?"

T-Nail didn't speak for almost ten seconds. Then he said, "Is that it?"

I didn't reply.

"What did you think that would do, Jacqueline? Shame me into fighting you one-on-one? I could easily snap your neck. And I know that's what you want. A quick death. But it isn't going to be that easy for you. You're going to watch Phineas die, while you both beg for mercy. Then you're going to die. We're not going to end this as equals. It ends with me in control, and you suffering."

"You're all here," I said to the hundred-plus gangbangers standing around us, "because this asshole cares more about revenge than he does about your lives. I haven't killed a single one of you. I had a rifle, and I aimed to wound. How many of you have died because of him? All because he was stupid enough to get shot in the spine and caught by the cops, so long ago some of you weren't even born yet. He's seeking honor? He has no honor. Has this man done a single thing to earn your respect?"

"I am War Chief," T-Nail said.

"You're a shithead," I said.

"I second that," Phin added. "I also second that you're weak, and you're a coward. Everyone here knows my wife would kick your ass. She already did it once. She'd do it again. You needed over a hundred guys to take out one female cop. That's how scared you are. Hey, you, with the hairy vest! Del Ray! Is this guy really the one you want running the show? I thought you were the General. Why is shithead here giving the orders?"

T-NAIL

The question Phineas asked hung in the air. T-Nail wasn't shamed by it. Words meant nothing to him. Jacqueline could whine until he cut her lips off, and T-Nail didn't care.

But something was going on with his men. Rather than feeling their fear and allegiance, T-Nail sensed doubt in their ranks. That Del Ray didn't refute the husband's accusation added to the traitorous vibe.

Dissention wouldn't be a good thing. And, truth told, the siege probably had taken a toll on the soldiers. There had been casualties. They were tired.

What they needed was something to cheer their spirits. A good leader knew when to use the stick, and when to use the carrot.

Now was a good time for the carrot.

"You men have done an admirable job, and you deserve a reward. Before we kill this bitch, let's run a train on her."

That got the cheers he was hoping for earlier.

He held up a hand for silence. His men immediately quieted down.

"But first," T-Nail said, "let's show her what it means to be a C-Note. Form the circle. Let's see how she handles a rum runner."

JACK

I knew what running a train meant.

Gang rape.

But the rum runner comment eluded me.

It didn't really matter. I was going to find out soon enough.

I was dragged across the floor, then shoved forward. The gang-bangers surrounded me and Phin.

"You want to be a leader, Del?" T-Nail shouted. "Lead the men in this."

The man with the scalps on his vest—the one Phin had shot in the ear—approached me. He didn't look overtly hostile. But he didn't look concerned for my well-being, either.

"What's a rum runner?" I asked him.

"You know what blooding into a gang means?"

"Beating a new member up to see if he can take it."

"Rum runner is that, but harder. Beat you until you can't even stand up."

"You ever stop to think that maybe your little club is a bit dysfunctional?" I asked.

Del Ray sucker-punched me in the jaw.

I fell onto all fours as the men cheered. I was only a few inches away from my husband.

"I didn't say it before," I told him. "But I'm saying it now. And I mean it. This is what I want. I'd rather they beat me to death than watch it happen to you. Ya-aburnee, Phin."

Phin's eyes teared-up, but his face was iron.

"No," he said.

"No?"

"Not today," Phin said. "You're the hero, Jack. You've always been the hero. And you aren't going to die first, because you aren't allowed to die today. You. Will. Not. Die." He winked. "Now go and beat the shit out of them, honey."

I was pulled away from him as the bangers hauled me back up to my feet.

He called me honey.

Phin called me honey.

One simple little word, uttered sincerely by the man I loved, and a tiny little bit of my hope had returned.

I twisted my arms, a standard judo escape, and rolled backward, away from the guys who'd grabbed me. Then I pointed at the man with the scalps on his vest.

"You. Fuzzy. You dropped something."

I pivoted, swiveling my hips, bringing my leg around in a reverse kick and connecting solidly with his face.

"It's your fucking teeth," I said. "Now who else wants some?"

Two men came at me. They were bigger. Stronger. Younger. But untrained. They left so many vulnerable spots open as they advanced, I had time to pick and choose. The first I uppercut in the jaw with the heel of my hand, the second I kneed in the groin, then chopped in the back of the neck as he fell.

Three down. A hundred or so to go.

Another man approached. A real big guy. Moving on the balls of his feet, his fists up like he'd spent some time in the gym. He came at me on my left, threw a quick roundhouse, then followed up with a jab that tagged me on the shoulder. I backed away.

"You've boxed," I said.

"Got a little training."

"You any good?"

"Good enough to beat your ass, bitch."

I kicked him in the chin and knocked him down. "Better go train some more, bitch."

Then it was three guys at once. The first came in low, lunging for the tackle. Smart. I wouldn't stand a chance if the fight went to the ground. I danced away from it like a matador, and got tapped in the chin. I whipped around, extending my arm and connecting with a backhand, then bunched up my shoulders and arms to weather a flurry of punches. When I saw an opening, I jabbed, then grabbed him by the ears and introduced his face to my knee.

By the way he yelled, his face didn't like the meeting.

Movement, peripherally. I ducked on reflex, and knuckles met the top of my head. My head won, and the guy backed off, screaming and staring at a hand that wasn't bent in the proper direction.

I got pushed in the back, and fell forward, onto the floor. Caught another glimpse of Phin.

He looked proud.

And then they were all over me, and the kicking began.

There was no way to defend against that. No way to block. No way to fight back. I tucked my head into my arms, curled up into a ball, and waited for them to stomp me to death.

And I was okay with that.

Not just because of ya-aburnee. But because of something my friend and ex-partner, Herb Benedict, said to me twenty years ago when I first encountered T-Nail.

The day you're no longer afraid is the day you'll die.

That day was today. Because I wasn't afraid. Val and Lund would take care of Sam. And if there was a heaven, the man I loved was going to find me.

But not if I found him first.

PHIN

Jack held her own for a while, and watching her, Phin had never loved anyone more. But there was only so much one person could do against a mob.

Then she went down, and they went at her like hyenas after zebra scraps.

Phin strained against the nails, and the pain finally hit. And it hit hard. Like charley horses, everywhere. Phin was able to pull for two seconds, then his body gave out.

They kept kicking Jack.

"Get up!" he yelled at her

Phin wasn't the hero. Jack was the hero. She needed to save the day, like she always did. That was her thing, not his. Phin couldn't even save those poor people at the Walmart. His best efforts just weren't good enough.

He tried to get up once more, pushing against the floor with his knees, trying to pry the nails out of the wood.

The wood was too strong. The pain won again.

"Get up!"

If it had been his wife nailed to the floor, she would have found a way out. She'd save him. That's what heroes did.

"GODDAMN IT, GET UP!"

That was when Phin realized he was no longer yelling at his wife.

He was yelling at himself.

No. He wasn't the hero.

But he sure as hell was going to help the hero.

Phin strained with more resolve than he ever thought he was capable of, and the nail heads dug trenches through his calf muscles, and then he pushed on his elbows and leveraged his forearms off the floor, turning the pain into strength and tearing his hands free. His feet stayed nailed, but Phin found a nearby length of rebar and wedged it under each shin, prying his shoes off the floor.

Then, somehow, he was stumbling toward the melee, howling like a berserker.

Phin didn't have Jack's fighting skills. But who needed skills when you were swinging a heavy iron bar?

He lost count of the skulls he cracked, and the mob sensed the danger and backed away, and then he was reaching down for Jack, trying to grab her hand to pull her up.

But she refused to untuck from the fetal position.

JACK

The kicking stopped. Then a hand was in my face.

A blood-covered hand.

I went to bite it. If I was dying, I was dying with this asshole's finger in my stomach.

And then I saw the wedding ring.

Phin.

"I thought your lazy ass was sitting this one out," I said, looking up at him.

"No way. You and me against the world. Remember?"

"I still hate that song."

I stood, and almost fell over. They'd beaten me up pretty good. Rum runner was an apt name for the ritual.

Phin looked even worse than I felt. He had blood on him, well, *everywhere*. But he still managed a smile for me.

"Let's fight until we can't fight anymore," he said. "Then keep fighting."

"The odds are terrible."

"You want to bet the odds? Or bet on us? What do you say, honey?"

I put up my fists. "My money is on us."

T-NAIL

This really hadn't turned out the way T-Nail had hoped.

Rather than get aroused, the men were even more uneasy than before. What the hell had happened to the youth of today? In T-Nail's time, gangbangers were tough. A few cracked skulls and this crew seemed ready to give up.

Fuck it. Time to show the kids how it got done.

He pushed the joystick on the Gyro, extending to his full height. Then he gripped his nail gun and rolled into battle.

DEL RAY

We only found one of his four missing teeth. And it was broken in half, probably not salvageable.

Looking around, he saw several of his men, down and bleeding.

Looking behind him, he saw the forest fire in the distance, closing in fast.

Enough was enough. He was getting his crew out of here.

"C-Notes!" he called, waving his hands. "C-Notes! It's time to—"

"Time to what?" T-Nail said.

Del had been so preoccupied he hadn't noticed the OG sneak up behind him.

"We're cutting out," Del said. "We spilled enough blood for your little revenge fantasy."

"Is that so?"

"Yeah. I'm going to the council. Laying it all out for them. I got a hundred witnesses who will all be happy to talk about what a shit job you've done."

"Here's something else for them to witness."

He raised his weapon and buried a nail in Del Ray's forehead.

HERB

Get out of the way, you assholes!" Harry laid on the horn. Then someone screamed and bounced off the front windshield.

"Not my fault," McGlade said. "I honked."

Herb sat in the passenger seat, viewing the scene with total awe. The forest fire had arrived, kicking up the Indian summer weather to regular summer temperatures, lighting up the trees around them. Gangbangers were everywhere, running this way and that way, on the roads and in the woods, some of them grabbing and climbing the Crimebago, trying to get inside. It was like...

"It's like an episode of *The Walking Dead*," Herb said, in awe.

"They're blocking my driveway. My house is still a few hundred meters away. I can't get through without running people over."

Herb was actually startled by McGlade's sudden humanity.

"If someone gets stuck in an axel it could blow the transmission," Harry finished.

He threw the RV into park, and hopped out of the driver's seat.

"Where are you going?" Herb asked.

"To the tank."

Then the side door jerked open, and a gangbanger launched himself into the vehicle, tackling McGlade against Homeboy's cage, all three crashing to the floor.

Herb already had his gun in hand. He swung it, clipping the hood on the side of the face, knocking him back outside.

Four more piled in.

Herb managed to hold onto his gun, but he got pinned against the refrigerator and couldn't aim. McGlade began to wail, and Herb thought they were tearing him apart until he realized Harry was yelling about everyone tracking mud on his carpeting.

More guys came inside. Herb always wondered how he'd fare in a zombie apocalypse, and now he had his answer. He would fail miserably.

On a positive note, at least he wouldn't be eaten alive.

"HOMEBOY!"

All movement stopped, and every eye zeroed in on the parrot. Free of his cage, Homeboy had somehow managed to climb the drapery covering the outside window, and he now roosted on the curtain rod.

"What the fuck is that thing?" somebody said.

"That's my parrot, Homeboy!" Harry announced, proud as any daddy. "And he's going to save the day!"

"HARRY!" Homeboy squawked.

And then the bird stretched out its featherless wings and leapt into the air—

—plummeting like a rock. He landed on the kitchen counter, where they'd tossed the baggie of cocaine taken from Chester, and immediately tore it to pieces.

A moment later the bird went rigid, and fell off the counter onto the floor.

"Dude, I think your parrot just OD'ed."

"Everybody stand back!" Harry ordered. Incredibly, they did. Perhaps seeing a naked parrot overdose on cocaine was just strange enough that continuing the attack became an afterthought.

McGlade gently picked Homeboy up, rested him on the couch, and put his fingers on his tiny, chest, beginning compressions.

"Stay with me, buddy." Harry said. "You're too young to die."

Then he leaned over and gave Homeboy the breath of life.

"That's just wrong," somebody said.

Herb had to agree.

McGlade's life-saving measures proved too aggressive, and Homeboy inflated like the world's ugliest balloon.

Then the dead parrot farted.

That was Herb's cue to get the hell out of there. The gangbangers who'd pinned him were transfixed on *The Harry and Homeboy CPR Show*, and Herb pushed his way to the front of the Crimebago.

"Hang in there, Homeboy! I'm charging the defibrillator!"

Herb was happy he wasn't there to see it.

"Clear!" McGlade yelled.

A collective groan filled the vehicle.

And so did an odor not dissimilar to roasted chicken.

Herb pushed out the driver's door. There were still gangbangers everywhere, and many seemed to be converging on the Crimebago. Even more concerning, the forest fire had gotten dangerously close.

It looked like a scene out of Dante's Inferno.

Herb hurried to the tank they'd towed for four hundred plus miles. He tried to remember how it worked, vaguely recalled Harry pointing to the top, and saw the valve handle.

He reached up and gave it a tug.

Six jets of water sprayed out of the nozzles on the sides with ten tons of pressure. Originally used as a street cleaner, the water tank also worked tremendously well for crowd control. The nearby gangbangers were knocked over. The ones further out didn't want to get wet, and stayed clear. And all the nearby flames sizzled and died out.

Secret weapon for the win.

Herb adjusted his grip on the SIG and went back around to the side door. He fired into the air, and everyone turned to look.

"Out! Now!"

One by one, the gangbangers filed out of the Crimebago. Herb climbed back inside and saw Harry still leaning over his expired parrot.

Homeboy appeared both squashed and burned. Apparently McGlade had pressed too hard on the paddles.

"I'm sorry about Homeboy, Harry."

"At least he died doing what he loved. Illegal narcotics."

"We need to go get Jack."

"I'm on it."

Herb followed Harry back to the cockpit, and McGlade started up the vehicle and hit the gas.

"I miss the little guy already," Harry said.

"Why?"

"Yeah, he was pretty awful, wasn't he?"

"He was the worst," Herb agreed.

"But let us not dwell on what he was or wasn't. Instead, let him be an example of the perils of meth addiction."

"He overdosed on coke."

Harry's shoulders slumped. "I hated that parrot."

The forest fire licked at the dirt driveway on either side, but the water tank kept it at bay, shooting hundreds of gallons of water in every direction, including in front of them.

And that's when the Crimebago got stuck in the mud.

JACK

Almost all of the gangbangers had taken off. I don't think Phin and I had scared them off with our fighting prowess, which had devolved to blindly swinging at anyone who came near. A careful, dedicated person with serious intent could have flattened us both without much trouble.

But intent seemed to be lacking. Maybe it had something to do with seeing T-Nail shoot their General in the head with a nail gun. That wasn't the best way to inspire loyalty in your troops.

For his part, T-Nail hadn't given up. But his tricked-out wheelchair continued to slow down. When he got within three meters of us, it stopped completely.

"Let's get around him, get away," I said to Phin.

Phin responded by collapsing next to my feet.

"I'm done, honey. Adrenaline wore off. I can't move."

"Don't be a baby," I said, reaching to help Phin up.

I collapsed right next to him. Since my whole body throbbed equally, I had to take visual inventory of my injuries using the one eye that wasn't swollen shut.

Left arm, broken.

Right ankle, broken.

Left leg, something pulled or torn.

Ribs...

I finally understood why Phin had been whining about his ribs. Cracked ribs hurt like hell.

As I studied my right arm, checking for damage, a nail magically appeared in my shoulder.

I stared at it, incredulous. It didn't actually hurt, but I knew that was normal. I'd heard stories of construction workers who had accidentally nail gunned their own feet to the floor, and didn't know it until they tried to walk.

This, however, was no accident.

"Jacqueline!" T-Nail roared.

"This guy." Phin shook his head. "I hate this guy."

"Jacqueline Daniels!"

"We can hear you, Terrance," I said. "Enough already. It's over."

"It's not over."

"It's over!" I yelled, feeling myself grow faint. "Your gang is gone. And it sounds like your battery is dead. What are you going to do? Kill us then crawl ten miles back to town? Don't be an idiot. You're going back to prison."

"I'm never going back to prison. If I die here, so be it. But you're dying first."

He fired again, and this one struck the floor a few centimeters from my hip.

I was too beaten up to even flinch.

"You talk about honor," I said. "You have no idea what honor is. You don't care about the world. And the world doesn't care about you. Nobody cares about you, Terrance. Your stupid revenge fantasy doesn't matter." I looked at Phin. "The only thing that matters is family."

"I got five hundred 20d nails," T-Nail said. "And I'm going to use every one of them on you."

He aimed the nail gun again. Phin tried to climb on top of me.

"Not the best time for sex, babe," I said.

"I'm going to shield you with my body."

"Maybe I want to shield you with my body."

"Maybe we both should just try to crawl out of range."

"I'd be up for that."

The next nail hit me in the calf, pinning me to the floor.

"Change of plans," I said, very close to passing out from pain. "I'm staying."

Phin nodded. "Then I'm staying, too."

We put our arms around each other and waited for the end.

T-NAIL

Not the best way to end things, but he still wound up alpha.

T-Nail wished he could be closer. To see the expressions on their faces as he put nail after nail into them. But he was fine with watching their slow demise from a few meters away.

Plus, his aim was improving. The next nail was going to go right into Jacqueline's belly.

Then there was a loud hissing sound, from behind him. T-Nail turned and looked down.

Del Ray, a nail sticking halfway into his forehead, had crawled over and cut the pneumatic hose going from the air compressor to the nail gun. He was currently hacking away at T-Nail's legs with a straight razor.

T-Nail whacked him in the head hard enough the kill him. Del Ray fell onto his face. T-Nail once again looked at Jacqueline and her husband.

He couldn't shoot them. But that was no problem. He'd do it the old-fashioned way.

By hand.

Undoing his straps, T-Nail fell to the floor and landed on his side. He shook off the impact, twisted forward, and began to drag himself toward Jacqueline and Phineas.

HERB

McGlade tried reverse for the fourth time then told Herb, "Get out and push."

Herb quickly exited through the passenger door.

"Put your weight into it!" Harry called after him. "That'll get us unstuck fast!"

But Herb didn't bother with trying to free the Crimebago. All he cared about was getting to Jack.

He ran as fast as he could, the mud sucking at his shoes, winded after only a dozen steps but more determined than he'd ever been in his life. He could see the house. It was only fifty meters away.

Then someone yelled, "Cop!" and the shooting started.

A whole lot of shooting.

Herb dove onto the ground, eating mud. Four gangbangers with machine guns cut the forest down around Herb.

Visibility was shit. The fire, and illumination from the Crimebago's headlights, reflected off the smoke and made it impossible to see more than a few meters ahead. Herb aimed where he thought he saw the nearest muzzle flash, squeezing the trigger twice.

He had no idea if he hit his targets or not. But he assumed not when four people returned fire, the rounds landing short and spraying mud into Herb's face.

Herb aimed again. He wasn't the crack shot that Jack was. And it had been months since he'd been on the range. And shooting while on his belly wasn't an ideal position.

But he couldn't die now. Not when Jack needed him.

Herb fired three more times.

They fired another hundred times at him.

No one was hitting anything. But they were getting closer.

He'd fired a warning shot in the Crimebago, so Herb only had four more rounds in his SIG Sauer magazine. But he had another full mag in his…

Oh, shit. When McGlade was rushing Herb out of the house, he'd forgotten to bring his spare mag.

Herb glanced behind him. Harry was nowhere to be seen.

"This is the police!" Herb yelled.

"We know!" they answered. "That's why we're shooting!"

They shot the shit out of the muddy driveway, just a meter from Herb's right side. He fired back, three times.

Leaving only one bullet left.

One bullet for four assailants.

Herb had failed.

His mind flashbacked to twenty years ago. The undercover operation where Jack had nabbed T-Nail. He'd been late then. He'd failed her.

And now he'd failed her again.

Then four shots rang out in rapid succession. But they weren't aimed at Herb.

They came from behind Herb. *Way* behind Herb. It sounded like a rifle, and it sounded far away.

"Hello?" shouted into the darkness.

No one answered.

"Nice shooting, babe!" he heard Harry yell. "You can get up, fatstuff. Threat neutralized."

Herb watched McGlade approach. He was carrying a flashlight, not a rifle.

"What the hell just happened?" Herb said.

"That's my specialist friend. The one I tweeted. She just drilled them all through their brain pans."

Herb was confused. "I thought she told you no."

"She's a spy, Dumbo. No means yes. She has to say that in case anyone is listening in."

"Why didn't you tell me that earlier?"

"Because I'm a dick," Harry said. "Want to see something cool?" He fished a quarter out of his pocket and tossed it straight up.

The coin never hit the ground. She shot it right out of the air.

"She's the best long distance shot in the world," McGlade said.

But Herb hadn't heard him say that. He was already sprinting toward the house.

JACK

I watched T-Nail pull himself toward me. Hand over hand. A blank expression on his face.

With my unbroken arm, I reached into my bra and took out the tactical pen, hiding it behind my back.

"Gotta give him points for determination," I said to Phin.

Phin didn't answer. He'd passed out.

When T-Nail was less than half a meter away, he stopped. "Every day, for the past twenty years, I've done five hundred pulls ups. I can bend a frying pan in half. Now I'm going to break every—"

"Blah blah blah," I interrupted. "So do it already. I'm sick of listening to your psycho ranting."

He lunged, grabbing my leg, pulling himself up to me until his huge hands wrapped around my throat.

The last time we'd been in this position, twenty years ago, I had poked a crack pipe into his eye. Unfortunately, it hadn't done any permanent damage.

The tactical pen worked much better. I stabbed it into his eye socket so hard it stuck there.

T-Nail howled, rocking my head back with a slap. He yanked out the pen.

Along with his eyeball.

He screamed even louder, reaching for my neck with both hands, squeezing.

As I blacked out, I realized the last thing I'd ever see was T-Nail's shish-kebobbed eye, resting on his cheek and dangling from the optic nerve.

T-NAIL

The pain was extraordinary.

And so was the rage.

T-Nail lost all control. His plan had been to take his time hurting Jacqueline. To drag it out over a few hours.

But he couldn't contain himself. He squeezed the cop hard enough to snap her neck and separate her head from her body.

HERB

Panic. Like a jolt of liquid electricity flushing through Herb's body, fueling every worst case scenario at once.

Jack was more than a co-worker. More than a partner.

She was his friend.

And he had to get to her. Fast.

Harry's house looked like it had been lifted up and dropped from a great height. Herb rushed around the perimeter, where several bonfires had been lit.

There, in the flickering light less than twenty meters away, he saw Jack being choked by T-Nail.

I can't fail her again.

Not again.

Herb didn't fire a warning shot.

He didn't announce himself as a police officer.

He just stopped, aimed his last bullet, and squeezed the trigger—

—blowing the top of the bastard's head off.

Jack flopped on her back, arms and legs akimbo.

"Jack!"

She didn't answer.

Herb ran to her, staring down at her motionless body.

"I'm too late. Oh, god, I'm too late."

Then her eyelids fluttered, and she stared up at him. "On the contrary, partner. You're right on time."

JACK

I chased the rest of the gang off," Harry McGlade said to me. "You're welcome."

"I never thought I'd be happy to see you, Harry. But I am."

"Well, I'm not happy to see you, Jackie. Damn, you look like hell."

"It's not all blood. Some of it is spaghetti sauce."

"Damn, you need to learn how to cook. The sauce is supposed to stay in the pan."

"So the gang's all here?" Phin had roused himself.

"Phineas," McGlade nodded at him.

"Harrison," Phin nodded back.

"We came in the nick of time to save your asses," Harry said. "Yet again. It's practically a full-time job."

"Thanks."

"That's what friends are for," Harry said. "Also, the two of you owe me three million dollars for trashing my house."

I heard a car drive up. Harry tugged out his gigantic handgun and pointed it into the darkness. But the woman in the Jeep was a familiar face.

"Chandler?" I said.

She shook her head. "No. I'm her better-looking twin sister."

I knew who she was. And she wasn't one of the good guys.

"This is Hammett," McGlade said. "Don't piss her off. She'll kill you."

Harry wasn't exaggerating.

"We appreciate the help," Herb said.

"You need to get in some range time, chubs," Hammett told him. "That was some really bad shooting."

"It was dark. And smoky."

"And I still hit them, through the trees, from one and a half kilometers away."

"Thanks." I kept my voice flat.

"I didn't do it for you."

"Well, thanks just the same."

"You've got some skills," Hammett told me. "You were doing pretty good in that gang fight, for about ten seconds. And nice move poking out that cyborg's eye."

"You saw that? Why didn't you help?

Hammett shrugged. "As I said, didn't do it for you. I did it because I was bored, and someone promised to tap my sweet ass."

"That's me!" McGlade said, raising his hand. "We'll be in the Crimebago. Nobody bother us for the next three and a half minutes."

"What about the fire?" Phin asked.

"Wind shifted," Hammett said. "It's heading the other direction."

Harry took Hammett by the hand, and they walked off.

"Are we sure we want to leave McGlade alone with that psychopath?" I asked.

Phin and Herb nodded. I supposed I agreed with them.

Moaning, from behind us. We all looked, and saw Del Ray sit up.

"Hold it!" Herb said, pointing his weapon.

I raised a palm. "Wait a sec, Herb."

The gangbanger got to his feet, wobbling a bit, then stared at us.

"Del Ray, right?" I asked.

He nodded. "You guys kill T-Nail?"

"Yeah."

Del Ray spat on T-Nail's corpse. "Dude was crazy."

"Says the guy with a bunch of scalps hanging on his vest," Phin said.

Del Ray looked down at his colors. "These are my dead homies."

"Excuse me?" I said.

"C-Notes. My gang."

"That's how you treat your homies?" Phin said. "Killing them and scalping them?"

"Naw. I never killed nobody. Never." He pointed to a scalp on his vest. "This is Jamal. Died on February tenth of last year. Robbed a liquor store, shot by cops. This here is Franklin. Gun deal gone bad, October eighteen, last month. This one..." he sniffled. "Lil' K. Died because this asshole cared more about revenge than he did about his brothers."

"Other people just save the ashes in an urn," Phin said.

"We're C's. No funerals. We don't pray over each other's graves. But this vest... it makes me remember. Remember my friends. And remember not to let the same mistakes happen again."

In a very warped way, that was poetic. "So, you're in charge of the C-Notes now?"

He nodded, then reached for the nail sticking in his head.

"Don't touch it," I said. "A doctor needs to do that."

"So, what now?" Del Ray asked.

I thought for a moment. It wasn't the easiest thing to do, considering how messed up I was. "I'm tired. Really tired. I want all of this behind me." I glanced at Phin. "*We* want all of this behind *us*."

"What are you saying?"

"I'm saying I don't want to put you in jail, waiting for the day you break out to kill me."

He narrowed his eyes. "So you want to make a deal?"

"We take you to the hospital, then go our separate ways. You don't bother me, I don't bother you."

"How about the mobsters who own this house?" Del asked. "They gonna bother me?"

That was perfect. I'd alluded over the intercom that the house was owned by dangerous people, and Del had ran with it. "I'll handle them. They'll leave you alone as long as I tell them to."

He nodded, then stuck out his hand. I didn't stick out mine.

"Where's our daughter, Del? Samantha?"

"Some of my crew went to pick her up. I told them not to harm her. I'll make sure she's okay."

"And how about Officer Knowles?"

"Never wanted to hurt the lady. When you put Samuel L. Jackson on the speaker, I was the one that pulled her away from T-Nail. She took off."

I held out my hand. We shook.

"We need to go find Tom and get you guys to a hospital," Herb said. "There's one in Rice Lake, about an hour away." My friend's face got serious as his eyes searched mine. "Are you going to make it?"

My good hand found Phin's and we laced our fingers together.

Are we going to make it?

I answered with as much certainty as I ever had about anything.

"Yes," I said. "We are."

PHIN

Hell yeah, we are."

Phin kissed her like it was the first time and the last time. He knew they'd be together forever. Knew it more than he'd ever known anything.

True happiness. What a lucky son of a bitch I am.

EPILOGUE

Months passed.

Wounds healed.

Life got back to normal. Better than normal. Jack was her old self again.

They were happy.

But Phin knew the happiness could vanish at any moment.

Not due to any trouble between them. Jack and Phin's relationship was stronger than it had ever been before.

The problem wasn't their marriage.

The problem was his wife's past. She had one more skeleton in the closet.

A maniac named Luther Kite.

If they were to ever be truly safe, truly happy, Kite would have to be dealt with.

And Phin knew how to find him.

THE END

A NOTE FROM JOE

I highly recommend checking out the Val Ryker series by my frequent collaborator, Ann Voss Peterson. Jack and Harry often have extended cameos in her novels, and both the Jack Daniels books and the Val Ryker books crossover with the CODENAME: CHANDLER series that Ann and I write together.

PUSHED TOO FAR

BURNED TOO HOT

DEAD TOO SOON

ABOUT THE AUTHOR

Joe Konrath is the author of more than twenty novels and dozens of shorter works in the mystery, thriller, horror, and science fiction genres. He's sold over three million books worldwide, and besides Jude Hrdin he's collaborated with bestsellers Blake Crouch, Ann Voss Peterson, Henry Perez, Tom Schreck, Jeff Strand, Tracy Sharp, Bernard Schaffer, Barry Eisler, Ken Lindsey, Garth Perry, Iain Rob Wright, and F. Paul Wilson. He likes beer, pinball machines, and playing pinball when drinking beer.

Visit him at www.jakonrath.com

Joe Konrath's
COMPLETE BIBLIOGRAPHY

JACK DANIELS THRILLERS

WHISKEY SOUR

BLOODY MARY

RUSTY NAIL

DIRTY MARTINI

FUZZY NAVEL

CHERRY BOMB

SHAKEN

STIRRED *with Blake Crouch*

RUM RUNNER

LAST CALL

SHOT OF TEQUILA

SERIAL KILLERS UNCUT *with Blake Crouch*

LADY 52 *with Jude Hardin*

65 PROOF *short stories*

FLOATERS *short with Henry Perez*

BURNERS *short with Henry Perez*

SUCKERS *short with Jeff Strand*

FLOATERS short with Henry Perez

BURNERS *short with Henry Perez*

JACKED UP! *short with Tracy Sharp*

STRAIGHT UP *short with Iain Rob Wright*

CHEESE WRESTLING *short with Bernard Schaffer*

ABDUCTIONS *short with Garth Perry*

BEAT DOWN *short with Garth Perry*

BABYSITTING MONEY *short with Ken Lindsey*

OCTOBER DARK *short with Joshua Simcox*

RACKED *short with Jude Hardin*

BABE ON BOARD *short with Ann Voss Peterson*

BANANA HAMMOCK

CODENAME: CHANDLER SERIES

EXPOSED *with Ann Voss Peterson*

HIT *with Ann Voss Peterson*

NAUGHTY *with Ann Voss Peterson*

FLEE *with Ann Voss Peterson*

SPREE *with Ann Voss Peterson*

THREE *with Ann Voss Peterson*

FIX *with F. Paul Wilson and Ann Voss Peterson*

RESCUE

THE KONRATH/KILBORN HORROR COLLECTIVE

ORIGIN

THE LIST

DISTURB

AFRAID

TRAPPED

ENDURANCE

HAUNTED HOUSE

WEBCAM

DRACULAS *with Blake Crouch, Jeff Strand, and F. Paul Wilson*

HOLES IN THE GROUND *with Iain Rob Wright*

THE GREYS

SECOND COMING

THE NINE

GRANDMA? *with Talon Konrath*

WILD NIGHT IS CALLING *short with Ann Voss Peterson*

TIMECASTER SERIES

Timecaster

Timecaster Supersymmetry

Timecaster Steampunk

Byter

EROTICA
(WRITING AS MELINDA DUCHAMP)

Fifty Shades of Alice in Wonderland

Fifty Shades of Alice through the Looking Glass

Fifty Shades of Alice at the Hellfire Club

Want It Bad

Fifty Shades of Jezebel and the Beanstalk

Fifty Shades of Puss in Boots

Fifty Shades of Goldilocks

The Sexperts – Fifty Grades of Shay

The Sexperts – The Girl with the Pearl Necklace

The Sexperts – Loving the Alien

WEBCAM

Someone is stalking webcam models.

He lurks in the untouchable recesses of the black web.

He's watching you. Right now.

When watching is no longer enough, he comes calling.

He's the last thing you'll ever see before the blood gets in your eyes.

Chicago Homicide Detective Tom Mankowski (THE LIST, HAUNTED HOUSE) is no stranger to homicidal maniacs. But this one is the worst he's ever chased, with an agenda that will make even the most diehard horror reader turn on all their lights, and switch off all Internet, WiFi, computers, and electronic devices.

Jack Kilborn reaches down into the depths of depravity and drags the terror novel kicking and cyber-screaming into the 21st century.

WEBCAM

I'm texting you from inside your closet. Wanna play? :-)

LAST CALL

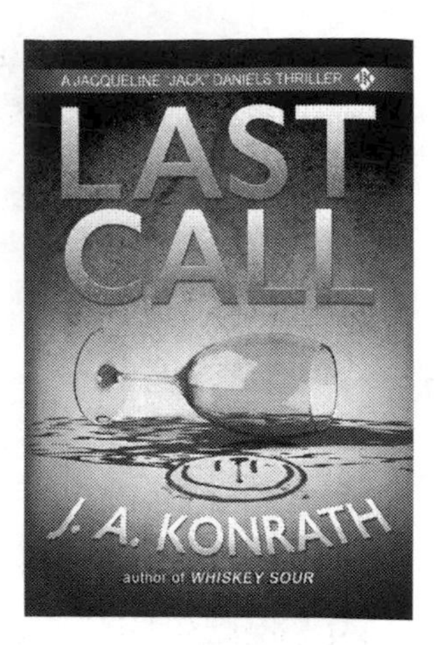

A retired cop past her prime…

A kidnapped bank robber fighting for his life…

A former mob enforcer with a blood debt…

A government assassin on the run…

A wisecracking private eye with only one hand…

A homicide sergeant with one week left on the job…

And three of the worst serial killers, ever.

This is where it all ends. An epic showdown in the desert, where good and evil will clash one last time.

His name is Luther Kite, and his specialty is murdering people in ways too horrible to imagine. He's gone south, where he's found a new, spectacular way to kill. And if you have enough money, you can bet on who dies first.

Legendary Chicago cop Jacqueline "Jack" Daniels has retired. She's no longer chasing bad guys, content to stay out of the public eye and raise her new daughter. But when her daughter's father, Phin Troutt, is kidnapped, she's forced to strap on her gun one last time.

Since being separated from his psychotic soulmate, the prolific serial killer known as Donaldson has been desperately searching for her. Now he thinks he's found out where his beloved, insane

Lucy has been hiding. He's going to find her, no matter how many people are slaughtered in the process.

All three will converge in same place. La Juntita, Mexico. Where a bloodthirsty cartel is enslaving people and forcing them to fight to the death in insane, gladiator-style games.

Join Jack and Phin, Donaldson and Lucy, and Luther, for the very last act in their twisted, perverse saga.

Along for the ride are Jack's friends; Harry and Herb, as well as a mob enforcer named Tequila, and a covert operative named Chandler.

There will be blood. And death. So much death...

LAST CALL by J.A. Konrath

The conclusion to the Jack Daniels/Luther Kite epic

WATCHED TOO LONG

Small town Wisconsin cop Val Ryker is about to move in with her longtime firefighter boyfriend when her old boss asks for a favor. Former Chicago Homicide lieutenant Jacqueline "Jack" Daniels, needs Val to babysit for a few days.

Val isn't comfortable around toddlers, but she accepts.

Then one baby becomes two, and some criminals from Jack's past come calling with child abduction and arson on their agenda.

Val might not know babies. But she knows a whole lot about putting up fight...

WATCHED TOO LONG by Ann Voss Peterson and J.A. Konrath

Some would kill for a good babysitter...